THE NEWMAN
RESIDENT

Charles Swift
Fifth East Publishing
2014

Fifth East Publishing, LLC
Copyright © 2014 by Charles Swift
All rights reserved.

ISBN: 0989979407
ISBN-13: 9780989979405

Library of Congress Control Number: 2014930059
Charles Swift, Provo, UT

To Denise,
for always believing

CHAPTER ONE

Richard walked down the steps from the school, careful to look benign for the hidden cameras. The Newman Home convinced parents it focused on teaching and nurturing and caring, but it also touted its security. No one in, no one out—not without permission from three bureaucratic levels. Drop your baby off, come back in 18 years, and he'll still be there, safe and secure and too smart for the rest of his life.

He walked toward the subway station, but when he got to the corner, he turned right instead of going straight. A bit risky, no question. When he made it around the corner he stopped, surveying the intersection and checking behind just to make sure he was alone. Hundreds of people filled the streets, honking in traffic or dodging one another on the sidewalks, so he couldn't be sure nobody was following him. Newman's Level Two Security blended in with the scenery, but he hoped he'd been around the guards long enough to sense if they were close.

Graffiti covered the seven-foot concrete wall surrounding the playground, an image of a school with dollar signs in the windows and the caption "Bring the children home." He dragged his fingers along the wall as he walked, as if to make sure the school didn't disappear before he could get to his spot. When he got to the hedges, he reached behind a bush and pulled out the old wooden crate, the word "whiskey" barely legible on the side.

Richard stepped up on the box and peered over the wall at about forty children in safari uniforms. Climbing ropes looked like jungle vines, a lion and giraffe watched over the slides and swings, little huts and bridges stood only a few feet off the ground but probably felt like tree houses and bridges high in the rainforest to the children. The kids he saw looked older than his son. He spotted a class, maybe around Christopher's age, on the lawn, under some young shade trees. Most of the children sat on the grass, listening to one of the Newman teachers. A couple of others were on a nearby bench, reading. Off in the far corner, a child was sitting alone, drawing or writing on a pad of paper, but Richard couldn't get a good look at his face.

Richard concentrated but just couldn't be sure the boy was his son.

"Hey, what do you think you're doing?"

Richard jerked around and saw a neighborhood security guard, his hand on his club.

"Got your fill of looking at little kids, buddy?"

"It's not what you think," Richard said, getting down and shoving the crate behind a bush with his foot. He backed away, keeping eye contact with the guard.

"Never is," the guard said, pulling out his club, "and I never care."

"I'm an attorney. City Ordinance 1465 says I have the right to be retained without the use of force until a police officer arrives."

"The use of deadly force," the guard said.

"Well, I can assure you—"

"Takes a long time to find a cop in this town now days, what with all the budget cuts and everything." The guard pulled out his club. "Anything can happen."

CHAPTER TWO

Opening title: RESIDENT CHRISTOPHER CARSON. FIRST STEPS. Richard paused the video on the title, wondering, once again, what kind of father would miss his son's first steps. He had turned off the Monet and the Picasso and devoted the living room screening wall to Christopher's video—a video almost six years old now. The Newman Home had sent more recent clips, but this was the moment he kept coming back to, time and again.

He sat on the floor, back against the white leather couch, pressing the ice compress against the back of his head. He made sure the sound was off, glanced one last time at the closed bedroom door, and whispered, "Play video."

Christopher was wearing the Newman summer uniform: khaki shorts and a shirt covered in little pockets. He looked like a happy explorer stumbling his way through a toddler safari. Such a little boy. How old was he when this video was made? Nine months? Ten? How could it be possible to walk that early? Seems like bone development or inner ear balance or something ought to be warning it was too early to walk. But here he was, taking his first steps.

Richard heard Carol start the shower.

"Slightly increase volume," he said.

Christopher leaned against the sofa, trying to decide if he should step forward or not. He stroked the soft fabric of the cushion, some sort of plush, almost furry, cloth, with a print of bright green leaves. Animals stuck their heads through the foliage, their friendly expressions both cartoonish and authentic. Nothing was repeated on the cloth: each leaf was unique, and there was only one of each animal. Seven in all: giraffe, elephant, gazelle, zebra, gorilla, leopard, and lion. Richard had memorized their faces and checked them each time he watched the video, half-expecting some change in an expression or an animal missing. A wallpaper print of tall grass covered the walls, almost making Christopher look like an ant on the jungle floor. The light in the room was gentle, easing its way in from a large window off to his son's left.

Christopher inched along, keeping his hand in constant contact with the cushions, until he got to the end of the sofa. He looked behind, like he was making sure he wasn't being followed, then back ahead. He moved his foot out, then slowly took his hand away from the couch. His face was tight with seriousness, concentration. Next, his other foot came forward. The sofa seemed far behind him now; he was on his own and knew it. His arms moved to keep his balance, and he stepped again.

Then he fell. He didn't just plop down on his padded rear, but toppled on his side. Hard.

Every time Christopher hit the floor, Richard's body jerked. He wanted to jump up and run through the screen to pick up his little boy. But, every time, he was beaten to it by a young woman who had been standing behind the video camera. She knelt down beside Christopher.

"Come on, Christopher," she said, "you can do it. Get up." She wore the faculty summer uniform that matched the kids' khaki uniform with pockets.

His bottom lip curled out, a sure sign that tears would follow. Richard had learned that face before they'd enrolled Christopher.

"No need to cry, honey."

It pleased Richard that she knew the sign. But it bothered him, too.

"Let's get up and have some more fun," she said.

Slowly, without any contact from the woman, Christopher sat back up. He crawled to the comfort of the sofa, then pulled himself up again.

The woman on the video, still kneeling, urged Christopher to walk toward her. Holding onto the couch, he glanced at the thick carpeting on the floor, then back at the woman. Richard braced himself for what was about to happen. Christopher looked directly at the camera, right into the lens. He didn't smile, he didn't cry, he didn't change his expression at all. But, just for that second or two, he looked directly into the eyes of his father, as if asking for encouragement or love or empathy, and getting nothing.

Richard had never said a word to Carol about the feeling of powerlessness that overcame him every time he experienced that moment in the video.

The woman picked up a small, furry lion from off-camera and held it out to Christopher, calling his name. It wasn't the Winnie the Pooh bear Richard had left with him when they'd enrolled him, but it was a beautiful, almost realistic-looking lion that matched everything else in the room. The little boy watched the lion as the woman moved it in tiny circles, then he let go of the sofa and took a step...then another...then finally took two more quick steps, almost tripping into the lion. The woman, smiling broadly and looking up at the camera, hugged Christopher and handed him the lion.

"That's wonderful," she said. "You're my little lion cub!"

She looked to someone off-camera, her smile gone. "Mark down four steps. Awareness level three."

"Richard."

"Switch video," Richard said, a little louder than he'd wanted. Now the wall was covered with the latest news on CNN. The President was signing something at a table, flanked by Senators from each of the four corporate political parties. Directly behind the President stood the Big Four—the CEOs of the four ruling corporations in the United States. All those political leaders spread across the screening wall like mildew.

"I thought you were going to bed," Carol said.

"I was," he said, "but I got caught up in the news."

Carol stood in the doorway, arms folded.

"So, what's going on in the world?"

"The President just signed an executive order," he said.

"For what?"

"She's extending the stay of the troops."

"That's odd," Carol said. "She looks awfully happy for a President who's making our troops stay longer. The Senators look pretty happy about it, too."

"Well, you know, 'Keep the Homeland Safe' and everything. If we fight them there, we won't have to fight them here. It's just—"

"Richard, that's enough," Carol said, coming into the room and standing directly in front of him, her back to the screening wall. "I saw this same clip earlier today. She's signing an addition to the Education Rights Bill, Richard, closing the last of the public schools."

"There were still public schools left?"

"That's not what we're talking about."

"Sure it is. Raise the bar on public schools, threaten to have private schools take over if the public schools fail, then don't give the public schools the funding they need to succeed. Result? The privatization of public schools. Corporations own our country."

"We're not talking about education policy—we're talking about how you're lying to me."

"I'd rather talk about something else."

"Pause video," she said in a commanding voice. "They called, Richard. You didn't bump your head on the subway, you fell on the sidewalk when the guard hit you."

"I didn't want to worry you."

"You didn't want to let me know you were at Newman again."

"What right do they have to stop a father from seeing his son?" he asked.

"The right you gave them."

"If I'd known—"

"Switch to previous video," she said. Behind her, the paused image of the woman hugging their son covered the wall, filling the room with stark light.

"Has she already given him the lion?" Carol asked without looking back at the screen.

Richard started to get up, but Carol gave him her cross-examination glare. He leaned back up against the couch and adjusted the ice compress.

"What's your problem? I mean, look at that," she said, pointing to the screen without looking at it. "He's loved, happy. He's well-cared for. He's one of the luckiest kids in the world."

"But don't you ever wonder why he didn't cry?"

"Cry? Why would you want him to cry?"

"He's just a baby, and he fell down. It must've hurt—he should've cried."

"You're the only person I know who'd be upset his son got up instead of crying. It's good to learn when you're young: you fall down, you pick yourself up."

"That young?"

"I give up," she said, looking down at the floor.

"I'd love it if you would," Richard said.

"Look—"

"Think of everything we've missed in his life. Reading to him…tucking him in…bandaging a scraped knee—"

Carol sat down on the chair. "How many times do we have to have this discussion? Have you ever thought maybe you're being a little selfish?"

"What?"

"It's all about what you've missed out by not having him here, but it's not his job to satisfy our needs. We're supposed to meet his."

"I grew up with a mom and dad. I had a great childhood. I just want Christopher—"

"I know," she said as she stood up. "But your experience isn't the only valid one, Richard. I had a nanny when I was little and went to boarding school when I got older. Summers were for camp. I want Christopher to have all the opportunities I had. And more."

"It'd just be three months. I could take a leave from work to be with him during the day and he'd be back in school before you know it."

"It takes both signatures," she said, leaving the room, "and they're not getting mine."

10

CHAPTER THREE

Carol always insisted they leave early enough to beat the standing-room-only rush on the subway so she could sit down and get some work done. Both she and Richard wore expensive suits, hers more expensive. Often people told them they looked like brother and sister. Carol had her briefcase on her lap, scanning a forty-page contract on her computer tablet, occasionally marking a sentence or paragraph. Richard sat next to her, staring straight ahead, holding a pen in his hand and balancing a black notebook on his lap. He felt like a man dressed up for his own funeral.

Richard kept picking at his novel in his mind. He had gotten to the second chapter a few months ago, but now he was back on the first, reworking it. He kept telling himself he was laying the foundation, that the first chapter had to be just right or the entire novel would fall apart. A month ago he heard writers should spill their words out on the page, get what they have to say out before them, then go back and craft their sentences later during revisions. Like a sculptor who plops down a lump of clay, then shapes it. Richard believed that. But, a couple of nights ago, he read that writers should craft each page, carefully, painstakingly, to avoid unnecessary, endless revisions later on. Apparently, spilling out the words meant laziness and bred too careless an attitude. Now

Richard knew that was true, so he was back at the first chapter. It had to be perfect.

"How's the chapter coming?" Carol asked, looking up from her document. They had barely spoken to one another all morning. But her question might mean things were better now.

"Making progress." He stared straight ahead, trying to look deep in thought.

"You know what your writing reminds me of?"

He looked down at the page. "Hemingway?"

"No. Law school."

"Ah, what every writer strives for."

"Remember at Columbia," she said, "how you used to fall asleep in class? You'd be in the middle of taking notes, and you'd just start to doze off. Your head would jerk back up, and there'd be this little squiggly line in the middle of the sentence. It basically looked like you were writing on the subway."

"At least I've improved. Back then, the scribbles made more sense than the words."

"You had the same problem in every class," Carol said, "but it was worse in Stuart's."

"Civil Procedure." Richard shook his head. "Nobody liked Civil Procedure."

"I did."

"I know."

Carol sat up in the subway seat, sticking out her chest and trying to look stuffy, professorial. Her voice deepened. "Wake up, Mr. Carson! Why are you wasting my time here? What in the world made you come to law school? Surely not love for the law."

"I remember that day," Richard said.

Carol slumped sheepishly down into the seat, trying to look like a scared law student. Her voice cracked. "No, Mr. Stuart. It was love for her."

Richard laughed. Anyone else might think his wife was being mean, but he knew this was her being playful. Teasing him was as close as she'd get to trying to make things all right after the fight from last night.

"And then you had to point to me. You couldn't have left it in the abstract, could you? I was so embarrassed."

"You loved it."

"Maybe a little."

The train stopped and another ten or so people climbed into the car. There was no more room to sit. The train started up again, the computerized conductor voice saying something Richard couldn't understand.

"Took the dean to get me back into that class," Richard said.

"And Stuart called on you every week for the rest of the semester."

"Now that, I learned in Constitutional Law, was cruel and unusual punishment. Torture."

"You learned Civil Procedure better than anyone else in that class."

"Except you."

She smiled. She still had her student award for Civil Procedure hanging in her office at home.

"Aren't you glad you didn't quit?"

They'd spent the first semester trying to understand what the law professors were saying, but they'd spent the second semester arguing about their future. He was determined to pursue his dream of writing the great American novel, and she was determined to stop him from quitting. She'd been more determined.

Richard knew he had to be careful how he answered this question, or their whole morning would fall apart. "What?" he said, motioning with his hands like a king over his kingdom, "and give up all this?"

Carol shook her head and went back to her contract, but she smiled.

Good, things were good again. He hated how any time they talked about their son these days, it ended up in a fight. How could two people who wanted the exact same thing—what was best for their son—be on opposite sides of the argument?

Carol's tablet chimed and a window appeared saying there was a call from Hunter. She rejected the call and went back to the contract.

"What's he calling for?" Richard asked. The second he spoke, he realized he'd made a mistake.

"Hunter can't call me?"

So much for the peaceful morning.

"It could be about Christopher. It just seems weird to reject the call."

"So, now I'm wrong to not talk to him?" Carol asked. "You need to make up your mind."

"You're always telling me that."

"Because it's always true."

CHAPTER FOUR

When the train stopped at Grand Central, Richard and Carol, along with everyone else in the car, hurried out. It was too early for the worst of the crowds, but people still made leaving the subway car and getting somewhere else a sort of competition. A few people waited on the platform to transfer to another train, but most herded themselves toward the stairs.

They passed by the four men in the Jamaican band, setting up their drums and preparing for their day's labor. This would probably be the band's last day at this stop. People were getting used to their music and feeling better about passing by without dropping any money in the drum case. Plus, televisions placed strategically throughout the subway kept everyone occupied. Why listen to a live band when you could watch one on T.V.?

Richard and Carol made their way up the stairs, winding through two or three tiled hallways. Digital posters covered the subway walls: *Wicked* still pulled in the crowds on Broadway, clips of the new Batman movie flashed across the poster screens, and ads for supposedly more powerful sprays to kill cockroaches invited the subway commuters to remember one of the many things they were trying to forget. Richard shook his head—they'd shipped ten people to Mars but they still couldn't get rid of cockroaches. They walked by several shops, still closed, and exited through the south doors not far from Park Avenue. They stopped there and gave each other a quick kiss. Richard watched as Carol started the two-block trek to the skyscraper that held Weatherford and Williams high above the rest of the world. The firm took up eight floors, and had other offices in Boston, D.C., Chicago, Atlanta, Dallas, Mobile, San Francisco, L.A., and a few other places Richard couldn't remember. As an associate, Carol played a major role in one of the most lucrative cases in the firm's history—the Druson case—and won it nearly single-handedly. She brought in millions for the firm and became the youngest attorney in New York to be advanced to partner.

Richard turned back into Grand Central and entered the main foyer, stopping for a minute to take in the sight. He loved this expansive room—its impressive height and width, its attention to detail, its determination to stay the same. He checked his watch against the clock over the information booth in the middle of the room. As always, his watch was a few minutes behind. More than once he'd told Carol he liked his watch a few minutes behind to remind him there were more important things in life than being a "slave to time." She'd given up trying to get him to reset it.

He scanned the constellations painted on the high ceiling overhead, like a sailor checking his bearings, hoping to find out where he was, wishing to know where he was going.

A large man from behind bumped into him, but Richard stood still, looking at the ceiling. When he looked down and started walking, he tried not to notice the homeless people sleeping along the floor. There seemed to be some sort of trouble in the corner. One subway police officer was talking to an old man wearing a tattered army jacket, aiming her club at him. Richard walked faster, but not fast enough to avoid hearing the moans from the old man after he'd been hit.

"How you doin', Mr. Carson?"

Richard liked to stop by Al's newsstand to chat and take a look at the magazines and papers before consigning himself to his desk. Al was probably in his sixties, but in pretty good shape. He wore a Yankees cap, worn around the edges.

"Good, Al. What's hot today?"

"Usual. The used-to-be-royal family's got its problems making the adjustment. Funny, I've never had any problem not being royal."

"Who wants to live in Buckingham Palace, anyway?" Richard glanced over the counter, looking at headlines. "Anything in the *Review*?"

"Circled one you'd like." Al reached from under the counter and handed him a copy.

"New novel?"

"Yeah, good one, too. Great title. It's a biblical allusion, you know."

Richard smiled. "Thanks, Al." He began scanning the review. "About a couple of boys growing up in Missouri. . . . This isn't a Huck and Tom rip-off, I hope."

"Literature don't do rip-offs. Writer like you ought to know that."

"My book is a growing-up story, too. In Vermont."

"I know, I know," Al said. "When do I get to read it?"

"Still on the first chapter."

"Get on with it, man! Rather read a good book than a perfect first chapter!"

Richard smiled and waved his card across the scanner disk. "Keep the change, Al."

Richard left Al at the newsstand and exited out to the street. He passed the usual individuals: the shoeshine man, headphones on, waiting for commuters; the short, round man always talking on his cell while he stood outside his computer shop; the three women in surgical scrubs who were always at the bus stop at this same time, wires running from their ears to their pockets. He remembered when he was a kid and they'd come to the city for the day. Even though it was always crowded with strangers who rarely spoke with each other, at least there was the potential. Sometimes these strangers would say a word or two, or even just give an encouraging nod. But now everyone was wired to something. There was always music to listen to or television or movies to watch or someone somewhere else to work out a deal with over the phone. No one was ever here anymore.

Richard hurried through his firm's lobby, reading the book review. Jones, Darrell, and Hubb had only one office, and it wasn't even as big as Weatherford's smallest branch. He closed the door to his office and sat at his desk. Something about the book caught his attention, like he was reading a review of the book he was writing before he'd even finished it. Two boys growing up long before they were ready, never having a real childhood. This was his story. Really, his son's story. He was the one who should be writing this.

He looked at the picture of the cover one more time, reading the title aloud. *"Death of the Innocents."*

CHAPTER FIVE

Richard needed to make up his mind. That's what Carol always said. And, to be honest, she was right. It was easy for him to analyze and evaluate and reflect; deciding and acting were the tough parts.

Richard had just finished reading the review about *Death of the Innocents* and was pacing in his office. It wasn't even ten yet, so it was too early to take a break, and there was no one at the firm he could talk to.

He looked over at his phone and said his wife's name. He wondered if she'd be too busy to pick up.

"Richard?"

"Carol. I've missed you."

"Me too. I mean, we haven't seen each other for over an hour."

"Okay, I got it, Counselor," he said. "Working on a big case?"

"Yamashita case. Worth 300 million dollars. We'll get a decent slice of that if all goes well."

"The Yamashita that owns almost half our bonds? That owns pretty much half our country?"

"You got it."

"I'm impressed. Sorry to spoil it for you, but I can tell you how the case ends." He sat on a couple of magazines near the edge of his desk. "You win."

Carol didn't say anything, but he could sense she was smiling.

"I'm still preparing for a deposition that's in less than an hour."

"I just wanted to see if we could grab some lunch."

"Isn't it a little early for lunch?"

"How about one?"

"I'm sorry. I've just got too much to do."

"How about dinner tonight? Your favorite restaurant."

"I'll be home late tonight. And, if I don't get off the phone, I won't be home until midnight."

Richard paused. "Do you really have that much to do, or is this about something else?"

"You know how it is," Carol said, "everyone has to bill just one more hour than everyone else. I've got to go. Don't wait up for me."

Richard was about to say something, but she hung up. He paused for a moment, then said his parents' names.

"Hello," his father answered, "how's the weather there?"

"How'd you know it was me?" Richard asked. "You haven't gotten Voice Recognition, have you?"

"Richard! Good to hear from you. I figured whoever was calling was somewhere near weather."

His father laughed. Richard didn't know anyone who enjoyed laughing more than his father.

"The leaves are starting to change."

"Summer hasn't even started yet, let alone fall," Richard said. "How could the leaves be changing?"

"You've got to be very observant, and sensitive. Imagination, faith, and a touch of prophecy help as well."

Richard smiled. "How're you doing, Dad? Used to being retired yet?"

"Oh, I still go down to the English Department every now and then and raise some Cain on campus. You know, they don't like someone who thinks the books mean something. They don't care about the author and the meaning—they only care about the latest theory."

"Hang in there, Dad," Richard said. "Don't give up the fight."

"Son, you know me, I don't give up fights. And I'm even willing to start a few."

Richard laughed. "How's Mom?"

"That old woman? Younger than ever," his father said. "Beautiful. Smart. She's thinking she'll retire in a couple of years, but I doubt the Physics Department will let her. Besides, I don't know what I'd do with her underfoot. She'll be filling the tub and trying to demonstrate wave theory to me all day. You want to talk to her?"

"No, I was actually calling you."

"You ought to at least say hello."

"Okay, put her on."

"Can't, she's at work."

Richard heard the laughing again.

"Dad, I was wondering if you'd read this new book, *Death of the Innocents*."

"By Fry? I have. About a couple of boys growing up in Missouri."

"That's the one. The reviewer says the book is flawed. That they grow up too quickly to be believable."

"No, I disagree. I think their childhood is taken from them. They never had a chance to grow. You ought to read it, son, it's a good book."

"That title haunts me," Richard said, looking down at the picture of the book's cover.

"It should. Herod...the babies he had killed out of fear for the future...it's a horrible story that continues to this day in all sorts of ways."

His father paused, but Richard sensed he should leave the silence alone.

"How's Christopher doing?" his father asked.

"Fine. We downloaded another video yesterday. I'll send you the link."

"I'm so tired of all the links I have in my life. For once I'd like to hold something in my hands."

"Ah, the good ol' days of DVDs," Richard said.

His father laughed. "Send me that link and we'll click on it until it wears out. We love to see that little boy. If he could just somehow get out of that blasted uniform."

Richard nodded. "I know."

"I don't know which is worse—watching those videos, or not watching them," his father said.

Richard could feel the void left now that the humor was gone from his father's voice.

"I guess I better get back to work, Dad."

"All right. Give our love to Carol. And our grandson, next time you see him. And keep some for yourself, son."

His father hung up without saying good-bye. Richard sat on the edge of his desk, staring down at the review. *Death of the Innocents*. He hoped he could find such a good title for his book. Of course, the boys in the book didn't really die, did they? They might as well have, though, because what life was worth living if its spirit has been robbed? No, no. It was better to be alive, even if things weren't exactly the way you wanted them. Nobody leads the life they were meant to. At least, not completely. "The mass of men lead lives of quiet desperation," Thoreau said, and he was right. But a man could live such a life and still call it good, couldn't he? It was a type of sacrifice. It was the price you paid for being an adult.

But should a child have to pay that price?

Richard got up from his desk and opened the door so hard it hit the wall. He almost ran down the hall, bumping into a first-year associate.

"Sorry, Steve," Richard said, not stopping.

"It's all right, Mr. Carson. I mean, Richard. I was wondering if we could meet about—"

"Sorry," Richard shouted from the end of the hall, "it's time I did something." He ran past the receptionist and out the door.

CHAPTER SIX

The subway was crowded. No matter what time of day it was, the subway was always crowded.

Richard climbed the stairs out of the subway stop and walked down the sidewalk. When he rounded the corner, there it was: The Newman Home. The building had housed the Essex & York Private School years before, but Newman had completely transformed it. Like most buildings in the area, there had always been bars on the windows, on the first floor to protect against intruders, and on the other six floors to protect against small children falling out. But Newman had special decorative railings made—with sculpted animals: the first floor had orange railings with giraffes; the second, gray with elephants; the third, brown with gazelles; the fourth, black and white, with zebras; the fifth, black, with gorillas; the sixth, yellow and black, with leopards; and the seventh, gold, with lions.

The dark sandstone on the front wall of the building, previously blackened by years of cars driving by, had been sandblasted weeks before "Newman" had been carved into granite. And the massive, cracking doors were replaced by two oak doors carved with jungle scenes.

"Welcome to the Newman Home," a pleasant, but computerized, voice said from somewhere near the front door, "where we develop minds for the future. Please wait here for security purposes."

Richard stood still on the porch, listening to the quiet whirr of the scanners making sure he was unarmed and healthy. He'd given up trying to see any cameras or microphones.

"Welcome, Mr. Carson." This was a real person's voice this time. "Please come in." A clicking sound indicated the door was now unlocked.

He grabbed one of the large door handles, shaped like a smiling python, and pulled open the door. A faint, robotic noise signaled some camera moving and refocusing. He stepped into the lobby and felt the cool breeze from the air conditioning wash over his face.

The only person in the lobby was a man in a safari outfit sitting behind a rounded counter, looking at a computer screen image projected above. Next to the counter was an oak door that led to the rest of the school. The walls were covered with bamboo, and massive African plants reached out from pots on the floor along the walls and from baskets hanging from the ceiling.

"Someone will be here to help you in a moment, Mr. Carson," the man said.

Richard took a few steps away from the counter and glanced around the lobby. The first time he and Carol had come here, she was still expecting, and the lobby had been crowded with other expectant parents waiting for the school tour. They had all been placed on the short list for their children's possible enrollment, and that visit had been the parents' first—and last—chance to meet the famous Dr. Newman. And it was the only time Richard had been through the oak door. He had been in the lobby a number of times, usually at the end of a quarter, when he and Carol and some of the other parents came to pick up their children for the quarterly visits home. The spring and fall visits were three days each, and summer and winter each had a week. Dr. Newman had explained that any longer would disrupt the entire education process. The parents always believed the experts. Hunter loved to repeatedly point out to him how some parents had even quit bothering to take their children home, wanting their children to make the most of their time at Newman.

The oak door opened and a man with a stern, square face, entered the lobby, followed by a much taller woman, six feet at least. The man stood off to the side.

Richard recognized the woman. He smiled when he saw her, not to be pleasant, but because he always found the way she moved amusing. Even though she was thin, she walked like a bear, awkwardly on its hind legs, looking for something it wasn't sure it would find. She and the man both wore safari uniforms.

"I'm Ms. Garrett," she said, "one of the Parent Representatives here at Newman."

"I need to speak to the superintendent."

"We told you yesterday the superintendent isn't available." Her lips quivered as she smiled. "Let's give me a try, shall we?"

Richard took a couple of steps back. "I want to talk with him about taking my son out this summer, for the quarter sabbatical."

Ms. Garrett looked at the man behind the computer. He'd been listening, but quickly resumed manipulating the projected computer image.

"No one has ever taken the sabbatical," Ms. Garrett said. "In fact, soon the policy will be written out of the book."

"Well, for now, it's written in, and I want to take advantage of it."

"I don't think it's a good idea."

"I'm not taking *you* home for the summer."

She turned and walked toward the oak door. "The superintendent's schedule is impossible. I'm sure you understand, Mr. Carson." She stopped at the door and faced Richard. "I'm sorry."

"No problem, I understand. Let me speak to Christopher then."

"Who?"

"My son."

She looked at the man behind the counter, but he was busy not looking back.

"Your son?"

"Yes."

"That's impossible. Here at the Newman Home we—"

"It's a school, not a home."

"You can't just come and meet anyone you have a whim to. Pulling him out of his class would disrupt everything." She opened the oak door. "I'm sorry, but we have the other residents to think of."

"And I only have one to think of." He walked up to within a couple of feet of her and heard the man behind the counter stand up. "Let me see him."

She shook her head. "Call the superintendent's secretary, Mr. Carson. Maybe you could meet with him sometime within the next couple of months."

"Look, Ms. Garrett, I'm an attorney. Don't get me mad."

"Everyone in Manhattan is an attorney," she said, "and they're all mad."

She slipped around the door and closed it after her. Richard turned the knob, but it was locked.

CHAPTER SEVEN

Richard left the school and headed for the playground. He wasn't worried this time about whether they knew where he was going or not. When he made it around the corner, he saw a man down the street, standing on the crate and staring over the wall. Richard stopped cold. The man was about his age, balding with a bit of a stomach. He looked like he'd never been outside before. He wore a gray flannel, double-breasted business suit.

Richard walked toward him. "What are you doing here?"

The man had been concentrating on the playground and almost fell off the crate when he heard Richard's voice. He jumped down and tried to straighten his suit.

"What were you doing?" Richard asked.

"I'm a child psychologist. I consult here. I was observing the children."

"No, you're not. I know the head psychologist here—he doesn't have people going around watching the kids from over a wall."

"No, I really—"

"Who are you?" Richard took a step closer.

The bald man looked behind him, then across the street. "I have a boy here. I just wanted to see him. That's all."

The man straightened his suit jacket.

"One time I think I might have seen him. But he was so far away, I couldn't be sure. That was a year ago, when he was three." The man pointed to the crate. "Here, take a look. Maybe you'll see your son today."

Richard climbed up on the crate and peered over the wall. Twenty or so children in their uniforms crowded in a circle, sitting on the grass and participating in some activity that involved clapping their hands in rhythm and reciting something he couldn't hear. No sign of Christopher.

"Wait a minute," Richard said, "how'd you know—"

He looked down and saw the man was gone.

CHAPTER EIGHT

I t was hot in Richard's office. Something was always wrong with the air conditioning. He leaned back in his chair and stared at his office ceiling, thinking. He had been out of the office much of the day, and now his door was closed. Some of the other attorneys would be wondering—and talking—about what was going on, but he didn't care. He hadn't even worried how he was going to explain a day with absolutely no hours billed.

He sat upright in his chair and looked at the photo in the brass frame on his desk, a picture of Carol, Christopher, and him, several years ago. Christopher was just a baby, sitting in his daddy's lap. Richard was smiling big, squeezing his baby, and the baby was giggling. Carol stood behind them both, arms down around his shoulders and holding her baby's hand. The Brooklyn Bridge dominated the background. Richard had always loved that bridge for some reason and had insisted the picture be taken there.

Christopher had been five and a half months old; two weeks later, he'd be going to Newman. Richard's parents kept insisting they take pictures throughout the day. It wasn't easy—not because they couldn't get Christopher to smile, but because they couldn't get him to stop giggling. Christopher had laughed and laughed, for no reason the adults could see. It was like there was some extremely funny private joke between him and his stuffed Winnie the Pooh bear. When Richard bought it, Carol had pointed out that he would be in Newman by the time he was old enough to have anything to do with the bear, and that the staff didn't allow stuffed animals from outside for health reasons—whatever that meant. But Richard put it in the crib every night. And, as far as he was concerned, the baby and bear adored each other.

They sent copies of the pictures to Richard's parents and Carol's mother. Carol's parents had divorced years before, and she had nothing to do with her father, but Richard had secretly sent him one. He'd never met the man, but he couldn't help feeling a grandpa had the right to see his only child's only child.

Two weeks after the picture was taken, the three of them were in the Newman lobby. The attendant kept trying to make Richard take Pooh Bear, telling him it would be discarded once the baby became an official resident, but Richard fought hard. His boy was going to keep it to comfort him on cold nights. The attendant took Christopher and the bear through the oak doorway and closed the door. Richard never saw the Pooh Bear again. He asked about it two or three times, but no one ever knew what he was talking about.

Richard placed the picture back on his desk. It was his favorite picture of his family, but he often found it difficult to look at it. Rather than reminding him of what he had, sometimes the picture would just accentuate his feelings that he'd lost his son—that, in a very real sense, he'd lost his family. The picture reminded him of a different photo he hadn't seen for years—one of his parents and their two sons, standing on the deck in the back of their Vermont home. His younger brother, David, was a junior in high school, and Richard had just started college. It was autumn, bright gold and red leaves covered the deck, and the four of them were laughing. They'd spent a half-hour trying to take the perfect family picture. His father had made some bad joke about something, they'd laughed, and the camera timer went off at just the right time. The perfect family picture.

He turned back to his computer and clicked on the video. Christopher was on the screen, now four or five years old, sitting on the floor of a classroom with six other children. They were surrounded by a rainforest wallpaper, bright green trees full of gorillas eating bananas and swinging on vines. The children wore their colder weather uniforms now, the same khaki, safari-style clothes, but with long sleeves and long pants. They watched one of the teachers as he used two hand puppets, a giraffe and a zebra, to teach about being polite.

Richard had almost memorized the video, so he busied himself with searching out details, hoping for clues—clues for what, he had no idea. For a moment, he focused on the pockets on those safari uniforms. The pockets never had anything in them. Shouldn't they have bulged a little here and there? These were little kids, for crying out loud. Shouldn't there have been a rock or a crayon or something in a pocket?

He studied the plush green carpet. Several of the children stroked the carpet as they watched the puppets. They would laugh, and sometimes laugh even more as they looked at one another, but they kept stroking the carpet. Reaching out to it. Feeling it. Richard kept watching the screen. Even though he'd seen this video many times, he still hoped something would be different this time. The children all seemed happy, but maybe a boy would frown for a second. Or maybe a girl would look distracted. He knew nothing would change, but he kept watching.

The phone rang. Richard picked it up without thinking, forgetting to look at the screen and see who was calling.

"Richard, are you there? This is Hunter."

Richard closed his eyes and took a deep breath. Hunter was the head psychologist at Newman, and one of Carol's friends from college. She felt like they owed the world to Hunter because he'd pulled so many strings to get Christopher into the school.

"Hello, Hunter."

"Look, I'll get to the point, Richard. Ms. Garrett told me you came by Newman today."

Richard didn't say anything.

"It's not a good idea," Hunter said. "The sabbatical. It's just not healthy for the resident to be taken out of the environment he's grown up in. Too disruptive."

"You didn't seem to mind taking him out of the environment he grew up in when you enrolled him."

"That's my point, Richard. We enroll them early so we don't have to waste time retraining them."

"I have the right to take him out on the sabbatical."

"Look, let's not talk policy, let's talk Christopher."

"Yeah, tell me about him. It's tough to know someone you never see."

"Richard, if I had the slightest doubt about the Newman Home, you know I wouldn't have my own son enrolled there."

Richard looked over at the paused image on the screen. All the children were frozen in their laughter, in their delight. All looking up at the teacher and the two puppets, a giraffe and a zebra. The children—their sweet, innocent, clean faces, paralyzed in pleasure as they watched two animals talking to each other.... What did a giraffe have to say to a zebra, anyway?

What did Richard have to say to Hunter?

"...but I'm part of something big," Hunter continued, "really important. And so are you. These kids are from the smartest parents...."

Richard noticed something he'd never seen before. Something stuck out of one of the pockets on Christopher's shirt. He looked harder, trying to make out what it was. It looked a little shiny. He zoomed in.

"It's a pen," Richard said.

"What?"

"A pen. I've got a video of Christopher on the computer. He has a pen in his pocket. No one else has one."

"So he has a pen."

"Maybe he draws with that pen." Richard pointed to the screen. "Or maybe he writes. Maybe he does something with it without having any official approval."

"Or maybe he just left a pen in his pocket."

"Maybe there's a rule that you can't have a pen in your pocket," Richard said, "and he's breaking the rule. Wouldn't that be great, Hunter!"

"Breaking rules really doesn't lead to much success in life."

"It could. Happy little clones. Look at them."

"I'm on the phone. I can't see them."

"That's the point. You don't even have to look at them, Hunter. They always look the same."

"They look like students at the finest private school in the world. What's the problem? How could you possibly find anything wrong with a picture of happy children? Just admit it: there's nothing wrong with Newman, you just miss your son."

"I do miss him," Richard said, "but that doesn't mean there's nothing wrong with Newman."

"You know what the studies show. Public schools failed a long time ago."

"If that's true, it's because we made them fail."

"It's taken government and business working as a team to save our children."

"Let's see, government mandates without funding. Vouchers. Privatization. They weren't trying to save our schools or our children. They were trying to create a new profit center. No child left behind? All the kids were left behind."

"Always the cynical lawyer."

"Newman tuition is the highest in the world, I bet," Richard said. "And there's all that fundraising. Makes you wonder if Newman isn't really about all the money."

"It's about the best education in the world. Worth every penny."

"I never went to a boarding school. I lived with those people... what do you call them?...oh yes, parents. Parents who loved me, who wanted what was best for me, who wanted to be with me."

"Newman parents love their children, too. That's why they enrolled them. They wanted what's best for their kids—the best education possible."

"Don't give me that spiel," Richard said, sitting up taller. "Those parents sent their kids to boot camp because they were too busy with their beloved careers to mess around with nuisances that had to be clothed, fed, and held. They have enough money to make their kids one less thing to worry about before staying late at the office or going out for dinner and a play."

"Or writing their novel?"

Silence.

"I didn't enroll Christopher so I could write my novel."

"Nobody held a gun to your head to get Christopher into Newman, Richard. You signed your name just like Carol did."

Richard slammed down the receiver. Hunter was an idiot. There was no way Richard agreed to let his son enroll in Newman so he could write. If someone told him he could have his son back if he gave up ever writing another word, he'd drop his pen and grab his son in a second.

The pen in Christopher's pocket now stood out in the picture. How could Richard have missed it before? He cherished the possibility, however slight, that his son had the same connection to writing that he did. He smiled. Maybe writing would be the key to bringing them together.

CHAPTER NINE

The secretary at Weatherford and Williams tried to stop him, insisting his wife was in an important meeting, but Richard walked past her. He finally had a plan for getting Christopher home and he didn't want anything to slow him down. He knew himself well enough to know he had to keep his momentum before he talked himself out of his plan. He opened Carol's office door without knocking, knowing he'd jump into the middle of whatever was happening. She was leaning against her desk, speaking with two attorneys who looked new to the firm, judging by the way they took notes on everything she was saying. Richard grabbed her hand and told her he was starving—they had to get something to eat together or he'd die. She complained, saying she couldn't leave, but she went with him. She usually liked to call the shots, but he knew she sometimes liked it when he'd step up and lead the way, almost leaving her in the dark. For a little while, at least.

He was still holding her hand as they came out onto the sidewalk. Traffic was heavy, as always, and the street was noisy. Nameless people crowded the sidewalk. Richard walked quickly, and Carol had difficulty keeping up.

They walked two or three blocks without saying a word. Whenever they passed a restaurant, Richard didn't even slow down. Finally, Carol let go of his hand and stopped.

"Richard, it's almost four o'clock. I grabbed a sandwich a long time ago."

"Then let's call it dinner."

"It's too early for dinner."

"For crying out loud, woman, live on the edge!"

"Where exactly are we going?"

"For the first time in your life, you're not going to know exactly anything."

He started walking down the sidewalk, leaving her standing. He turned at the corner and looked back at her. She was smiling, but stopped when she saw he was watching her.

"I hope we're not going to eat vegetarian hot dogs again," she shouted after him. "I hate green hot dogs."

She caught up with him just as he was about to turn a corner. Richard paused for a second, as though out of respect or reverence, as he looked at the massive building straight ahead. The gigantic lions kept watch over one of the few places in the city where a person could find books that weren't just on screens.

"We're going to eat dinner at the library?" Carol asked.

Richard nodded and almost ran toward the library. He knew what he was doing, but he had no idea how to do it. How was she ever going to go along with this? Carol again tried to catch up, and finally got to him when he paused at the top of the steps. The two entered the library and headed straight for the huge reading room.

There were several rows of tables, with a number of people scattered among them reading or writing. Richard sat down at a table near the back, and Carol sat next to him.

"What shall we order?" Carol asked. "I've heard they've got great sushi."

"What was the reason I gave Stuart for going to law school?"

Carol paused. Richard studied her face, worried for the least little sign she would build up her walls and refuse to talk.

"You told him you went to law school because you loved me," Carol said.

"That's what I said. And it was true. You know that, don't you?"

"Yes."

"You wanted to marry a guy who'd get a real job."

"Someone had to wake you up from your dream."

This wasn't the conversation he'd written in his head on the way over to her office. Richard looked around the room, watching the people sitting on the benches as they waited for the books they'd requested to be brought to the desk. They looked like intelligent, busy people, and here they were sitting and waiting. People seemed to waste half their lives waiting for things, but books were actually worth waiting for.

"But, Carol," he said, "I hate my real job."

"I know you don't like it, but—"

"No, Carol, no. I don't don't like it. I hate it. I hated law school. I hated my summer jobs. And I hate being a lawyer." His voice was getting louder with each sentence. "I don't like pumpernickel bread. I don't like shirts that scratch my neck. But I hate being a lawyer, Carol. I hate being what I am."

"Okay, okay," she said, trying to quiet him. "You made your point." She glanced around the room. "Look, maybe you hate your job, but I didn't force you to go to Columbia. It's not my fault you—"

"I'm not saying it's your fault. I take full responsibility."

"Oh," she said. "Well, good. Because it really isn't my fault."

41

"It's not about fault. But it *is* about doing something because of love."

"What are you getting at?"

Richard picked up a book not too far away on their table. He held it in one hand and shook it, like a preacher making his point with the Bible.

"You know how you're always telling me I analyze things too much? That I need to get to the *doing* part of life?"

She nodded.

"It's time for me to quit thinking about writing and to write."

"You are a writer," she said. "You're writing that novel."

"No, I'm a lawyer. One more lawyer, helping people with money keep it or get more. I want to be a writer. Full-time."

Carol sat back in her chair. "Why now? Why can't you just keep writing part-time like you always have?"

"I read a review about a book this morning and kept thinking this is my story—this is our son's story. I need to write our story, Carol, and quit letting other people do it."

Carol took a deep breath and looked away.

Richard put the book down on the table and sat back in his seat. This conversation was not a complete success, but he'd never get up the courage again to make it this far. He couldn't let either of them leave that room until he'd said everything he'd needed to. His body wanted to lean across the table, to get closer to Carol as he said what he was about to say. But he stopped himself. He needed the space. The buffer.

"Earlier today I spoke with Jennifer," Richard said. Carol turned and stared at him and he kept looking straight into her eyes. "I got a leave of absence approved."

"What? You quit?" Her face filled with red.

"A leave of absence, just for the summer. Nothing's finalized. I told her I'd need to talk with you first."

"How generous."

She got up to leave, but Richard grabbed her arm.

"We've gotten expert at walking away from conversations. From each other. Let's finish this one, okay?"

"We need your salary, Richard. How—"

"I know, I know. But we can make it for the summer. The issue isn't money, it's my chance to live the life I want to live. I've given law years and years of my life. I'm just asking for one summer."

Carol looked down at her hands, then off to the side, taking her time. "It's that important to you?" she asked.

"The chance to write is as important to me as law is to you. One summer will give me the chance to get past the first couple of chapters and really get into the book."

She folded her arms and stared across the room. "What if you can't get the book published? Will you want to start another one?"

"Maybe. But I won't take another summer off."

"What if—"

"What if I do get the book published? What if it becomes a best seller, and I make millions?"

"Then it would be a real job." Carol smiled.

"Just one summer. I promise."

Slowly, Carol reached over and picked up the book Richard had been holding. She looked at it for a second, then handed it to him. "Go for it, Richard."

"You're serious?"

"Don't give me a chance to back out."

"I won't, I won't. Let's do it." Richard reached over and held her hands.

"Don't be so quick on the gratitude," she said. "Show it to me with a best seller."

"I owe you one."

"And don't think I'll forget that," she said as she stood up.

Richard touched her arm. "Just a minute," he said, "there's one more thing. I'm not quite done."

"Well, I am. I've got a three hundred million dollar suit calling my name. Loudly. We can talk on the way back. And this time, I'm taking a cab."

She started walking away, and Richard's only option was to follow her. Now, as they were walking back toward the library entrance, he worried he wouldn't have the courage to finish what he had to say. Maybe he should stop there. The whole plan might be too much. Carol had just compromised more than he'd ever seen her do since they met. She gave him her blessing to actually not make any money for three months. Maybe it wouldn't be fair to ask any more of her.

But this was his last chance.

They were now on the street, and Carol got a cab and climbed into it. He climbed in after her.

"So, what's the one more thing?" she asked. "And be careful—don't push your luck."

Richard looked at her, then out the window. He wished they weren't sitting so close together.

"It's related to my taking the summer off to write. But more important. I've been thinking about this for a long time as well. I know how you feel, but—

"Richard, what is it?"

"You've got to promise to keep an open mind about—"

"I'm starting to lose my patience."

"It's Christopher."

Silence.

"What about him?" Her voice shook.

Richard turned from the window and looked into Carol's face. She didn't look angry, like she had when he first mentioned taking the leave of absence for the summer. She looked afraid. Her bottom lip quivered, just a little. He took a deep breath.

"He really should take that quarter sabbatical," Richard said. Just the saying of it infused him with courage. "Now that I'm going to be home for the summer, there's no reason he can't be, too."

Carol looked away for a moment. The cab had stopped in traffic, waiting for a delivery truck that was backing up. She opened her door, nowhere near her building, and turned back to Richard.

"This little field trip was never about your writing," she said, her voice quivering. Her eyes were piercing, but her face looked pale, vulnerable. "It was about getting Christopher home."

"Everything I said about my writing was true," Richard said, looking up the street. A bus stopped and several children in their school uniforms got off. He looked back at his wife. "But, I have to be honest, Carol, I'll do everything I can to get our son home where he belongs."

She walked away.

CHAPTER TEN

"**N**ext," Richard kept saying, hoping to find something worth watching.

CNN: Interview with the man who had just been appointed to the new cabinet post, Secretary of Corporate Alliance.

CBS: Report on the President's speech about the great success of privatizing schools.

ESPN: Cage fighting again.

It was almost eleven and Carol still hadn't called. She usually didn't get home until nine, but she always called if she was going to be later. He landed on some local cable station: blustery people in turn-of-the-century clothes dancing with their pets.

"Off."

He knew she was tough, that she could attack in the courtroom like no one else, that she was a trial lawyer twenty-four hours a day. When he'd devised his plan, he'd seen it as building a logical case for bringing Christopher home. He'd never thought she'd look so betrayed. He'd expected her to be bothered, perhaps even angry, but to see her so hurt—that was something he wasn't prepared for.

The locks on the front door buzzed as they opened. Richard jumped up and looked around the room, then sat back down and picked up whatever book was on the nearby table. He heard footsteps coming down the hall towards the living room.

"Sorry I'm late," Carol said, as she headed for their bedroom. "I'm exhausted."

This was it. The first step in her apology ritual. Or was it more of a game?

"Okay," he said. But this was too important to be left to a game. "Carol, I'm sorry about this afternoon. I shouldn't have sprung on you everything I've ever thought. I should've given you a chance to breathe."

There was a long, tense pause. Richard wanted to fill the void, but waited instead for her response.

"I shouldn't have lost my temper," she finally said, as she turned to face him.

Lost her temper? She hadn't lost her temper—she'd fallen apart.

"You know," he said, "we took summers off every year when we were kids."

"I didn't go home," she said. "I went to camp and had a great time, making friends, learning things."

"It's just one summer, Carol. It won't be that big of a disruption."

"You're really that clueless?"

She turned and walked into their bedroom, but he followed after her.

"Clue me in, Carol. Let's get to the bottom of this."

She turned to him, her face firm and resolute. "Look, of course, I'm worried about messing up our son's future with this wild goose chase of yours. I don't want to see him fall behind because of the sabbatical, or maybe even get released from Newman for becoming uncompetitive. But there's more to what happened today than that."

"Uncompetitive? You don't seem to see—"

"Do you want me to tell you what's going on or not?"

"You're right." Richard fell back into a chair. "I'll just listen."

Carol sat on the bed. "You know how messy my parents' divorce was. I was just a kid, but I knew what was going on. I heard a lot of ugly things a kid shouldn't ever have to hear."

He nodded.

"One of the things Mom said over and over was this: 'You can never trust a man. All men want is control over women.' I don't think that—not for a minute. But, sometimes, I really do *feel* that way. So when you did what you did today, I felt manipulated. I felt betrayed."

"I'm sorry. I never meant for you to feel that way." He sat on the bed next to her and held her hand, glad when she didn't pull away.

"Do you have any idea how difficult it will be to write and have him home at the same time?" she asked.

"No, but I want to find out."

"That's not all you want to do."

"What do—"

"Everything goes back to your brother, Richard. You know that."

"No, I don't know that. In fact, I would—".

"You two were so close, such good friends. And, then, you lost him. He was gone from your life. And ever since then you've been afraid of losing the people you love. You're afraid of losing Christopher."

Richard knew she was right at some level. He took a deep breath.

"Nobody wants to lose someone they love," Richard finally said.

"Of course not, but you analyze everything to death because making a decision means losing the other alternatives."

"Maybe, but not this time. I've made my decision. I've given you what you want for years. Why can't you give me what I want for three months?"

Carol closed her eyes and took a deep breath. "Look, I made that little trip to the library for you. There's a trip I want you to make with me. Then we'll decide."

CHAPTER ELEVEN

Richard, Carol, and Hunter stood in a dark room, looking through a one-way mirror at a Newman laboratory that was also fairly dark. Hunter had made it clear that no parents had ever been to this room before, that he could get in trouble if the superintendent found out, that if it hadn't been for his friendship with Carol he never would have considered doing this. Carol kept nodding and thanking him; Richard tried his best to ignore him.

Two scientists were in the room with them, and several others were on the other side of the mirror, connecting electrodes to eleven children calmly seated at their individual desks.

"Neuroplasticity," Hunter said. "That's what this is all about. It's how we live up to our motto: Developing minds for the future. We've known for years the brain changes when a person learns— that it forms and develops throughout life. When people practice an activity, their neural networks reshape themselves in response. The same goes for when they access memories. People aren't born with a brain they're stuck with for their whole lives. They can develop what they're born with. They can become smarter."

"But there's nothing really new about that," Richard said. "Like you said, we've known this for years."

"True, but Dr. Newman has discovered how to observe and measure these neural changes. Any school can test how students do on exams, measuring how well they recall information or even,

51

if we're lucky, how they can synthesize it. But the Newman Home can literally measure the changes in the brain and see what can be done to stimulate more such changes."

No one had said anything about this when they'd enrolled Christopher, and Richard was bothered by all of it. He didn't like the idea that scientists at the school were scanning the children's minds and trying to manipulate the natural process of learning. What ever happened to learning being about exploration and personal growth? Wasn't a good school supposed to be instilling a love for learning rather than an experiment for it?

But this was just the sort of information that would bolster Carol's enthusiasm for the school. What could be better than teachers actually being able to know if students are learning and how to help them learn more? In fact, the more he thought about it from her perspective, the more he began to wonder if he was the one mistaken. Was this something to be concerned about, or not?

"Why aren't the kids nervous about being hooked up?" Richard asked.

"We do this type of research with all the residents," Hunter said. "They're used to it."

"That's not very comforting."

"Richard, there's absolutely no risk to them. They're being prepared for the electroencephalography portion of the research. You know, EEG. What we've actually developed here is an ftEEG, for Functional Transference Electroencephalography. Nothing you'll find anywhere else, but it's still quite safe."

"I don't remember approving this for our son."

"All Newman parents give their approval when they sign the enrollment papers. They agree to let their residents participate in research in improving education."

"I remember that part of the contract," Carol said.

"I do, too," Richard said, looking at his wife. "But I never dreamed it was anything like this."

"The only risk is the tiniest bit of skin irritation underneath the electrodes," Hunter said. "Perfectly safe."

The eleven children were arranged in a semi-circle in the lab. The center desk was empty. There was nothing on their desks, nothing on the walls, nothing on the ceiling. The lab was dark enough that it was impossible to see any detail in the children's faces.

"It's such a sterile environment," Richard said.

"This is one of the most advanced classrooms at the Newman Home," Hunter said. "In the world, to be honest. You'll see in a moment."

Several panels on the right rose up, revealing shelves of what looked like large bicycle helmets. The scientists eased the helmets onto the residents' heads, making minor adjustments until they pushed a button on the side that appeared to tighten the apparatus around the head.

"Looks like—" Richard said.

"Still perfectly safe," Hunter said. "These instruments are called afMRI machines, for Advanced Functional Magnetic Resonance Imaging. You know what MRI machines do. Well, these allow us to observe the brain activity of each of the residents."

"How are they different from fMRI machines?" Carol asked.

Hunter smiled. "I'm impressed you know about fMRI. Like fMRI machines, these can detect changes in blood flow in the brain. These machines are much smaller, though, and can detect much more subtle flow changes. They are also compatible with these special electrodes you see connected to the residents. The biggest advance—the one that's most important—is that these babies aren't restricted to detecting blood flow when combined with the ftEEG. Because of the research under Dr. Newman's direction, we can literally watch what happens in their brains in very specific, useful ways as the residents learn. I'll show you."

The scientists left the lab, and Hunter pushed a couple of buttons on the control panel. The lights in the lab dimmed down. Simultaneously, identical holographic images of the solar system emitted from each desk with holographic notebook keyboards beside them. The children began studying the images and making notes in their notebooks by moving their hands in the air, interacting with the keyboards.

"Each resident has a monitor here in the control room," Hunter said. "The monitors allow us to observe what's going on in their brains as they learn, and computers record and evaluate the data."

Each monitor had an image of a resident's brain with different colors appearing and disappearing. White lines, like bolts of lightning, appeared on the brain images. Some would appear and then fade, but many grew brighter and thicker.

"Watch the monitors," Hunter said. "The colors represent blood flow. When we see a specific section of the brain filling with red, for example, that means that that portion of the brain is being stimulated. The resident is tapping into that portion of the brain while learning what we've placed in the hologram."

"Nothing new," Richard said. He found all of this fascinating, but that was the last thing he was going to admit to anyone.

"Basically, nothing new," Hunter said, "though we could argue that the precision and effectiveness are new. But, here's the really new stuff." Hunter pointed to the white lines appearing in the brain images. "These lines represent synapses. We can actually see the neurons forming synapses—we can identify where these are being formed, how strong they are, and how they relate to what the resident is doing."

"You can see the residents making connections!" Carol said.

"Exactly. And with our computer analysis, we can determine what we need to do to help them learn more, and to do so in shorter amounts of time."

"Amazing!"

"Let's shake things up a bit," Hunter said, pushing a button.

The holographic images of the solar system paused, then disappeared, but the notebooks remained. Within a few seconds, new images came up from the desks—three-dimensional shapes of different colors. The residents would stare at the shapes, sometimes point to two or three of them, then enter something in their notebooks. Soon, the notebooks disappeared and the residents started moving their hands in the air, grabbing the shapes and arranging them in new patterns.

"Notice the changes in blood flow and synapses building," Hunter said, pointing to one of the monitors. "After the lab work is done, our scientists will analyze the data, indentify the peaks of learning, and help us tweak the exercises we've developed to strengthen the residents' capacities for learning. All beyond cutting edge."

After a couple of minutes, Hunter pushed a button and the holographic images paused. The lighting in the lab remained dimmed.

"See, Richard," Carol said. "This is what the Newman Home has to offer our son."

"Life as a lab rat?"

Carol rolled her eyes. "We've got to give Christopher every advantage we can."

"Watch this," Hunter said as he pushed another button.

The door to the lab opened and a scientist walked in, followed by a young boy in his safari school uniform. His back was to the mirror. He sat in the center desk and the scientist connected the electrodes and the afMRI machine. Hunter pushed more buttons and the holographic images of shapes resumed. The students went back to manipulating the images. The new student was still, studying the shapes and colors, then quickly moved them in patterns with both hands, almost as if he didn't have to even think.

"Keep your eyes on monitor number six," Hunter said.

It was obvious this student's brain was much more engaged than any of the others'. There was more blood flow in more areas of his brain, and the synapses were forming quickly.

"We've just barely started," Hunter said, pushing another button.

A second holographic image appeared, but only in front of the boy sitting in desk number six. The new image displayed various rocks and minerals to be identified and categorized. The boy used one hand for the shapes and one for the rocks, not slowing down in the slightest. The brain image on his monitor was bursting with color and synapse lightning. It was like fireworks.

"I can tell you from past experience with this resident's results," Hunter said, "the synapses will be greater in both number and strength than any other residents."

"So, what's the point?" Richard asked. "What does this really tell us about the boy?"

"This resident is one of the smartest at the Newman Home, Richard. He *is* the smartest. Not just now, but out of all the students we've ever taught here. And, even more important, he has the greatest potential for developing his brain—learning more than any other resident we've seen, and learning it more quickly."

"I guess that's great, if you believe your child is nothing more than a brain with legs," Richard said. "I'm sure his parents must be very proud."

"That shouldn't be hard to find out," Hunter said. "You're his father. How proud are you?"

CHAPTER TWELVE

"3 0 Miles of Books," the sign said, and Richard felt like he'd walked all of them.

Richard had been in The Strand Bookstore for hours, sitting on the floor, trying to be out of the way as much as possible. He leaned up against the wall with a copy of *David Copperfield*. Stacks of books he'd taken down from the shelves surrounded him, like a wall of sandbags to keep out a flood.

Was Carol right? Was he only thinking of himself when it came to bringing home Christopher for the summer? She was convinced he wasn't thinking of her, but he knew the demons she fought from her childhood, her sense of never having been in a real family, her confusion over her parents always looking for a way to not be with her. She always insisted the way she was raised worked best for her, but the look in her eyes as she spoke told him otherwise.

For him, wanting to have their son home for the summer was all about Christopher. What made the sabbatical decision all the more difficult was that, for her, it was all about Christopher as well. Their experience at the lab in Newman was palpable proof of what she'd been saying for years about that school and their son. That place would give him the life he deserved. It would help him reach his potential—no, it would give him the potential he was capable of, then help him surpass it. To take him away from that environment, even for three months, would be to take him away from his future. How would he ever catch up to where he could have been?

They'd argued, of course, but the fight ended with Carol's promising him that she would sign the papers for the sabbatical if he could tell her to her face that it was the best thing for their son. Not the best thing for Richard, she'd emphasized, but for their son.

Richard's cell phone beeped, letting him know he'd received an e-mail from his father. He'd called him after the lab performance and spoken with him for over an hour. His father had a way of helping him not only figure out what would be the best thing to do, but also see things he'd never seen before, understand things he'd only felt.

Richard had e-mailed his father a copy of Christopher's brain scan image, full of color and bright white lines like a snapshot of some festival. When he'd sent it to his father, he'd titled it, "What it looks like to be brilliant."

He tapped the e-mail and saw a different image: one of Christopher sitting on his lap, before they'd enrolled him into the school. The little boy had his entire hand wrapped around his daddy's finger, smiling. Underneath the picture was the title his father had given it: "What it looks like to be loved."

Richard knew what he had to do.

CHAPTER
THIRTEEN

C arol and Richard sat in the top row of the darkened auditorium. Along with fifty other couples, they listened to Ms. Garrett explain each slide on the screen. Richard kept tapping his foot, wishing the presentation would all be over so they could see Christopher. The superintendent had agreed to let Christopher take the sabbatical, but insisted that Richard and Carol participate in the prospective parent orientation again.

"Forcing us to sit through this propaganda blitz isn't going to change our minds."

"Be patient. And remember, when we finally do get to meet with him—"

"You do all the talking."

"Right."

Richard leaned back away from his wife. He felt sorry for the parents—they'd probably visited the finest private schools in the city, or at least read their literature, and their children weren't even born yet. They'd most likely already chosen a college.

Slide of a typical brownstone.

"The Newman Academy was founded almost 40 years ago as one of the finest private boarding schools in New York City,"

Ms. Garrett said. "From its very first year, the waiting list was long. Dr. Newman implemented the most advanced educational techniques of the time, relying on cutting-edge technology, like computer-modified learning models, while teachers in public schools were still cleaning their chalkboard erasers."

Slide of toddlers in navy blue uniforms.

"After several years of remarkable success, including the addition of four new academies in New York state, Dr. Newman asked, If these techniques work for older children, then why not younger? That simple, yet profound, question inspired the birth of the Newman Home."

Slide of "The Newman Home" etched over the entrance of the building.

"Children could now be enrolled at six months. Finally, children would be raised by experts, and parents could rest easy at night, knowing their children were being given the best care possible. As the residents got older, their cognitive abilities—from grasping abstract concepts to calculating complex mathematical problems to interpreting textual significance—improved dramatically under our program. Who knew even toddlers could perform so well on the most advanced standardized tests? Dr. Newman knew!"

Applause. Extended applause, in fact.

These were the parents who had made it to the short list for enrollment into Newman. Maybe ten of these couples would actually get to enroll a child at Newman, but all the couples in the auditorium most likely considered themselves extremely fortunate to have gotten this far.

A rapid arranging of several slides into a collage of a number of buildings that looked almost identical to the one the parents were sitting in, each with "Newman Home" etched over its doors.

"Today," Ms. Garrett said, "the Newman Home System boasts twenty homes throughout the northeast. Each home provides the finest empirically-proven, child-centered education for children from infancy through high school. Our master teachers are certified in the most advanced techniques used by the National Educational Certification Board, the governing body of all education in the United States. Regular independent testing of our residents has proven they have superior cognitive development and extraordinary expertise in the areas that matter most: math and sciences."

Slide of a male student, wearing a Yale sweatshirt, looking into a microscope in a lab full of other college students. Slide of two young women wearing their crimson graduation robes in front of the statue of John Harvard. Slide of a man and a woman, dressed in crisp, blue business suits, standing in front of the New York Stock Exchange.

"Without exception, Newman Home graduates succeeded at the most prestigious universities in the world. They have progressed to the finest graduate schools, and are now internationally-recognized leaders in the worlds of business, law, and politics."

Slide of a man in a dark blue suit, holding a leather briefcase, standing outside the entrance to an office building.

"David Anderson, head of The Anderson Group, one of the leading accounting firms in the country."

Slide of another man, looking similar to David Anderson, standing on the steps of the United States Capitol.

"Andrew Stockman, United States Senator."

Slide of a woman, in judicial robes, sitting at a desk.

"Ann Stanton, United States Supreme Court Justice."

The parents applauded, so proud of all that their children were about to gain in facts and dates and formulas and skills. But why didn't they see what they were about to lose? The chance to rock their daughter to sleep when she became scared because of the thunder...lying on the floor beside a crib that held a restless boy who couldn't get to sleep...opening the world of *Winnie-the-Pooh* to a new generation of explorers in the Hundred Acre Wood. Richard looked down at his hands. These were memories of his youth, not of Christopher's. Christopher had always been too independent during his visits to need such attention. Or, at least, to show that he needed it.

Slide of the building in which the parents were meeting, featuring faculty, administration, and the students, all in safari uniforms. Some students held baby residents in their arms.

"Parents used to say it was too bad children didn't come with an instruction manual," Ms. Garret said. "Well, now they do. The Newman Home faculty and staff know the instruction manual by heart for one simple, yet profound reason: we wrote it!"

"Everything in this place is simple, yet profound," Richard whispered to Carol. She gave him the look.

"As you know," Ms. Garrett said, "Dr. Newman has been working with the President, Congress, and corporate leaders to receive the required governmental approvals and financial backing to expand the Newman Home system throughout the country. If all goes as planned, we will begin to even further expand our educational system by the end of the year. It won't be long before you find a Newman Home in every state!"

"Making millions more off children," Richard said to Carol while the parents applauded.

"You can't put a price tag on an excellent education," Carol said.

"Why do they even do this orientation? They don't need to sell Newman. These parents have been begging to get their kids in here."

"And if they didn't invite them, you'd complain about a lack of transparency. They're giving the parents a chance to tour the home."

"Then why don't they let us see all of it?"

"See what I mean? There's nothing they can do to please you."

Slide of a sweet, little girl and a handsome boy in Newman uniforms sitting on a bench, looking at their computer tablets.

"Let's be honest for a moment," Ms. Garrett said.

"It's about time," Richard whispered.

"The Newman Home is not for everyone. Many parents are nostalgic about pampering and smothering their children because it makes them feel indispensible. But Newman parents put their children first. They want their children raised by experts. They want the best teachers, the best classrooms, the best curriculum, the best classmates for their children. The best parents understand that Newman residents grow up to be the best adults."

The audience stood, applauding as though their children's futures depended upon their enthusiasm. Ms. Garrett spoke a command to the lectern, and the screen raised to reveal a one-way mirror, almost the entire height and length of the wall. On the other side of the mirror was the classroom with the plush green carpet and rain forest wallpaper from the video of the teacher with the hand puppets. Ten children sat at their desks, watching their teacher as she wrote an equation on the white board at the front of the room. There was a number of other equations already on the board.

"The quality of our instruction is unsurpassed," Ms. Garrett said. "Here, Dr. Martinez, one of our science teachers, is explaining how scientists considered the Higgs particle to be definitive until the collider experiments recently proved the Higgs field more complicated than it needed to be. How many of you understood the latest theories of physics when you were nine?"

Polite laughter made its way through the audience.

"Here at Newman, we stress learning through competition. The latest research is conclusive: competition motivates learning.

As we like to say, 'Without competition, you're left with a monopoly of ignorance.' At the end of each trimester, we administer standardized examinations which certify what the residents have mastered. These examinations go beyond what any other school uses anywhere in the world. They drill deeper into the students' knowledge and their ability to extrapolate from that knowledge. Other school systems have taken a look at our examinations and concluded they are advanced in their ability to examine what the students know—and that they are too difficult for the schools to use with their students."

Slide of words covering the screen, "The Newman Home: Developing Minds for the Future."

There was applause throughout the auditorium, coupled with pleased laughter among the parents. They had made the right decision.

A freckled boy with bright red hair sat in the back of the classroom, staring straight into the one-way mirror, licking his fingers and trying to plaster a cowlick down in the back. The teacher was consumed with writing on the white board, and the other children had their backs to him.

A small wave of suppressed giggling made its way across the audience. Rather than laughing, though, Richard studied Ms. Garrett for her reaction.

Ms. Garrett faced the parents, trying not to move her lips as she gave a command to the lectern. Just as the curtain began to close, the teacher turned and saw the boy, still struggling with his hair. She glanced at the mirror, then back at the boy. The teacher spoke, and the boy jumped and turned straight ahead. None of the other children looked back at the boy, and the curtain closed.

The lights in the auditorium gradually came up.

"Now, if you will please follow me," Ms. Garrett said as she straightened her safari shirt and led the way to the exit.

"Aren't you glad you're not his father?" Carol said, standing up. "How embarrassing."

"I guess."

"Come on, let's meet with the superintendent."

Richard didn't move.

"Don't you want to meet with him?" Carol asked. "What's wrong?"

"Nothing. It's just strange, that's all."

"What?"

"Well, why didn't any of the other children look back at the red-haired boy when the teacher said something? Wouldn't that have been the normal reaction?"

"I don't think—"

"It didn't look like the teacher yelled. What could she have said that scared him so much?"

"It's called 'life,' Richard," Carol said. She headed toward the exit where a Newman host was waiting to take them to the super-intendent's office. "Don't make a big deal out of it, okay?"

Carol left the auditorium with the host. Richard stood up and walked down the steps to the stage. He looked back, but he was alone. After he climbed up onto the stage, he parted the curtain with his hand but couldn't see anything through the one-way mirror. Then he put his ear up against the cold wall, thinking he heard something. He wasn't sure, the sound was too muffled, but it sounded like a child crying.

CHAPTER FOURTEEN

Hunter opened the door to the superintendent's office, but only slightly.

"Are you two sure about this?" he whispered to Richard and Carol. "It's not too late to keep Christopher with us."

Carol was about to reply, but Richard pushed the door open so the superintendent could see them. He didn't want to give Carol a chance to back out. Hunter introduced them to the superintendent, and everyone sat down.

"What did you think of the orientation?" Hunter asked.

Carol spoke quickly. "It was nice to go through it again. It looks like you almost have the funding you need to expand."

"We're getting closer," Hunter said. "Have most of the key players on board."

No one said anything. Richard looked at his watch, his eyes following the second hand.

"We appreciate your taking the time to meet with us," Carol said to the superintendent. "I'm sure you're no less busy than Dr. Newman."

The superintendent smiled and scooted his chair back to cross his legs. "He and I work very closely together. He used to introduce himself as the mad scientist, and me as the man who made the experiment a reality."

"No one asked me if my son could be the subject of an experiment," Richard said.

"Pardon me?" the superintendent said.

"You have a lot to be proud of," Carol said. "And the Newman Home *is* an experiment, in the sense that it's something that's never been done before."

"Exactly."

"In fact," Hunter said, "I think it's fair to say it's no longer an experiment. We've arrived at irrefutable scientific conclusions. I wanted to show you both something." He pointed to a wall. "Brain scan." A large image of a human brain appeared. "More than any other—"

"Superintendent," Richard said, "what's the next step to taking our son out for the sabbatical? I'm sure he's waiting for us."

"Actually," the superintendent said, "I'm not entirely enthusiastic about this sabbatical."

"No one around here seems to be," Richard said.

"That policy is a relic from the early days when parents weren't accustomed to having their young children enroll in school full-time," the superintendent said. "We quickly found that even regular visits home made it more difficult for the residents to progress cognitively, but we were not as quick to rewrite the policy. No one has ever requested a sabbatical before, so we simply didn't think there was an urgency to correct the policy."

"I find it difficult to believe no one has ever requested one before."

"Three months is a long time for a resident to be out." The superintendent picked up his ruler. "I don't know if he will be able to keep up with his peers once he returns. Emotionally and

academically. Our first concern must be the welfare of the resident, not the whims of a parent."

"That's what I was trying to tell you a minute ago with this
brain scan," Hunter said, pointing to the image on the wall. "When
a resident is away from the stimuli we offer here, even for a short
period of time, there's a decrease—"

"Look, maybe you don't understand what's going on here,"
Richard said to the superintendent, ignoring Hunter. "Our decision has been made. Christopher—'the resident'—is going to
reside with us for a while. We aren't going to torture him into
forgetting everything he's learned. In fact, we may even teach him
something. He's taking the sabbatical."

"Of course, Mr. Carson," the superintendent said. "I'm mere-
ly concerned that you're dragging the resident into your fantasy
world of playing and story writing."

"Just give us the papers. It's time to get our son home where
he belongs."

"I'm sorry, Superintendent," Carol said. "Perhaps it would be
best for us to simply sign the sabbatical papers and be on our way.
We've already read the papers and are familiar with their content.
I'm afraid when my husband is this determined, there's not much
left to say."

The superintendent pulled the papers out of the drawer. "Just
to be certain, you both realize that while it takes both signatures
to receive the resident for the sabbatical, only one signature is required to return him before the sabbatical is over. This is in keeping with the original contract when you enrolled your resident."

Richard and Carol reviewed the papers and signed them. She
thanked the superintendent, shaking his hand, then turned to
Hunter, who seemed to shake her hand a little too long and nod,
just a little.

After they left the office, Richard could hear the muted sounds of Hunter and the superintendent talking after the door closed. The superintendent's secretary looked up from her desk and the host, sitting on a sofa nearby, stood up.

"Thanks for letting me do all the talking," Carol said out of the corner of her mouth.

"Anytime."

The host led them through the halls until they got to the oak door. Richard and Carol walked into the lobby where he paced while she sat on the couch to wait. Every few minutes he would complain about it taking too long and she would remind him it hadn't been that long. Finally, the oak door opened and Christopher stepped through. Alone.

Instead of his uniform, he wore blue jeans and a brown corduroy shirt Richard had bought him during his last visit in the winter. They still looked new, though small for him now. "Newman Home" was embroidered on his safari backpack.

Christopher looked at his shoes, not moving. He didn't look up at his parents, and his left hand, dropped to his side, shook.

Richard kneeled down next to him so their faces could be close. "Hi, Christopher. How are you doing?"

"Hello, Richard," Christopher almost whispered, still without looking. "Hello, Carol."

"Hello, Christopher," Carol said. "Are you okay?"

"Have I done something wrong?" Christopher asked.

"No, Christopher," Richard said. "Why do you say that?"

"Why am I going to your apartment before the break?"

"You haven't done anything wrong. We just want you to be home with us. Right, Carol?"

Carol was looking away, trying to keep her composure. She took a deep breath.

"It'll just be for a little while," she said. "You'll get to come back before you know it."

"Good. I can't fall behind in my studies."

"Don't worry about your studies for a while, okay?" Richard said, standing up. "Let's just go home."

Richard held out his hand for his son, but the little boy never reached up to hold it.

CHAPTER FIFTEEN

hristopher just stared at the floor as Richard locked the front door to their apartment. On the subway ride home, he had tried to have a conversation, but Carol was in no mood and Christopher would only nod at anything said to him. Carol took the bags of takeout to the kitchen while the other two went to the bedroom down the hall.

"I think you'll really like your room, Christopher. I got it all ready for you."

"Thank you, Richard."

Richard opened the door and turned on the light. The boxes and stacks were gone, and the small room almost looked large with just the bed and dresser. There was still nothing on the walls; the Brooklyn Bridge photograph on the dresser of the three of them was the only thing in the room that made it look like something more than a room in a boarding house.

"How do you like it? There's a lot more room with the boxes cleared out, isn't there?"

"Richard, how long will this visit be?"

"What do you mean?"

"I need to make my plans," Christopher said. "And to make my plans, I need to know how long this visit will be."

"Didn't they talk to you about what was going on?" Richard asked.

"No. One of the hosts got me out of class this morning and took me to my personal area. He made me change into these clothes, took away my safari uniform, and then took me to you. No one told me anything. I'll get my uniform back, won't I?"

Richard sat down on the bed and pulled his son closer to him. "You're taking the summer sabbatical. That means you will be home with us for three months. This month, next month, and August."

Christopher's eyes opened wide. "Then what?"

"Then you'll go back home," Carol said, standing in the doorway. "And, if you want to go back sooner, just let us know."

Richard stared through her. He couldn't name what he felt, he was afraid to, but it was like when he'd first met his future mother-in-law and sensed that he was being condemned by a one-woman jury. Or on the first day—no, the first entire month—of law school. It wasn't hatred, or fear, or even anger, though they were all part of what he felt.

"I'd like to go back home now," Christopher whispered.

Richard looked up at Carol. She wouldn't look at him, and she wouldn't look at their son. Then it came to him: betrayal. When he'd met his future mother-in-law and when he'd started law school he'd felt Carol was betraying him. And now the feeling had returned.

"You'll go back," Richard said, "if that's what's best. Right now, you're visiting us. You can at least stay a week, like you do at Christmas. Then we can talk about Newman if you want. For now," Richard said, standing up, "you need to get unpacked."

Richard unzipped the safari backpack and took everything out: a pair of underwear, two pairs of socks, and a pad of paper with a pen. Christopher grabbed the paper and pen and sat back on his bed. Richard put the clothes in the drawer and opened the closet. The boxes and files and magazines were stacked so high and tight they left no room for even the small bag. He'd have to move all the stuff to the basement tomorrow.

He placed the bag under the bed instead. His son held the framed picture of the three of them as though studying a relic discovered at some ancient burial site.

"Do you need anything before we get dinner ready?" Richard asked.

Christopher kept looking at the picture. "How am I supposed to keep up with the other residents if I'm gone so long? I won't know anything when I get back home."

Carol shook her head and left. Richard knelt down next to his son.

"It's going to be all right," Richard said. "You'll remember everything. And you'll learn a lot with us. You'll see."

Without looking up, Christopher motioned with his finger for Richard to come closer. "Do you promise?" Christopher whispered.

Richard had put the takeout in serving bowls to make dinner look more special. Each of them picked at the orange chicken and rice like scientists in a lab. Once in a while, someone actually took a bite.

"How do you like your dinner?" Richard asked.

"Thank you for preparing it."

"I wasn't sure you liked Chinese food, but you didn't seem to know what you wanted when I asked."

"They never ask us what we want to eat at home," Christopher said. "We just eat what they give us."

"I imagine this is better than what you had to eat at the school, isn't it?"

"The school?"

"Yes, Newman."

"No," Christopher said, "the food back home is actually very good."

"Oh." Richard took a drink and went back to rearranging his food on the plate. "So, they have pretty good food at the school?

"Yes."

Richard smiled, but then quit when he couldn't figure out what to say next. Chinese? he thought. What a stupid choice to get for a little boy. Hamburgers, tacos—anything would've been better. He looked up at his son, but he didn't look back. Then he looked at his wife, but she was looking down as well. She hadn't said a word when they were setting the table.

After dinner, Christopher went to the room while Richard and Carol cleaned up. When they were done, they found him sitting on the bed. He wasn't looking at the picture or reading or getting undressed. Just sitting.

"What are you doing?" Richard asked.

"Thinking."

"Oh." Richard looked at his wife, but she kept her eyes on their son. "Well, I guess it's time for you to go to sleep," he said. "It is, isn't it? I don't want to make you go to bed too early."

"No, it's time for me to go to sleep."

Richard could feel the time pouring over him in some sort of molasses way. "It's good to have you here," he said, trying to leave the room. "Good night. Let us know if you need anything."

"Thank you."

"Good night," Carol finally spoke.

"Good night, Carol."

"Sleep tight," Richard said as he was closing the door.

"What do you mean?"

"What?"

"What does 'sleep tight' mean?"

"I don't know. It's just something my folks used to say to me every night. Haven't I said it to you during your visits?"

"No."

"I'm sure I have."

"No. If you had, I would've asked you about it before. What does it mean?"

"It means to enjoy your sleep," Richard said as he closed the door, hoping to escape any other explanation.

"Thank you. I'll do my best."

After he closed the door, Richard turned to speak to his wife, but she was already at her office door down the hall. He walked towards her.

"It's always a little awkward the first night," Richard said. "It'll get better soon."

"No, this is different. Before, he knew he'd be back home soon. He doesn't know what's happening this time. He's scared."

"You're making too big a deal—"

"I've got some catching up to do," she said as she closed her door.

"So do I," Richard said.

He walked back to Christopher's door, putting his ear up to it. He thought he could hear crying and put his hand to the door-knob, but the sound stopped.

"Christopher, are you okay?" Richard asked.

"Richard, I'm asleep."

CHAPTER SIXTEEN

"I'll be home late tonight," Carol said from the front door. "Don't wait up."

Richard sat back down at the kitchen table. Christopher stood next to the stove like he was guarding it from thieves, his left hand twitching. Richard wanted to run over to his son and hug him and talk to him and listen to him. He wanted to grab that hand and hold it so tight it couldn't twitch, or so tight the twitch would leave his son's body and enter his. But he didn't want to do the wrong thing, so he just stayed in his chair.

"Christopher."

The boy didn't move.

"Christopher. It was an accident. You didn't mean to spill the milk on her."

Christopher turned, his eyes so blank, so empty—it was like the boy wasn't even in the room. Worse, it was like he wasn't anywhere else, either. He was nowhere.

"Christopher, let's finish breakfast."

"No, thank you. I'm not hungry."

"You didn't eat much for dinner last night."

"I apologize for not eating enough—"

"No, don't say that. I was just saying you must be hungry."

"I'm sorry for saying 'I apologize'."

Christopher walked out of the kitchen and into the living room. Richard stood in the kitchen, rubbing his forehead, trying to come up with something, anything. His father always made being a father look so easy, so natural, but he couldn't make it through the first morning without everyone being upset.

He found Christopher on the couch and offered to turn on the television for him, but his son wasn't interested. Richard looked around the room as if there might be some cue card that would tell him what to say. Writing dialogue was hard enough; saying it at times like these was impossible.

"Richard?"

"Yes?"

"I slept tight."

"What?"

Christopher looked up at his father. "I slept tight. Just like you told me to."

"'Sleep tight' isn't an order." Christopher looked away again. Richard knelt down near his son. "But I'm glad you slept tight. It's good to have you home with us."

Christopher looked at Richard out of the corner of his eye like he wasn't sure he believed his father.

"Well," Richard said, "one thing I've been wanting to do is call Grandma and Grandpa and let them talk to you. They were excited when I told them you'd be home for the summer, and they'd kill me if we didn't call."

Christopher looked shocked.

"No, I mean they'd be disappointed."

Richard picked up the phone. The phone rang only once when Richard's mother picked it up.

"This had better be Richard Carson, or I'm throwing this phone in the fireplace," she said.

"You don't have a fire going in June, do you?" Richard asked.

"I don't need a fire, your father and I have been burning up wondering if you'd remember to call us. Now, let me talk to that grandson of mine."

"Hey, I just barely got on the line, don't—"

"I can talk to you forever, but I've only got the summer with that little boy. Put him on!"

There was quite a bit of his Texan grandmother in his mother, especially when she wanted to make it clear things weren't going the way she'd wanted them to.

He looked at his son and pointed to the phone. "You're on speaker now."

"What am I supposed to do?" Christopher asked.

"Just talk to her. Be yourself."

Christopher moved closer to the phone. "Hello, Mrs. Carson."

"Who am I talking to, the bank? You call me Grandma, okay?"

"Yes."

"How are you doing, Christopher? Grandpa and I have missed you an awful lot. Have you been getting our letters?"

"No."

There was a pause. "Well, we've been writing you, and can hardly wait to see you. Remember when we came down to New York on one of your visits? We went to that place near the water, sort of like a shopping mall, and Grandpa took the picture of you and your mommy and daddy in front of the Brooklyn Bridge? Do you remember, honey?"

"No. But I believe that photograph is in the room I'm staying in."

"Honey, Grandpa wants to talk to you. Just a minute. Bye, bye. I love you."

"Good-bye."

"Hey, little buddy," Grandpa almost sang into the phone. "How's my favorite grandson?"

"I don't know."

"That's you, Christopher. You're my favorite grandson."

"Do you have other grandchildren?"

"No, but that doesn't mean you had to be my favorite. You're my favorite because I like you."

"Oh. I'm fine. How are you?"

"Doing a lot better than I was a few minutes ago, I tell you. Is it good to be home?"

"Here?"

"Well, yes. With your mom and dad."

Christopher didn't answer.

"Are you going to be coming up to see us? You've never been up here before, but this time you've got a longer break."

"Where do you live?"

"Vermont. The most beautiful state in the country. You'd love it. You can run around all day and never see the same tree twice."

Christopher looked up at Richard. "Are we going to Vermont today?"

"No."

"No, we won't be visiting you," Christopher said to his grandfather.

"What!"

"Hi, Dad. Christopher just asked if we were visiting *today*."

"Then you will?"

"Well, I don't know yet. A lot of it depends on Carol."

"Don't wait too long, son. Time slips by pretty quickly without saying a word. What are you and your son going to do today?"

"I don't know. We're trying to figure that out."

"Good grief, Richard, the boy probably doesn't have a toy to his name. Go to the store."

"He does need some new clothes."

"I said toys, not clothes. But if he needs those, get them, too. Get out there and spend some time together. Grow some memories."

"You're right, Dad."

"Let's talk again real soon. Take care of yourself. And take care of that grandson of mine."

"Will do."

"And talk to Carol about when you can come up to visit."

Richard hung up the phone. Christopher just sat on the couch like he was waiting for someone to tell him what to do.

"They really think a lot of you, Christopher. They're anxious to see you."

"Does Carol have parents?"

"Yes. Yes, she does."

"Have I met them?"

"You've seen her mother a few times, but not many."

"I don't remember."

"I didn't think you would." Richard looked around the room again, trying to think of what to do. "You know, this is ridiculous, you can't wear the same winter shirt and pants all summer."

"Why?"

"I think it's against the rules."

The little boy looked directly at his father, scared.

"Not really against the rules," Richard said, "just hot. It'd just be real hot. You need something more comfortable. What kind of clothes would you like?"

"Should I wear clothes like yours?"

"If you want to." Richard looked down at his Yankees T-shirt and faded jeans. "These are my writing clothes. And my reading clothes. And my watching TV clothes. In fact, I can do just about anything I want in these."

"They are very," Christopher paused, "versatile."

Richard nodded. "I guess so. After years of getting up almost every morning and binding myself with suits and hanging myself with ties, I figure I can wear what I want now. And you can, too. You don't have to dress like someone on safari anymore."

"I like my safari uniform."

"That's nice, but you get to be yourself now. You're not some big game hunter in Africa. You get to be a little boy.

"But I like being a Newman resident."

CHAPTER
SEVENTEEN

The air was calm and humid. Richard and Christopher walked along the outside wall of Macy's. He wanted to hold his son's hand, but he wasn't sure if Christopher was too old for that. As they neared the revolving doors, Richard stopped his son to look at one of the display windows.

"Macy's has the absolute best windows in the world. Remember last Christmas when we came down and saw Santa's workshop?"

"No." Christopher stared at the display: three female mannequins wearing knit tops and cotton shorts, supposedly heading for the beach for an afternoon of fun. "No, I'm sorry, but I don't remember. Was it this exact window?"

He didn't remember all those elves hammering and sawing and putting toys together? And the little train that chugged around a big Christmas tree in the corner or the Mrs. Claus that was bringing out some freshly baked cookies for Santa and all his helpers? How could he not remember when it was just a few months ago?

"It's no big deal. Let's just go in."

Christopher hesitated at the revolving door, his body swaying as he tried to get in rhythm. He finally stepped in, but he didn't quite keep up and was pushed along in the door until he got to the other side. Richard caught up with him in a few seconds, and they made their way through the crowded store.

Once they got to the boys' department upstairs, Richard realized he had no idea how much to buy. He wished he'd asked his mother or father for suggestions; Carol wouldn't have had any idea. After trying to figure out how frequently he'd wash and what Christopher could wear between washings, he finally decided on four pairs of pants, seven shirts, sneakers, and a handful or two of socks and underwear. If he was wrong, they could always come back.

Christopher asked why he couldn't just get all jeans and T-shirts, but his father pointed out that even he had slacks and nicer shirts in his closet. As they looked through some shirts on hangers, Richard noticed a man who'd been looking through the shelves of shirts for several minutes. Hoping for some help, he wondered if the man could possibly be the clerk when a thin twenty-something man who looked like a model came up and offered his help. The clerk helped them pick out a few shirts and a couple of pairs of pants, then Richard and his son went to the dressing room. When they came back out, the clerk had another handful of clothes for the boy to try on.

After a few more trips to the dressing room, Richard waved his credit card over the scanner, trying his best to avoid seeing the total. Carol had already made it clear they'd have to watch costs now that they didn't have his salary. As the clerk folded the clothes one by one, placing them in the shopping bags, Christopher kept looking all around as though they were in some sort of fascinating museum of life. Of course, he'd taken Christopher to stores before on his break, but his son seemed to be looking through different eyes this time.

"There's a T.G.I.S. sale over in the toy department today," the clerk said, handing Richard the bags. "Some good buys."

"T.G.I.S.?" Richard asked.

"Thank Goodness It's Summer. Of course, parents always say the opposite about summer, don't they? That's why they invented summer camp." The clerk winked.

Richard took the two large bags from the clerk, and he and Christopher headed for the escalators.

"What's summer camp?" Christopher asked.

"During the summer, some parents send their kids to camps out near some lake or something."

"Do you want to send me to camp?"

"No," Richard said, "absolutely not." For the first time since bringing him home, he saw the beginnings of a smile on his son's face. "But I would like to check out that toy sale. What do you say?"

Richard let his son lead the way, interested to see what toys might appeal to him. They'd never bought him any toys for Christmas or birthdays, since he couldn't take them back to Newman. Christopher walked past the dolls and the baby toys, which wasn't too surprising, but he also didn't spend any time at the cars or the guns or the action figures. The boy went through the entire department without even stopping.

"Are you all done?" Richard asked.

"Yes. I saw everything."

"Don't you want to get anything?"

Christopher shook his head. "I don't know what most of those things are."

"Here, let's look together, a little more slowly this time."

Richard took him over to the action figures. After all these years, there were still the classics: Batman, G.I. Joe, Harry Potter. Plus, there was a good supply Richard didn't recognize, like some boy who looked like he was armed for the mother of all battles and several aliens that must have been from the same movie.

Christopher picked up a couple and looked at them closely, less like a little boy and more like an archaeologist with a piece of pottery, and Richard noticed out of the corner of his eye the same man he'd seen in the clothing department. The man pretended to look at toys, but so awkwardly Richard knew it was all pretense.

"What are you supposed to do with these?" Christopher asked, pointing to some G.I. Joes.

"Well, you kind of...you take one, and then you get the other... you sort of crash them together a lot. Like they're fighting. You make up things about them and play with them."

"Oh."

"Let's take a look at the cars. Maybe you'll like those."

They walked over to another aisle, Richard keeping an eye on the man. He wore a dark blue suit, so Richard figured he wasn't from the school. But you could never be sure; Level Two Security was hard to spot. Anyway, why would the school send someone to spy on them? Spy? Talk about being on edge.

"Now what do we do?"

"Well, you have your classics. Matchbox cars are more like little replicas of actual cars. And you have Hot Wheels—they're sporty cars. Then you've got these HoverMods that don't even have wheels because they can float on bursts of air."

He picked up a HoverMod and showed his son how it could hang about an inch in the air and move forward. As Christopher was fascinated by the car, Richard looked up again and caught the man staring straight at Christopher. The man turned around and walked to another aisle.

"Here are some games. Why don't you take a look at them for a minute?"

"Where are you going?"

"I just need to ask that man something. I won't go far." Richard left the bags of clothes near Christopher and walked around the corner. The man was pretending to be looking at some dolls when Richard grabbed him by the shoulder, turning him around.

"Hey, what are you doing?" the man said.

"What's going on here? You've been following us ever since we got here."

"I was hoping you'd recognize me."

Richard inspected the man's face. It was round in a familiar way, and the man was going bald. He was a little paunchy, like he spent too much time behind a desk.

"You're the man at the school. The guy using my crate."

The man relaxed a little and tried to smile. "That's right."

"What do you want? Why are you following us?"

"I just wanted to talk with you, but I wasn't sure how you'd react."

"Talk about what?"

"Your son, Christopher."

Richard stepped back, his jaw tightening. "How do you know his name? What do you want?"

"I want to know how you got him out. I've been trying for months. Just for the sabbatical, that's all I wanted, the sabbatical." The man's eyes were moist now. "How did you do it?"

"My wife and I just filled out the papers."

"We've done that, three times. But something always happens, and the sabbatical doesn't come through. Here," the man reached into his coat pocket and pulled out a business card. He scribbled something on the back. "Tonight, at twelve o'clock, a support group is meeting at this apartment. Come and talk to all of us."

"Support group? Why midnight?"

"They're dangerous, Mr. Carson. You can't meet in the middle of the day and talk about them."

"Who?"

Perspiration dripped down the man's face as he looked around. "Look, we've talked too long. I've got to go."

"What's this all about?"

"Please come tonight. And don't tell anyone about the meeting. Not your son, not your wife, not anyone."

The man turned away from Richard and headed for the stairs. He looked back once, then hurried out of sight. Richard looked after him, long after he was gone, then read the card. Harold Solomon. Accountant. Why was this accountant holding secret midnight meetings? Richard didn't know what to do. Part of him just wanted to forget about the man, but another part wanted to run over, grab Christopher and go back to the apartment and stay there.

He turned the card over. Handwritten in black ink were another address and phone number and the words, "Richard, let us help."

CHAPTER EIGHTEEN

Christopher picked out Scrabble at the store, one of the old versions, with wooden tiles and a board—the same kind Richard had played with as a boy. They spent an hour after dinner playing. After Christopher went to bed, Richard had tried to get some writing done. But two and a half hours, and nothing. Not a chapter, not a page, not a paragraph. He'd always hoped having his son home would give him peace, ease the turmoil that stopped him from finding the words. But his thoughts were more bound inside tonight than ever before.

"Who's Harold Solomon?"

Richard jumped out of his chair. Carol had opened the front door and come into the office without his hearing a sound.

"Don't do that!"

"Somebody's got something to hide."

Richard opened his mouth to defend himself, but she smiled. He put his arms around her waist and pulled her close, kissing her. Life was good again.

"Welcome home, Counselor."

"I move we call it a day and get to bed," she said.

"No objection."

She left the room and he stayed in the office for a moment, listening to her footsteps going down the hall. The scent of her perfume was still in the air. He closed his eyes and breathed deeply. He could never remember the name of the perfume, but it always excited him, making him want to hold her.

He glanced down at his notebook and the only words he'd written, large and bold: Harold Solomon. He'd almost forgotten about his strange stalker-accountant. He scratched out Harold's name, then followed the perfume trail to their bedroom, where he found Carol putting on her nightgown.

"How was your day?" he asked.

"I've got too many cases. We need to hire some more attorneys." She walked into the bathroom. "But as long as they can get everyone to work ridiculous hours, they'll never hire enough to get us to normal workweeks. Remember when 80 hours a week was considered normal?"

"Christopher and I had a good day today."

His wife pause before she turned on the water to wash her face.

"I think this is going to be an excellent summer," he said.

"It's just the first day," she said. "Let's see how things go."

"What's that supposed to mean?"

"Nothing, Richard, just let's take things one day at a time."

As she dried her face, an emptiness came over him, pushing out any feeling of hope that she would give this sabbatical a chance. What was she thinking? What was she planning?

"You won't believe this," he said as they walked back into the bedroom, "but your mother called."

"Oh, I forgot. She left a message on my cell."

"She said she'd be in the city tomorrow and wanted to eat lunch with you."

"I'll call her in the morning and set something up," Carol said.

"I went ahead and invited her to dinner tomorrow night. We'll eat early so she can make it back to New Jersey before it gets too dark."

Carol stopped. Richard had seen that expression before, watching her perform in the courtroom. And he'd felt sorry for the witness.

"You did what?"

"Don't worry, I'll get takeout. Nothing fancy. I think she was just surprised to be invited."

"I'll cancel."

"What do you mean? I've already invited her."

"You know I don't like her coming here," Carol said. "I feel like I'm having a judge over to my own home."

"I thought it'd be good for her to see her only grandchild. I don't know how long it's been since she's seen him."

"Did you tell her he's here now?"

"No, I thought it'd be a nice surprise."

Carol marched back into the bathroom, closing the door after her. Richard heard water running in the sink.

"Don't you want your mother to know Christopher is here?"

No answer.

"Are you just planning to keep him a secret all summer?"

Still no answer.

"Answer me, Carol, what's going on here?"

CHAPTER
NINETEEN

O ff in the distance a police siren pierced the night air. It felt much later than it actually was. Richard stood on the corner, looking up at his living room window, then back down at the front door of his apartment building. The light was still on in the living room, and the only person who'd left the building was the lanky man in 610 who'd come out ten minutes earlier. At first Richard stuck around to make sure Carol didn't leave Christopher alone in the apartment, but deep down he knew she wouldn't do that. After their fight he'd told her he was leaving to get some air. She'd nodded and turned off the light by the bed. This was the first time she'd been alone with Christopher since they'd sent him away to school.

"What are you doing here?"

Startled, Richard turned and bumped into a short, round neighborhood security guard, clinching his club. He'd seen the man, walking the neighborhood around East 63rd, fingering his club and occasionally saying something into the band around his wrist, but they'd never spoken to each other before.

"I'm with Bulldog Security. You are required to respond to me."

"I live here."

"On this corner? At midnight? Don't think so."

"No, really. I live in that building over there." He pulled out his wallet and showed the guard his ID. "I'm just heading out."

"Better get heading then."

The guard just stood there, sticking out his chest like he was expecting a fight. Richard wondered if he should go back home, but he turned around and headed down the street. After a while he made it to Park Avenue and turned to look behind him. The guard was long gone.

Richard passed the Christian Science Church on the corner. Didn't he have an aunt who was a Christian Scientist? Or a great aunt? Yes, Aunt Ellen, a smiling woman who would always remind him to look on the bright side. "No matter what you look for," she'd tell him, "you find it. So look for the good."

As Richard turned south on Park Avenue, he pulled Harold Solomon's business card out of his jeans pockets. "Richard, let us help." How could they help? What did they need to help with? None of it made any sense to Richard, but maybe the meeting would provide some answers.

He stepped into the street and hailed a cab.

The cab took him to an area of the city Richard knew well from his Columbia days. They drove through the low 100's, the Morningside Heights area. All the shops on the first floor of the old apartment buildings were closed. This section of Broadway wasn't all that far from the theatre district, but worlds away. No stars, no glamour. A bagel store...a bookstore...maybe a dry cleaners or a shoe store. And, every so often, a cheap place where Columbia students could grab a slice of New York style pizza. All run-down and maybe a little scary to someone from a nicer part of town. But, as a student, Richard never gave the area a second thought. For him, the worst local dive was better than the law school library.

Past the wall surrounding Columbia, the cab turned left on 122nd, heading for the Hudson, then right on Riverside Drive. Some of Richard's classmates used to joke about this being the most religious section of the world per square foot. Within a few blocks were the Cathedral of St. John the Divine, Union Theological Seminary, Jewish Theological Seminary, Riverside Church, and who knew what else scattered among the neighborhood streets.

Richard wished he'd been here a little sooner to hear the midnight bells. He hadn't really gone to church since he was a kid, but as a law student he'd spent hours trying to study in Sakura Park so he could be near the Riverside Church tower when the bells rang.

The cab stopped at a dark apartment building on Riverside, just half a block up from Sakura Park. Richard paid the driver and got out of the cab. He was the only person on the street. He walked up to the front door of the building and rang the buzzer to apartment 512. There was no answer, so he rang the buzzer again. Finally, he heard a faint voice over the static.

"Who is this? We're in bed."

"I'm sorry. I was told there would be a meeting here."

"Who told you?"

"Harold Solomon."

There was a clicking sound, and the door opened.

CHAPTER TWENTY

There was no counter or security person, only a camera mounted near the doorway. The staircase was out in the open, fairly safe, so Richard took the stairs. He kept asking himself why this building seemed so familiar, and finally, as he got to the fifth floor, he remembered that one of his law school classmates had lived in this building with his wife and son. They weren't friends—Richard couldn't even remember the guy's name—but they'd studied together once for the Criminal Law final in his apartment here.

Richard was about to knock on the door to 512 when the peep hole darkened. Someone was looking at him. Richard heard someone say, "It's him," and then the door opened. It was Harold.

"Hurry up. Come in," Harold whispered.

Richard came in the apartment and waited while Harold locked the four door locks. The apartment was dark, with little light coming from the living room down the long, narrow hall. The hardwood floor sloped off to the left, and the walls were thick with chipped plaster. Harold walked around Richard and motioned him to follow.

Richard was surprised to see six other people in the living room: four women and two men. They all sat on the floor, serious and secretive looking, but it was too dark to really make out any faces in the light of the single lamp. Nobody got up when the two came in.

"Go ahead and sit down, Richard," Harold said in a low voice. "We're glad you came. Let me introduce you to everyone." Richard found a piece of the floor to sit on, and Harold sat next to him.

"Like, just tell us who *he* is," a man sitting in a dark corner off to the right said in a rough voice. "He can find out who we are later, if he needs to."

"This is the man I was just starting to tell you about," Harold said, "Richard Carson. He's a lawyer, but he's staying home full-time right now to work on his novel." Richard looked up at Harold, surprised. He didn't like some stranger knowing so much about him. "His son—"

"Let's leave my son out of this," Richard said. "I didn't come to talk about him. I just came to listen."

"Then listen to this, man," the rough voice said, "your son is what this is all about. Too late to leave him out."

"His son is Christopher," Harold said, "six years old, and his wife is Carol, a successful, well-respected attorney. They got Christopher out on the sabbatical."

This last statement obviously meant a lot to the group, as everyone immediately started talking with one another.

"Look," Richard said, purposely not whispering, "what's this about? What are you, a bunch of thirteen-year-olds playing around with a secret club or something?"

Richard started to get up, but Harold touched his knee and looked at him, pleading for him to stay.

"What have you got," that same coarse voice from the corner said, "that's more important than this?"

"It's my fault," Harold said. "I figured if I told him very much he would think we were delusional or something and would never meet with us. Let me tell you what's going on, Richard."

Richard looked around the room, trying to see faces. "That would be nice," he finally said, quieter. "But you're a bit late if you were trying to stop me from thinking you're delusional."

"All of us have children at the Newman Home," Harold said, "just like you. There are other concerned parents, but we don't meet all together because we don't want to attract attention. Too big a risk."

"Now that's what I mean, Harold, this bit about risk. I've hated that school since the day I looked at their brochure, but I'm not holding meetings in dark rooms at midnight. Don't you think you're all a little...uh...."

"Paranoid?" Harold asked.

"Well, yes."

"Let me ask you something," Harold said, "when you saw me at Macy's two or three times before we finally spoke, what were you thinking? You seemed a little nervous."

"Well, I wasn't—"

"Honestly, what were you thinking?"

Richard looked down at his hands. "I wondered if you were from the school."

"A little paranoid, Carson?" the coarse voice said. "I mean, like why didn't you think he was a store cop, or just some guy having a tough time shopping, or even some mass murderer who stalked his victims in department stores?"

"Okay," Richard said, "all that proves is that I had an irrational fear."

"No, all that proves is that you have good instincts," a woman across from Richard said, almost to herself. "Let me give you some evidence." As she leaned forward, the light from the lamp illuminated her face. She was very white, even pale, and she had beautiful, soft-looking skin. She had arranged her long black hair into a tight bun, but instead of making her look stern, it somehow made her look compassionate.

"I'm Rebecca Solomon. Harold and I have a son, Joshua. He's a handsome boy. Big, brown eyes, so dark you can't see the pupils. Thick black hair that curls if you let it grow long enough. And believe me, at Newman, they don't let it grow long enough."

Rebecca took a deep breath before she continued. "We enrolled Joshua at the Newman Home, convinced we loved him so much we were willing to give him up for a while. Like the story of Hannah, I suppose. We borrowed the extra money from Harold's parents. We wanted what was best for Joshua, not what was convenient for us. I'd always wanted to stay home with our children. We wanted to give him the best education, the greatest chance at being happy and successful. Besides, if it didn't work out, we could always take him out."

Richard nodded. "I'd always held onto that hope, but my wife sees it differently."

"That's just it. Harold and I saw it exactly the same. Any problems? Bring Joshua home. So, we enrolled him. We downloaded our videos. He came home for a couple of quarterly visits. Everything seemed like it was going well for the first couple of years."

"Then we were blessed with Sarah," Harold said. "And we brought Joshua home for his first Hanukkah with his little sister."

"Did he not treat her well?" Richard asked.

"Oh no, no, he was wonderful to her," Rebecca said. "That wasn't the problem." She stopped. For a moment she didn't even try to say something, as she struggled to keep her composure. Harold offered his hand, and she held it. No one else spoke.

"He was well behaved," she said. "He ate everything we placed before him. He wasn't fussy, didn't jump on the furniture, no tantrums. For two days Harold and I spent every waking minute with our son and daughter. We took them places...we played with them...we hugged them and kissed them."

"Then what was wrong?" Richard asked.

"He never kissed back," she said, staring straight at Richard for the first time. "He would put his arms around us, he would put his lips against our cheeks, but there was nothing there. He would speak only if spoken to. We wanted our little boy, not a well-trained dog."

"His eyes," Harold whispered, shaking his head.

"Ah, his eyes," she said. "Those big, brown, loving eyes. Empty. He wasn't seeing everything for the first time anymore. He wasn't even looking anymore. It's difficult to explain."

"I know what you mean," Richard said. "I've seen that look."

"We returned him to the school and tried to resume our lives, but we couldn't. We felt horrible, couldn't bear having him away from us. After a week, we called them and said we'd decided to withdraw him. They said we couldn't. We had a contract. They said that he was happy at Newman and only seemed distant when he was at home, with us. We told them to keep the money, we wanted our son. They finally agreed and said it would take a couple days to process the papers."

"So, what happened?" Richard said.

"He's almost ten now, and he's still in the school. We can't even take him out for quarterly visits anymore. We have to visit him there. Sometimes, Harold and I take turns trying to see him at the playground."

"I don't get it," Richard said. "They can't keep him against your will, not if you both want to take him out."

"You have no idea how connected the school is to everyone in power, do you?" the coarse voice said. "Get a clue, Richard."

Richard stared at the corner, trying to see the face that belonged to the voice, wishing he'd just keep quiet.

The shadows covered Rebecca's face as she leaned back.

"We called every day," Rebecca said. "We contacted the city. We had our lawyer contact the school. One day, while Harold was at work and I was home alone with Sarah, someone from the school came to our apartment with a social worker. They had papers. Psychiatrists had examined Joshua and concluded we had done some sort of damage to him during his visits. They had a video of him talking about how we mistreated him."

"They left us a copy and we watched it over and over" Harold said. "Can you imagine what it's like to hear your little boy say such things about you, like you're monsters? We weren't fit to be parents, they said, and the social worker was going to visit our home repeatedly, unannounced, to make certain we changed. Otherwise, the state would take our daughter away from us."

"They can't do that—" Richard said.

"They can do whatever they want, man," the voice rasped.

Everyone was quiet.

"It was like *Sophie's Choice*," Rebecca said. "Try to win our son, we lose our daughter."

"We fight in ways we can," Harold whispered. "That is part of what these meetings are about. We meet. We talk. We read. We watch. We have Sarah with us, and someday we'll have what we need to get Joshua back. I don't know how yet, but someday we'll get all our children back."

CHAPTER TWENTY-ONE

One by one, each parent talked about how they were connected to the Solomons and to Newman. The grandmother, Joan, said she had placed her granddaughter in the school when her daughter and son-in-law had lost their lives in an auto accident. She soon regretted enrolling the girl, but when she mentioned her concerns to Harold, her accountant, she realized she'd better not try to take her out—at least for now.

Sandra, an attractive woman in her late twenties with short blonde hair, said she and her husband had enrolled their little girl in Newman because of how enthusiastic their neighbors, the Solomons, had been when they were considering the school. But after seeing what had happened with Joshua, Sandra wanted to take their daughter out. Her husband, though, said there were two sides to every story and that the Solomons may have exaggerated their situation.

The next people to speak were a couple, Paul and Lauren. Paul's was the coarse, sarcastic voice, but now Lauren did most of the talking. When Paul did speak, he was quiet, almost reverent. They were both Ph.D. students at Columbia; he was studying philosophy, and she was studying biochemistry. The group was meeting in their apartment. The two had a daughter and had made arrangements with a friend, whose husband was also attending Columbia, to babysit her while they were in their classes. After just a couple of months, though, the babysitter's husband dropped out of school and they moved away. Paul and Lauren tried a series of other arrangements for taking care of their daughter, but none worked out. Finally, Lauren's parents offered to pay the costs of Newman for their granddaughter.

"That was three years ago," Lauren said. "But like the Solomons' boy, our daughter just seemed to be losing her spirit. I guess we didn't really notice it at first—maybe we were too busy. Anyway, we decided to un-enroll her, you know, talked to some friends, started figuring out how we could trade off working on our dissertations. But about a month ago, we met Rebecca in the park with her little girl. She told us what had happened with their son, and we started attending these meetings."

"So, you stopped trying to get your daughter out?" Richard asked.

"Not at first. We kept telling ourselves that our case was different."

"But then we heard about Joseph's son," Paul spoke up, "and that put a new light on everything. I think it did for everybody."

"Joseph's son?" Richard asked.

Paul looked at his wife, and neither spoke. Richard couldn't catch anybody's eye.

"It's past two," Harold said. "I think it's time we break. Should we meet next week—"

Richard heard a new voice: "I will speak about it." A man emerged from the shadows and moved closer to the lamp, where everyone could plainly see his face. "He would want me to speak of it, if it can help.

"I'm Joseph Thomas. I'm a professor at Harvard Law and have a home in Cambridge. Almost eight years ago, my wife and I had a son, Samuel. Joanne died in childbirth."

"I'm sorry," Richard said.

"That left me alone," Joseph continued, "with a wonderful little baby, and a new academic career, and a law practice on the side. He didn't have a mother, and how could I give him what he needed? I talked to several experts, spent weeks researching what was best for Samuel. I read about the Newman program here in New York and contacted the school." Joseph rubbed his hands together. "Newman admitted him. They said he was like a little leopard, fast on his feet because he was fast in his mind."

"Everything is about the jungle over there," Richard said.

"More than you realize," Joseph said. "He looked so happy in the videos, so I figured he was reserved at home because he wasn't used to the surroundings. But when he came home last Christmas, Samuel wasn't a little boy anymore. He was getting increasingly distant. More and more it just seemed that what was happening at Newman was some sort of experiment. I told the superintendent I was removing my son from the facility."

Joseph paused and looked around the room. He took a deep breath.

"Looking back," Joseph said, "I wish I'd just kept him home after the visit. But he was back at the school, and the superintendent argued with me. He said I was making a mistake. He had his head child psychologist talk with me—"

"Hunter Jenkins," Richard said.

Joseph smiled slightly. "Yes, Dr. Jenkins. He showed me studies, videos of happy Newman residents, everything you can think of. He even tried to convince me I had an obligation to prove an African American child could succeed in the school. 'If you take

him out,' Dr. Jenkins said, 'how will another black child get in?'
After several weeks of this harassment, I finally barged into the
place and demanded my son. They told me the papers would be
finalized the next week. I told them they had to be ready the next
day. This was six weeks ago."

No one was looking at Joseph now, except for Richard.

"I went to the school first thing in the morning to pick up
my son. A couple of guards—excuse me, *hosts*—took me to the
superintendent's office, and he told me the news. Samuel had run
away."

"Run away?" Richard said. "That's impossible. That place is a
fortress."

"That's what I said. But the superintendent claimed Samuel
was so upset he'd be returning home with me that he ran away.
He said the security is designed to keep unwanted people out, not
to keep residents in. He claimed he tried calling me, but I hadn't
answered. And he said he'd called the police."

"We can tell Richard about this next time," Harold said.

"No, I need to tell him now," Joseph said, shaking his head. "I
left the facility and called the police. I knew the school had never
called me, but the police wouldn't say if they'd been called or not.
They said they'd keep an eye out for Samuel. I called my family,
my friends, everyone I could think of. Some of them drove down
from Boston and helped me look all over Manhattan. We searched
every place we could. For two days, we searched. I even hired two
private detectives. But nothing."

Joseph took a deep breath, looking down at his hands.

"Somehow, the Solomons heard about my situation and contacted me about a month ago. I came to a couple meetings and listened, but I was searching for my son—I didn't have time to trust

strangers. Things changed two weeks ago, and I had something to say. I had nothing left to lose."

Joseph paused again.

"The police found Samuel," he said, "not far from the George Washington Bridge, lying beside the Hudson. Face down."

CHAPTER
TWENTY-TWO

When Richard got back to the apartment, his pillow and a blanket were waiting for him on the couch. He hurried for his son's room and made sure Christopher was safe, then collapsed on the couch. He was exhausted, but still had trouble getting to sleep until about four-thirty in the morning. When he woke up it was almost eight, and Carol had already left without saying a word.

He went to Christopher's room and opened the door. Christopher was sitting up in his bed, spelling out words with the Scrabble game, waiting for his father to wake up. All he wanted to do that morning was be with Christopher, sit next to him, try to talk to him, but it just wasn't that easy.

After breakfast, the two went back to Carol's home office so Richard could get some writing in for the day. Christopher brought his Scrabble game and played on the floor while his father struggled over getting something down in the notebook. At noon, he still had nothing to show for the morning. Nothing on the page. He wasn't surprised. Nothing in his life seemed to be working. Nothing with his son. Nothing with his wife. Nothing.

Richard went over every word from the meeting the night before. He couldn't stand not knowing what his son must have gone through at the school. His childhood had been stolen from him. And what would his son have to go through when he returned? The superintendent would be angry with Christopher for having been the only child to leave on sabbatical before they'd ended the policy.

Forget Newman. What about now? Was Christopher safe now?

All Richard could think of was some sweet, innocent boy named Samuel, lying face down by the river. He didn't want to look at Christopher and see Samuel.

But he couldn't become paranoid, like those people last night. Maybe it was some horrible set of coincidences that brought those people together with such painful stories. After all, there were a couple of hundred kids at this Newman. Out of all those families, some were certain to have negative experiences, but that doesn't mean all of them would. That doesn't mean he had to.

Joseph had shown Richard a photo of Samuel. He was a beautiful, healthy, intelligent boy—full of wonder at one time, his father had said. Full of life.

The phone rang and Richard figured he should just let voice mail answer it. Maybe he should screen all the calls. But what was the point of having his son home if they had to live in fear? He ran into the living room and picked up the phone.

"Hello."

"Hello, son."

"Dad. How're you doing?"

"Fine, fine, fine, fine, fine. Your mother's fine, I'm fine, the house is fine, and if we had a dog, he'd be fine, too. What we want to know is, how are you and our grandson doing? We were just talking about you two and felt like we ought to call. You know, grandparents' intuition."

"We're doing fine."

"Go get Christopher, would you, son? We'd like to talk to him." His father called out across the room. "Hey, Grandma, get on the other phone. Christopher's coming on."

"Hello, is this Christopher?" Grandma asked.

"No, this is me," Grandpa replied.

"I know you're not him. I want to talk to my grandson. Is he there?"

"Don't you want to talk to me, Mom?" Richard asked.

"Sure. How are you doing?"

"Fine."

"Great. Now get my grandson."

"Just a minute," Richard said.

He put down the phone. Richard had been excited about taking Christopher to Vermont to be with his grandparents, but after last night, he was afraid of that, too. Maybe he could find some way to keep Christopher home for good—make the sabbatical last forever.

He called for Christopher to come to the phone.

"I'll be back in Carol's office if you need me," Richard said. He didn't want to hear his son getting closer to his parents, only to have everything fall apart at the end of the summer.

Richard sat down near the Scrabble board on the floor. This was no life for a little boy, spending all morning moving tiles around. Something on the board caught his eye. He noticed a word, then another. Just as he was about to kneel down to get a closer look, he heard Christopher coming down the hall and sat back in the chair. Christopher seemed a little brighter now, a little lighter.

"Do they want to talk to me now?" Richard asked.

"No. They hung up."

"Oh. How are they?"

"They're doing well."

"What did you talk about?"

"About you." Christopher sat down on the floor and mixed up the Scrabble tiles. "About what you were like when you were a little boy."

"Why would they talk about that?"

"I asked them."

Christopher looked down at the board, slowly spelling new words with the tiles. Richard wondered why Christopher would be asking about his childhood. And he wondered why he'd never told his son any of his own stories.

"Can you use contractions in Scrabble?" Christopher asked.

"No."

"I didn't think you could."

Did most six-year olds play Scrabble? This was good. Christopher was enjoying being with words, playing with them. Maybe the school wasn't so—

"Would you like to play Scrabble?" Christopher asked.

"No, I really ought to get back to my writing."

"Oh." Christopher messed the tiles up, then started putting them back into the box.

Richard closed his eyes. What would his father do now?

"But you know," Richard said, getting down on the floor next to his son, "this game is really all about writing, isn't it? Let's play!"

Christopher smiled and started getting the tiles out. Richard let him take the lead, so they didn't play the game so much as spend time spelling together.

"You know," Richard said after a few minutes, "I've got an even better idea. There's a place I want to show you that's full of words."

CHAPTER TWENTY-THREE

"**W**hat do you think?" Richard asked as they walked past row after row of wooden tables in the library's mammoth reading room. Sunlight filled the room through the arched windows.

"I've never seen so many books," Christopher said.

"They've tried hard to not let it change too much. This is a place you come to read books—not skim texts on screens or stare at holograms, but books."

"I need to read a book."

Richard smiled. "Let's see what we can dig up."

They found several books for Christopher and a place at one of the tables. Richard started reading one of the books he got about Vermont while his son sat across from him, lost to the world in a collection of stories about King Arthur and his Knights of the Round Table.

After a half hour, Christopher looked up and watched his father.

"What are you thinking?" Richard asked.

"Nothing," Christopher said as he looked down.

"Really, what are you thinking?"

"I guess I wondered why you need to read books about Vermont if you lived there."

"It's for my book."

"But you remember Vermont, don't you?"

"You can't always trust what you remember."

Christopher nodded, then went back to his book. Richard opened another book and scanned the table of contents. He turned to about the middle of the book, then began reading. Occasionally, he'd take a couple of notes on his notebook and look up at his son. It was like Christopher had left the library, left New York, the twenty-first century. A light in his eyes transformed that shell of a person who'd obediently sat in his bedroom the first night back into an excited six-year-old boy.

After three hours, Christopher closed the book, finished. Richard looked up. "Did you like the book?"

"Yes."

"What was it about?"

Christopher held up the book so his father could read the title.

"I know the name of it, but what was it about?"

"King Arthur. And Queen Guinevere. And Sir Lancelot, of course. And swords and lances and horses and helmets and shields and the castle. Camelot. You can't forget Camelot."

"That, my son, is something I will never do."

They checked out several books and left the library. Richard couldn't decide if they should take the quick and dirty route home or the cleaner and safer route, and Christopher had no opinion. Richard finally decided on the subway to give him more time to write back at the apartment. As they headed for the station, Richard noticed up ahead a man and a woman entering a restaurant. They were several yards away, and their backs were to him, but they both somehow seemed familiar. The man had his hand on the woman's back as she went into the restaurant. Everything seemed slow motion to Richard. He'd seen Carol wear that dark blue dress and scarf a month ago.

CHAPTER TWENTY-FOUR

Time for bed. At least, Richard thought so, but he wasn't sure what time his son should be going to bed. He'd been reading on the couch while Christopher was doing something in his bedroom. When he peered around Christopher's door, he found him lying on the floor, sound asleep, next to his Scrabble game. His son had changed into a brown T-shirt and blue jeans, like he was trying to wear all of his new clothes in one day. Christopher was asleep, but he didn't look at peace. Maybe he really wasn't happy here. Maybe he needed to go back. Maybe the kids really were as happy at Newman as Hunter always claimed they were.

He picked up Christopher, realizing once again how unused to being a father he was: he had this big boy in his arms, sound asleep, and the bed was still made, not ready for anyone to lie in. Richard laid him on the bed, on top of the covers, and took off his new sneakers. He got a blanket from the closet in the hall and covered him. On his way out, he turned around at the doorway, looking at his son one last time for the day. He wished he could close the door and lie next to his son and keep the world out. If there were just some way to stay in that room, the two of them, and not have to deal with anyone or anything else. No blank pages, angry wives, experimental schools. Just a father and a son. Together.

Richard looked down at the floor and saw the Scrabble board. The tiles seemed carefully arranged, so he knelt down to get a closer look.

THE STORY NEVER CHANGES

He closed the door and went back to the couch, worn down. What story never changes? Had his son written that for his father to read, or was he just playing around with words? He thought they'd made some progress the day before, spending time together shopping. But that strange group meeting last night changed everything. The entire world had shifted a degree on its axis, and now everything was different. Before, he could always hope and pray that Carol would change by the end of the summer, that Christopher could stay home and share his childhood with his parents. Now, that dream brought its own nightmare. Even if they both decided to keep him home, what would the school do? Would they try something like they'd done with Joseph's son? Or was his death even Newman's fault at all? Maybe Samuel really did run away.

The front door opened around nine and Carol came into the living room, wearing her dark blue dress and scarf.

"Glad you didn't have to work too late," Richard said. "Were you pretty busy all day?"

"Chained to my desk. I should've worked later." She looked at her watch. "Where's Christopher?"

"He's in bed."

"Good."

Carol sat down and took off her shoes. As she rubbed her feet, she looked up at Richard.

"Get much writing done today?"

"Let's not go there."

"Go there? We don't have to go there. We live there."

Richard leaned forward towards his wife. "Okay, Carol, let's talk. What are you really upset about?"

"If you don't ever write, then the book will never get done. And if the book doesn't get done, we don't even have a slight chance of making any money off it."

"That's not it. Come on, what is it?"

"Don't worry," Carol said, standing up, "I'm not counting on a dime."

"Okay, I'll play along. It's money."

"It wouldn't hurt—"

"Cause if it is," Richard said as he stood up, "maybe we could save a little by cutting out some expensive restaurants."

"I don't eat out a lot."

"Sorry, I jumped to conclusions. Maybe you didn't have to pay."

"What are you getting at?"

"I saw you and some other man going into a restaurant today."

"What were you doing, spying on me?"

"Did you have a good dessert?"

"Look—"

"Who was it? Someone from work? Someone at your gym?"

"I don't have to—"

"Wait a minute," Richard said, falling back into the couch. "It was Hunter, wasn't it?"

"So I ate lunch with him," she said. "He's just helping me figure out this Christopher thing. He is a psychologist, you know."

"'This Christopher thing'?"

"Don't play stupid."

Carol left for their bedroom, pulling the door behind her. He heard the door lock.

"I don't know how much longer I can take this," Richard said, looking up at the ceiling.

"Maybe I should return home."

Christopher was standing in the hall, holding his Scrabble box like most boys would have held a teddy bear.

"What do you mean? You are home."

"To my home."

"This is your home, son," Richard said, walking toward him.

"But I only make you two unhappy."

"Oh, son," Richard said as he knelt in front of Christopher, "you make me happy every day."

The little boy closed his eyes. His left hand started twitching.

"Let's get you back to bed."

"I didn't ask to come to this place," Christopher said, "or to be left in that room alone with the game. And I didn't ask to be born. At least not to parents who don't want me. I want to go back home where I belong."

Christopher ran into his room and slammed the door. Stunned, Richard slowly walked over to the door and knelt down.

"You don't really want to be a resident again, do you?"

"I like it there," Christopher said between sobs. "The teachers are nice. They call me their little lion cub. But Carol doesn't want me here. You don't want me here. What am I doing here?"

"I want you—"

"Don't lie to me, Richard. I'm just a kid, but I'm not stupid."

"Christopher—"

"Just send me back home."

"Son—"

"Go away."

Richard slowly got up. He leaned against his son's door. His heart told him to not go away, to go into his son's room and talk with him. He had no idea what he would say, but maybe the words would come. He just kept hearing those words: "Go away." Why didn't he ever know the best thing to do?

Richard listened. He could hear Christopher trying not to cry, or at least trying not to be heard. Maybe he should try one more time.

"Christopher. I really didn't mean—"

"Go away."

He went away.

CHAPTER
TWENTY-FIVE

"**W**hat's going on?" Richard whispered into his cell phone.

"Richard, I didn't know you cared."

"Look, Hunter, you know what I'm talking about."

"What's your problem?"

"Today. Lunch. I saw you two."

"Are you serious?" Hunter laughed. "This is about lunch? Look, Carol and I have been friends for a long time. We're big kids now. We can go to lunch like adults without anyone worrying about us."

Richard paced around the home office, trying to figure out what to say next. He wasn't even sure why he called and felt stupid; of course, Carol would never cheat on him. Hunter, he wasn't so sure about. But something wasn't right with this.

"I just don't like—"

"Look, we're not having an affair," Hunter said. "I'm a happily married man, just like you."

"That's not what I'm talking about."

"Then what are you talking about, Richard?"

"I'm talking about...about...I'm talking about what you and Carol were talking about."

"What?"

"That's my question," Richard said, stopping in the middle of the office. "What did you talk about today at lunch?"

"Nothing. Just friends talking—"

"You were talking about Christopher."

"Sure, a little, but—"

Richard parted the curtain. The street light was still out—had been for at least a month. "What are you two planning?"

"You're getting paranoid, my friend."

"You're dodging the question. What are you and my wife up to?"

Hunter hung up.

CHAPTER
TWENTY-SIX

I t was dark, maybe one or two in the morning, but Richard was still just sitting on the couch looking at the closed blinds.

This was not the life he'd planned on living—certainly not the one he'd dreamed of living. He'd always wanted to be a writer, ever since he wrote his first story when he was about Christopher's age. And he'd wanted to marry and have children. Now he was a writer, a husband, and a father, but he was failing at all three—the words wouldn't come, his wife avoided him, and his son told him to go away. He'd hoped this summer he and Christopher would become close, inseparable, and Carol would realize how important it was to have him home with them. He didn't expect her to be completely won over by the end of the summer, but enough to want to keep Christopher and try being a family. It might take a little longer with her, but by Christmas he'd figured she would be glad the three of them were together. Now he wasn't sure if there was any reason for hope at all.

Richard got up from the couch and decided to see if Carol had unlocked the bedroom door. He walked by Christopher's room and listened again. Nothing. Not a sound. He opened the door and looked in.

Christopher was still in his clothes, asleep on his bed. His curtains were open, and the moon gently lit the room. Richard looked around the room at the bare walls and thought how much it appeared to be the room of someone who wasn't planning to stay for very long. There were no posters or pictures or calendars, and the only thing on the dresser, the picture of them at the Brooklyn Bridge, was turned now, facing the bed.

Richard took the blanket from the foot of the bed and covered his son. He was afraid of waking Christopher, but he reached down and stroked his son's hair.

"I apologize," Christopher whispered, without opening his eyes.

Richard pulled back. "I'm sorry. I thought you were asleep."

"We weren't allowed to speak that way back home. I shouldn't have done it here."

It was late, they both needed their sleep, but Richard knelt down next to the bed. "What happened when someone did?" Richard asked.

Silence.

"Please tell me."

"The adults took those kinds of residents away," Christopher said, his eyes still closed.

"Where? Where would they take them?"

Christopher winced a little, and Richard quit stroking his hair.

"I'm sorry. You don't have to talk about it." Richard started to stand up, but Christopher grabbed his hand.

"Please don't stop," Christopher said.

Richard resumed stroking his son's hair. It was thick and dark brown, like his.

"I don't know," Christopher said. "The residents would come back to class the next day and not talk that way anymore."

Maybe they could finally talk, in the dark. Eyes closed. Richard looked up at the moon and thought he felt warmth coming from it.

"It's good to tell me how you feel," Richard said.

"I thought if I went back home, you and Carol would be happier."

"You belong here. We all just need to be patient while we make the adjustment."

Christopher turned on his side, facing the wall, his eyes still closed.

"Why doesn't she like me?"

Richard stared down at the wooden floor, so linear, so straight and properly lined up and perfectly placed.

"She loves you. Very much. And she's showing it the only way she knows how."

"How?"

Richard smiled. "This may not make much sense, but she's fighting for your future, trying to give you what that school claims to give kids. That's what she does when she cares about something. She fights for it."

"What is she afraid of?" Christopher asked.

"What do you mean?"

"People fight when they're afraid, don't they?"

"I don't know." Richard thought. "Maybe. Maybe people fight when they're afraid."

"What are you afraid of, Richard?"

Richard looked down at Christopher's face. His eyes were still closed, and he looked so much like a little boy, but he talked so old. He shouldn't have to be old at such a young age.

"I better let you get some sleep now," Richard said. "You dream about what you'd like to do tomorrow, then tell me in the morning. Let's make it a good day tomorrow." He adjusted the blanket around his son.

"Do you know what I'd really like to do tomorrow? I'd like to get a notebook, just like yours."

"What would you do with that?"

"Write."

"Really?"

"Of course," Christopher said.

"You know, Christopher," Richard whispered after a moment had passed, "one day I was at the playground and saw a boy writing. Did you ever write out on the playground?"

He could see his son's body tense a little.

"We don't have to get me a notebook if you don't want to."

"No, no, that would be great. We'll get you one."

"Just like yours."

"Just like mine."

Christopher turned in his bed so he could face his father, but he kept his eyes closed. "Tell me about the book you're writing."

"Well," Richard said, "it's about a boy. It's about being a boy. About growing up and having to deal with the world around you."

Christopher smiled, something Richard rarely saw.

"What? Why are you smiling?"

Christopher stopped. "I'm sorry."

"Don't be sorry. It's good to smile."

Christopher smiled again.

"Yes, I like that face," Richard said. "Now, why are you smiling?"

"How do you know what it's like to be a boy?"

Richard chuckled. He told him what it was like for him to grow up in Vermont with his parents and brother. He lost himself in the details of the TV programs they watched together, places they liked to visit, until he could hear his son's breathing get deeper. He looked so at peace, so happy to be with this father.

He continued to stroke his son's hair, feeling close, when he felt something under his finger. Just below the hairline on the side of Christopher's head, not far from his ear. Richard pulled back the hair just a little and saw it. A thin, red line remaining from an incision of some kind.

CHAPTER TWENTY-SEVEN

Harold Solomon called with what he said was urgent news, but he refused to tell Richard over the phone. They had to talk in person, he insisted. Richard had been lying on the couch for about an hour, trying to figure out a way to fall asleep. He checked on Christopher and saw that he was asleep. Then he checked their bedroom door, but it was still locked. He figured he'd be gone for just a few minutes and Carol would never know he'd been gone, but he left a note on the table saying that he had left just in case she woke up.

He made it down to the street and found a cab. The traffic was light. He sat in the back of the cab and thought about how he hated those kinds of calls—no one ever called that late with good news. When he was twenty years old, home from college for Christmas break, the phone rang at about two o'clock in the morning. Richard had almost held his breath to try to hear what it was about, but he could only hear the low mumblings of his father talking two rooms down. He'd heard his father hang up the phone, then start talking quietly to his mother.

He couldn't hear anything for a while, then his father left the bedroom and ran down the stairs, getting into the truck. Richard waited for his mother to come in, but she never did. Finally, he walked into the hall and heard his mother crying. Her bedroom door was open.

"What's wrong, Mom?" he asked.

She didn't answer.

"Is it David?"

She nodded.

"Is he...okay?"

She told him David was alive, but in trouble. Richard didn't know what to do. He'd wanted to sit by her and comfort her, but he didn't feel strong enough. So he backed away from the door and returned to his room. He sat in his bed, pulled the covers up to his waist, and waited for an hour, then two, hoping to hear the garage door open.

The cab driver turned on Water Street and pulled up to South Street Seaport. Richard paid him, got out of the cab, and finally found Harold in front of a small souvenir shop.

"What couldn't you tell me over the phone?" Richard asked.

"Let's walk a little," Harold said.

The men started walking along the pier. Despite the late hour, the Seaport was crowded with people drinking too much and talking too loud at the outdoor restaurant tables. A large yacht, with an alternative-techno band and a deck full of screaming dancers, made its way along the pier to dock.

"Do you remember Sandra?" Harold asked.

"Yes. The one whose husband didn't see anything wrong with Newman. They're your neighbors."

"Right. Their daughter is Tanya. I don't think they ever told you her name."

Harold kept walking, without saying anything, until they got to the end of the shops. They turned the corner and stood next to the railing, just a few feet from the water. The Brooklyn Bridge was brightly lit, looking old and big and powerful as it spanned the waters.

"So, what happened?" Richard asked. "Is she okay?"

"Sandra couldn't take it any longer and called the school. She said she wanted her little girl to come home for a couple of days, even though it wasn't time for a quarterly visit. They refused, of course. Then she went down there and demanded to see her daughter. Not take her out, just *see* her daughter in the lobby. They told her to wait a minute while they got her, but instead they phoned her husband. He came down to the school, angry and embarrassed, and took Sandra home. She was almost hysterical. Then the next morning...."

Harold looked up at the Brooklyn Bridge for a long moment.

"What happened?" Richard asked.

"Then the next morning, Sandra and her husband got a phone call from one of the school psychologists. She said Tanya was in the hospital suffering from a nervous breakdown."

"A nervous breakdown?"

"How many little children do you know have nervous break-downs? She said when the school had told her daughter her mother had come to visit her, the little girl fell apart. That's why they'd called her husband."

"Had they told the husband that the girl was having a nervous breakdown?"

"No. He hadn't heard anything about it until the phone call the next day."

"Didn't that strike him as suspicious?"

"It gets worse," Harold said. "The superintendent convinced the social worker at the hospital the parents shouldn't be allowed to visit the girl until she's stabilized—whatever that means."

"How can a hospital tell parents they can't see their own child?" Richard asked.

Harold shrugged. "That school's awfully powerful, Richard."

Richard moved his hand along the railing, looking across the river.

"How is Sandra doing?"

"She's holding it together, barely," Harold said. "Her husband is completely supportive of the school, though. He thinks the psychologist is right."

Richard leaned against the railing with his back to the bridge. "So here's Sandra, sitting at home waiting to hear how her daughter's doing, blaming herself for her little girl's supposed breakdown—"

"And her husband blaming her," Harold said.

"And her husband blaming her, and she can't even see the little girl and find out first-hand what's really going on."

"Still think we're paranoid?" Harold asked.

"What if it's true, though? What if she really had a breakdown?"

"Richard, come on."

"I know. I'm not taking their side, I'm just confused. I don't want to be looking for bad guys under every rock."

"So which is worse, Richard, that the school is lying to the parents to keep them away from their daughter, or that the little girl is so estranged from her own mother that the thought of being with her sends the girl into hysterics?"

CHAPTER
TWENTY-EIGHT

Video #47: Christopher, about three years old, sits in a circle with his classmates, singing a song about animals.

Video #62: Christopher's class is on a field trip to Central Park. They stop every few feet while one of the teachers points out characteristics of a plant. The children appear fascinated.

Video #133: The children are presenting their science fair projects. No parents are in the audience, because no parents were invited to watch.

Richard spent the rest of the night studying Newman videos on his computer, hoping to find some answers. He didn't even know what he was looking for. In a way, every videotaped moment looked perfect. And, for some reason, that made him worry.

But then there was Tanya. He'd never met that little girl, but he couldn't help but be obsessed with her circumstances. How could the idea of seeing her mother make her fall apart? No, Richard was right to be so concerned. Maybe he couldn't exactly put his finger on the problem, but there was plenty to be concerned about.

As he watched the sun rise, the answer he'd been looking for finally came to him: his parents. He'd take his family to visit his parents. Today. They had to get away from everything and be together. Get to know each other.

"You can always unlock the door," Carol said as she sat next to him on the couch. "You know where the key is."

"If you lock the door, it's for a reason. If you want me in our bedroom, it's up to you to unlock it."

Carol rubbed her eyes. She looked like she hadn't gotten much sleep, either.

"Carol, when you get a chance, check something on the back of Christopher's head." He bowed his head down and pointed to where she should look.

"What is it?"

"I'm not a doctor. Just look at it, would you?" As soon as he spoke, he felt bad for sounding so irritated.

Carol sighed. "How did we get here, Richard?"

"I'm not sure, but I think I know how we can get out."

"He belongs back at his home," Carol said, learning forward. "It's what's best for him and for us."

Richard shook his head. "He needs more time with us. With family. We need to take him to visit my folks."

Carol laughed a little, then paused. "You're serious?"

"Why not?"

"Think about it," Carol said. "He's going back home at the end of the summer—if not sooner. It's going to be hard enough for him to make the transition back to Newman without having to add your parents and their home. The last thing we want is for him to get attached to your parents."

"Shouldn't he spend some time with his grandparents?"

"Grandparents!" Christopher came running into the living room. "We're going to go see my grandparents? Really?"

"How can we not go now?" Richard asked Carol. "This is the happiest I've ever seen him."

"This is a big mistake, Richard. It's taking him in the opposite direction."

"We all need this."

Carol shook her head. "Unlike some people around here, I can't just play whenever I want." She stood up. "Looks like another big decision you've made before we really get a chance to talk about it."

"Hey, Christopher, come over here for a minute," Richard said. He motioned for Carol to come closer. "I just want to see something." He pulled back the hair on the back of his son's head and showed his wife.

"Just a scratch," Carol said.

"Way too straight for a scratch," Richard said. "Christopher, do you remember getting hurt or cut or something back here?"

"No. I feel great."

"Richard," Carol said, "sometimes a scratch is just a scratch."

"And sometimes, it isn't," Richard said.

CHAPTER
TWENTY-NINE

Richard and Christopher boarded the train. They could have chosen the Lightning Bolt and gotten to Vermont in half the time, but they agreed to take the older train and spend more time. On the Bolt, the scenery moved by so quickly it was difficult to know what was out there.

The train slowed as it passed through some small Connecticut town, Richard wasn't sure which. One of those quiet, calendar-perfect New England villages. Richard loved small towns like this—clean, trimmed, proper—and often dreamed of moving to one. "What do people do here for a living?" he'd ask Carol. "Commute" was her standard reply.

Some people who lived there also worked there, he knew: they stocked shelves in stores or made sure people got safely on the trains or accepted deposit slips at banks. And standing at a bank window, greeting neighbors and helping them grow their savings accounts, seemed a universe above practicing law. Of course, he didn't need Carol to tell him he was being romantic, idealistic. Being a teller in a village bank wouldn't be the most exciting of lives, but he couldn't help but wonder how important excitement was supposed to be in life.

He pulled his notebook out of the pocket on the back of the seat in front of him. He had wanted to buy a new fountain pen, a rather expensive one, to be honest, to kind of commemorate his starting out as a real, full-time writer, but Carol had pleasantly suggested he buy one with royalties. She had a point. He spent a lot of energy trying to write, but all he had to show for it were dozens of rejection slips for his short stories and a stalled novel manuscript. She'd sometimes call writing his "hobby." He'd once told her, "Lawyering is how I earn my living; writing is how I earn my keep." He thought he was being profound, but she laughed and said, "Then you'd better work harder if you want me to keep you." It was early enough in their marriage that he'd laughed too.

"How's your writing coming?" Christopher asked, pulling out his notebook and pen.

"What?"

"How is your writing coming?"

"Okay, I guess. How about yours?"

"Fine."

"And what did you say you're writing?"

Christopher started putting the notebook away.

"Okay, okay, you don't have to tell me," Richard said. "Just curious."

Christopher opened the notebook and started writing. Before they caught the train that morning, Richard had made sure they'd stopped to buy a notebook for Christopher. He insisted on having one exactly like his father's. Richard bent over his own notebook, writing, and noticed his son checking once or twice to make certain Richard wasn't trying to read what he was writing.

This was a strange feeling for Richard, father and son, sitting next to each other, writing in the same kind of notebook. He felt almost as though there were two of him, that sitting next to him was a smaller version of himself.

"Will I ever know what you're writing?" Richard asked.

"I don't know," Christopher said. "Maybe if you're good." He looked up and smiled.

CHAPTER THIRTY

It was past nine when the bright red Jeep Cherokee, only a year old, drove up the gravel driveway of his parents' good-sized, two-story home. The front light was on, waiting. Richard climbed out of the passenger's side, and his father, in his corduroy shirt and blue jeans, climbed out from behind the wheel. His father's thick white hair, combined with his deep blue eyes and knowing face, made him look almost prophetic.

"Has it changed?" his father asked, smiling.

"Not a bit."

"Is that good?"

"Perfect."

The house was part of the land, like it hadn't been built but had grown there over years like the giant pines and cedars surrounding it. The outside was roughly hewn wood, never painted, and a wide, wooden deck traveled around the entire house. Richard scaled the rock chimney with his eyes like he'd done with his feet so many times as a boy.

"I've missed this place," he said. "A year's too long to wait."

"It's missed you, too."

Grandpa opened the back door of the Jeep. "Come on out, little buddy," he said. "We can't bring the house to you."

Christopher climbed out, staring at the house.

"Isn't it great out here, Christopher?" Richard asked.

Christopher looked up at the trees.

"What do you think?" Grandpa asked.

"It's the most beautiful place in the world," Christopher said.

"Oh, isn't this wonderful!" Grandma hurried down the steps from the house. She was in her mid-sixties, but that didn't stop her from walking with a spry jump in her step. Her hair was long and grey, with a good share of white, pulled back in a ponytail. In her red flannel shirt, jeans, and leather hiking boots, she looked like she'd fallen off a page from that month's L.L. Bean catalog. She was clearly excited to see her son and grandson, but the person she ran up to was Grandpa, giving him a kiss on his lips and squeezing his arms. They looked at each other, talked to each other, held onto each other not like newlyweds, but like a husband and a wife who had shared forty years of life and were grateful for it.

"Now, where is that grandson of mine?" she asked. Christopher had taken a few steps back as she'd come down the steps, but she ran over and knelt in front of him.

"Hello, Mrs. Carson," Christopher said, holding out his hand to shake hers.

"What?" Grandma's voice sounded shocked, but she was smiling.

"Mayday! Mayday!" Grandpa said. "I told you, little buddy, I told you. It's Grandpa and Grandma. If you don't want to sleep in the shed, you'd better learn that quick."

"Hello, Grandma."

"Put that hand away," she said as she pulled him up to her and hugged him tight. "I'm not letting go until you hug back," she said. He brought his arms up around her and hugged her.

"I'm happy to be here," he said quietly.

"Not as happy as I am, honey."

"Now," Grandma said as she stood up, "where's that man you call your father?"

"Mom," Richard said as he hugged her.

"It's been too, too long," she whispered in his ear as they hugged.

"I know. It's good to be home."

They held each other's arms. "I'm sorry Carol couldn't make it," Grandma said, "but I'm glad that didn't stop you two men from coming."

"She's very busy."

"Come on, Grandma," Grandpa said as he pulled the bag out of the back of the Jeep, "it's almost tomorrow. I'll put the Jeep in the garage later."

He led the way up to the house. Richard tried to take the bag from his father, but he wouldn't hear of it, barreling through the front door, knocking the bag against the walls. Grandma and Christopher followed. She reached down and took his hand, holding it as they walked up the steps.

"Is it really almost tomorrow?" he asked.

"Yes, in less than three hours it will be tomorrow."

"Then where will today go?"

"Not to worry, it doesn't go anywhere," Grandma said. "It just becomes one of the yesterdays. Those aren't cheap, either. It's taken me years to have as many yesterdays as I have."

They stepped into the entry and she closed the door behind them. Grandma and Christopher, still holding hands, climbed the stairs to the second floor and found the two men standing in the hall, looking at the pictures that lined the walls.

"Remember the other one you took of us that same day?" Richard said to his father, pointing to a picture of Richard and his parents with Christopher in front of the Brooklyn Bridge. "We've got it up in Christopher's room."

Christopher came up to take a look.

"And I haven't seen this for years," Richard said as he took a different picture off the wall and looked more closely. "I'm not sure I even remember why we took this." It was a photo of two eleven-year-old boys—Richard and his best friend, Andy—leaning against each other, hair messed up, dirt on their face, backpacks beside them. They were each outdoing the other's grin. "What were we doing?"

"You've been breathing that Manhattan acid air too long, son. Don't you remember the way you talked and talked about how you wanted to camp out, alone, once school let out? Just the two of you, for a whole week. Your mother and I kept saying you were too young. Finally you wore us down, and we said you could do it."

"If you camped here," Grandma added.

"Now I remember. Who wanted to camp in their own yard?"

"That's why we built the house on four acres," Grandpa told Christopher, "so the boys could be in the woods without having to leave home. Anyway, your daddy and Andy packed everything up, wouldn't even let me help, and took their long hike a few yards back into our woods. And how long do you think your brave daddy roughed it with his friend?"

"I don't know. Did he last for a week?"

"More like one night! Those boys were jumping at the chance to get warm and have Grandma's cooking for breakfast."

"That's when we took this picture of our own Lewis and Clark," Grandma said.

"Well, it was cold," Richard said. "And when we woke up we realized all we'd packed for breakfast was a can of pork and beans."

"And no can opener!" Grandpa said.

"Who's that?" Christopher asked, pointing at a different photo. It was a picture of Richard's brother, about sixteen years old, sitting on the railing of the deck, the woods behind him. His jeans had several holes, and he wasn't wearing a shirt. There was no smile on his face, and it looked like he was working hard to make sure one didn't show up. "Is that you when you were a boy, Richard?"

Richard looked closely at the photo, then looked away. "We need to get you to bed," he said.

"That's a good question, Christopher," Grandma said. "That's your daddy's brother, David."

Richard sighed.

"Richard has a brother?" Christopher asked.

"He never told you about his brother?" Grandpa asked. Christopher shook his head no. Grandpa looked over to Grandma. "You need to meet your uncle, little buddy."

"Now, I'm not—" Richard started.

"It's almost tomorrow, Grandpa," she said, then smiled. "You've got a grandson to spend tomorrow with."

"You're absolutely, positively, correctalamente, my dear. Come on, buddy, help me carry this bag to your room. We got it all ready especially for you."

Christopher helped Grandpa carry the bag down the hall. As they got close to a room, Grandpa told Christopher that it would be his, and he and his grandmother went in first. Grandpa waited for Richard to come.

"Richard, I want you and our grandson to have a wonderful time here," his father said quietly as he followed Richard into the room.

In the bedroom was an oak student desk and chair, a bookcase full of books, a baseball and mitt on top of a tall oak dresser with a bat in the nearby corner, and even a couple of new Batman and Spiderman posters. And what a bed! It was piled high with pillows and covered with a thick, plush, inviting red and brown comforter. Such a bed would make getting up in the morning, especially a cold morning, very difficult.

"This used to be your daddy's room," Grandma said. "We thought you'd like to sleep in it."

"It's changed," Richard said, still staring around at the walls. "Not a lot, but some."

"Of course," Grandpa said. "This is a bedroom, son, not a museum." He knelt next to his grandson. "So what do you think?"

"This is very nice and spacious. You're very kind."

"Now boy, quit talking like you're a text book. You're home—act like it!"

"Don't listen to that old owl, honey," Grandma interjected. "You can talk any way you want. So long as you call me 'Grandma' all the time."

"Life's too short to talk like you're being interviewed for a job, for Pete's sake," Grandpa said. He turned Christopher around so they were looking eye to eye. "That's right, little buddy, you talk anyway you want. Not the way they told you to talk."

There was an uneasiness, but just for a few seconds, then the boy smiled. "I can talk any way I want?"

"Take it from me, an old English professor. You be yourself. With which a preposition you may even end a sentence."

"Then, may I ask you a question?"

"Sure little buddy, shoot."

"Those big pictures of those two men—"

"Yeah, we got those posters just for you."

"Are they friends of yours?"

"Batman and Spidey?" Grandpa said. "You bet they are! We go way back. In fact—"

"Not tonight, Grandpa," Grandma said. "This boy needs to go to bed. You'll have to forgive him, Christopher. Grandpa's so excited to have someone in the house his own age, he can barely stand it. Your daddy will be in the room right across the hall. You won't get scared by yourself, will you, sweetie?"

"No, I will be just fine."

"What?" Grandpa said, trying to look stern.

"I'll be okay," Christopher said. He looked up at his grandpa and smiled.

"And if you get scared," Grandpa said to Richard, pointing at him and talking in a little old lady's voice, "you just crawl in bed with my little buddy here. He'll protect you. Okay, sweetie?"

CHAPTER THIRTY-ONE

I t took three tries, but Richard finally got Hunter on the phone.

"Look, can't you take a hint?" Hunter said. "I'm not picking up. It's late. I don't want to talk to you."

"It's not that late," Richard said. It was that late, but he didn't want anyone in the house to know he was making a call so he'd waited. He stood by the window in the bedroom with the lights off, looking at the forest behind his parents house. "This is important."

"I'm getting tired of these phone calls, Richard. You got your sabbatical. What do you want now?"

"Neuroplasticity."

Hunter paused. "There's an article about that on our site. You should—"

"I have. But tell me more."

"Well, it's like I told you at the lab. The brain is a living organ. It changes when we learn and—"

"What is Newman doing with neuroplasticity?"

"That's in the article. He's developed exercises that enhance the residents' ability to learn and develop their brains. Their minds. People used to say teaching was an art. Believe me, it's science, all the way."

"You're so careful to not tell me anything that's not in the article."

"Richard, what do you want? If you want to learn more about it, you've got a computer."

"That's just it, Hunter. I can find plenty about neuroplasticity. What I can't find is anything about Newman's agenda."

"I told you, we have mental exercises—"

"There's got to be more to it."

"Sorry to disappoint you, but that's it. I've got to get going. We're not all on vacation, you know."

"Like, is Newman doing anything that would require an incision of some sort?"

There was a long pause.

"Hunter?"

"Is that what this is all about? Sorry we didn't tell you, Richard, but Christopher had a little fall at the playground a while ago. Nothing serious. The nurse took care of it in no time."

"Why hide it?"

"We weren't hiding it. It just seemed so insignificant we didn't even think about telling you. Those kinds of scrapes and bruises happen all the time."

"What about his left hand? The twitching?"

"Maybe you should bring him home so we can take a look at him. Sounds like he's having problems with you he didn't have with us."

Richard hung up.

CHAPTER
THIRTY-TWO

The morning sunlight felt warm and comfortable as Richard walked into the kitchen. He'd set his alarm for five so he could write, but he didn't even remember shutting it off. He leaned against the doorway and watched his mother stacking dishes at the breakfast table, her back to him. The sunlight...the waffle iron on the counter...a couple of the oak cabinet doors left open just a little...and his mother in her own world, humming.

His mother turned to take the dishes to the sink and saw him. She smiled right away.

"You're up! I'm so glad you slept in. You needed to get more of that New York air out of you so you can breathe better up here." She put the dishes near the sink and gave Richard a hug.

"Am I going to get a hug every time I come into a room around here?" Richard asked.

"No, this is the last hug I'm going to give you. I just won't let go."

They both smiled, then started loading the dishwasher together.

"As soon as I'm finished here," she said, "I want to fix you a big Vermont breakfast. What would you like?"

"I'm the one who slept in. I'll fix me something later."

"Nonsense."

"And don't worry about Christopher—he never eats much for breakfast."

"Oh, that must be the city, son. He already ate with Grandpa and me."

"He actually ate something?"

"Not something—everything. Two eggs, toast, waffles, bacon—the whole works. Your father was glad it wasn't his turn to cook."

"He never eats like that at home. Not even that big of a dinner."

"City living will do that to you."

His mother pressed the buttons on the dishwasher while Richard walked over to the table.

"Where is he, anyway?" Richard asked.

"Can't you hear them laughing? They're having a great time in the back."

Richard walked to the French doors leading to the deck in the back. He reached for the knob, but when he heard shouting and laughing, he pulled back and parted the curtain. About thirty yards from the back of the house was the old stump and ax he remembered from when he was a boy. Wood was stacked near the stump, only three or four split pieces on the other side. Richard heard more laughter and finally spotted Grandpa and Christopher farther back, near the edge of the trees. Grandpa was chasing Christopher, and neither of them could run very well because they were laughing too hard. Finally, Grandpa caught up with the boy and tackled him. Christopher laughed and kicked his legs, trying to get free.

Richard watched, like he'd just walked into a theatre in the middle of a fascinating scene. He tried to figure out what he'd missed, feeling deep within himself that he was a spectator, that he was watching something far away, separate from himself, something he was no more a part of than he would be of that movie.

He moved away from the door, numb.

"What's wrong, honey?"

"Oh, nothing."

His mother looked out the window over the sink and laughed. "They're not getting any more wood chopped than you and your father ever used to. Go out there and give them some help."

"No, I think I'll go for a walk."

"Richard, go out there and have some fun with them."

"I really don't walk enough, Mom. City living will do that to you."

"Can't I at least get you something to eat?"

"I'm really not that hungry." As he passed through the kitchen he noticed the Jeep keys hanging on a hook near the doorway. "Do you mind if I borrow the Cherokee? It'd be nice to go for a drive."

"Don't get enough driving in the city?"

Richard stopped and looked at his mother. "What?"

"Nothing."

"You're giving me that look of yours."

"What look?"

"The one where you're shaking your head in disappointment without moving it an inch. How do you do that, is it with your eyes?"

"It's more in the forehead," she said as she turned back to the sink.

Richard looked back at the window to the backyard.

"What's his secret, Mom? What's yours? You're both so comfortable, so easygoing with Christopher."

She turned from the sink and studied her son for a moment as though she were weighing her words, trying to make certain they were something of substance, but not too heavy. Then she smiled. "We're not perfect, you know that. But it's nice to hear, anyway. It's good to have you home, son."

She started to turn back around, but his voice stopped her. "Mom, what's the secret?"

"There's no secret, honey, you just have to be sure you're on the same side of the door as your children."

He looked at the keys, looked at the window over the sink, heard the laughter. "Sounds easy, but sometimes the door has been slammed and locked. And not necessarily by you or your kid." He turned to leave.

"That's when you climb in through the window," she said just before he left the kitchen.

CHAPTER

THIRTY-THREE

Richard enjoyed the feel of driving the Jeep, like he was being set free. There were a few houses along this road, but they were far apart. That didn't stop the neighbors from being neighborly, it just stopped them from tripping over each other. And that made for long friendships. He was getting near the Bedfords' home, where his best friend Andy had grown up.

As he rounded the curve, he saw the house and stopped. He had spent so many months on his novel, trying to capture what it meant to be a child, and here he was looking at it. There was the long wooden porch that had been such a large part of his childhood.

Hundreds of times, Richard had ridden his bicycle down the road, rounded the curve, and found Andy sitting on the edge of the porch waiting for him. Richard would ride his bike onto the lawn—despite Andy's mom trying to look stern when she told him not to—and drop it by the cedar because they were always in such a hurry to do something. Anything. Sometimes they'd crawl under the porch and pretend they were spies or soldiers or whatever they felt at the moment. Sometimes they'd bring games out on the porch—one of their favorites was Risk—and play all afternoon.

He pulled away from the house and headed down the road. It had been a long time, but Richard and the roads knew each other well, and now they were leading him through the hills. He wasn't thinking of his driving or of the scenery, he was just going. Andy's house was a mile behind him now, and Richard turned past the last house on the road. There was a "Dead End" sign, but he knew to turn again and let the Jeep's tires find the ruts of an old path that led up the side of the hill. It was a path his bicycles, then his motorcycle, had taken him up many times, alone.

Richard stopped the Jeep. He climbed out and walked to the round, ancient rock. He sat down, absorbing the scene before him. This wasn't a Vermont postcard scene. There was no small, white church with towering steeple, no covered bridge or centuries-old mill with a water wheel. He could see no trace of a person in any direction from that hill; even the path ended a hundred yards from the top. All you could see from the hill were trees...sky...dirt. And it certainly wasn't some sort of hill of mythological proportions, dominating all others like Mount Olympus. He could see from his rock at least two, maybe three other hills that were taller.

Years before, in his own, private ceremony, Richard had given the hill a name. He'd never told anyone, not even Andy or his parents. Its name was the one thing he felt as he was growing up that only he knew. Though others certainly knew the hill, they didn't know the name. And without the name, they'd never know the hill.

This was where he'd come when he was younger to write, to think, to dream, to laugh, to pray. He felt that the last time he'd done any of those things very well was the last time he'd sat on this hill.

He stood up, in front of his rock, and looked out once more upon the rolling hills before him. True, he loved the colors here in the fall, but in summer everything seemed more peaceful, more humble. Everything was green, and nothing appeared to be trying to outdo the others with spectacles of color.

"Ktaadan," said a voice from behind him.

Richard turned sharply. There he was, just a few feet from Richard, in jeans, hiking boots, flannel shirt, and blue jean jacket.

David.

"I called the folks," David said. "Mom told me you'd gone for a drive. It wasn't hard to figure out where you'd be, big brother. Ktaadan."

Richard started walking toward the Jeep, not even looking at his brother. He stared at the earth in front of him as he walked, feeling the anger build.

David grabbed his brother's arm. "Don't go, Richard."

Richard pulled away and stared his brother in the face. "How do you even know about this place? How do you know the name?"

"Have you blocked that out, too? You brought me here, when I was fourteen, the day before you left for college. We sat on the rock together, and you told me the name."

"I would remember that," Richard said as he turned back toward the Jeep. "That never happened."

"Yes it did, Richard," David shouted. "You can't take that away from me."

Richard stopped. He hadn't heard his brother's voice for almost five years, but he felt like he'd just heard it the day before. "I told you the name?"

"The mountain Thoreau wrote about in *The Maine Woods*. The mountain where he was shaken up by nature and had to confront those awful, powerful feelings. After you left for college, I bought a copy and read that chapter over and over. 'What is this Titan that has possession of me? Talk of mysteries! Think of our life in nature, daily to be shown matter, to come in contact with it, rocks, trees, wind on our cheeks!'"

"'The solid earth.'" Richard said. "'The actual world. The common sense.'"

The brothers recited the last few words together. "'Contact! Contact! Who are we? Where are we?'"

"Who are we, big brother? Where are we?"

"You know what happened, David."

"I made a mistake."

"Is that what you call it? Dropping out of college to be a full-time junkie—that's a mistake? Getting busted for drugs, dragging Dad out of bed to dig you out of jail while Mom cried herself sick at home—that's a mistake? Then all that wasted time as an addict, living in a hole somewhere, never making anything of yourself. You broke their hearts," Richard said. "You almost killed them."

"No, I hurt them. I hurt them bad. But you're the one almost killing them."

Richard grabbed David by the jacket and threw him down to the ground. He jumped on top of him and held his brother's arms hard against the earth. "You liar!" he yelled, inches from David's face. "You're the one! You're the one!"

"If you really believed that, you wouldn't be yelling."

Richard got off of his brother and sat on the ground next to him. David sat up, rubbing the back of his head where it had hit the ground.

"Are you clean?" Richard asked, studying the grass in front of him.

"Almost four years."

"How could you do that to them, David?"

David stood up and started walking down the hill. "I give up, big brother."

"Do you have any idea how hard it was to lose my little brother?"

His brother turned, shaking his head. "Sorry, big brother, that doesn't wash anymore. The hurt comes with the caring, and caring is risky. It always is."

David walked out of view down the hill. Richard wanted to call after his brother, but didn't have the words.

CHAPTER
THIRTY-FOUR

"What's the deal with David?" Richard asked when he walked into the kitchen.

"Well, hello to you, too," his mother said. "He said he'd know where you'd be."

"Did you know he was here? Does he live here now?"

"No, no, no, but I wish he did. He owns a music store down in New Haven, near Yale."

"Music store? They got rid of those years ago."

"I know," she said, "but he's making this version work. Collectors can buy records and CDs, or you can listen to music and download it there for a discount. People buy from him because he knows his music, how to connect them with artists they'll care about. Like a bookstore for music. You ought to go there sometime." She opened the dishwasher and started putting the dishes away in the cabinet. "He also works on computer programs at night. He's very gifted with the computer, Richard. Already sold an app."

"Sounds like you keep in touch with him."

"He calls at least once a week. We have good talks."

"Did you tell him I'd be here this weekend?"

She turned. "Of course I did, is there anything wrong with that?"

"Sorry."

"David always asks how you and Carol and Christopher are doing. When he found out you were coming, he said he'd come up and stay with the Taylors." She pointed her finger at Richard. "It's shameful both of my sons are in town at the same time, and they can't stay in our home together."

Richard walked over to his mother and hugged her.

"I'm sorry, Mom. I didn't mean to interrogate you."

She pulled away. "He's a good boy, Richard, you should give him a chance."

"We had a talk."

"You did? Did everything go all right?"

"I guess." He saw the hope she was feeling. "I don't know, I'm not as good at forgiving the prodigal son as you and Dad are."

"Just remember, he's our prodigal son, not yours."

"I'm part of the family, too."

"Absolutely. And which one are you in the parable?"

He didn't really mean to, but he smiled. "You've never been known for subtlety, have you, Mom?"

"Not if I can help it."

Richard left his mother in the kitchen and stepped out onto the front porch. He leaned against a post for a moment, taking a deep breath and savoring the crisp, pine air.

"Time to get a move on," Grandpa said. "We've got some of those memories to make."

Richard smiled. "One question: all those times you and I chopped wood, did we have plenty out here? I don't remember."

"Always."

"Then why were we chopping wood?"

"It's a secret," Grandpa said, winking. Grandpa turned to the side of the house and shouted, "He's ready!"

Christopher came running around the corner of the house, hose in hand, aiming right at his dad.

"Let's go, buddy!" Grandpa shouted as he grabbed part of the hose.

Christopher paused, smiled, then turned the nozzle wide open, drenching his dad in seconds.

"You're it!" Christopher shouted as he and Grandpa dropped the hose and ran. They left the nozzle turned on, so the hose danced all over the yard, spraying water in every direction. Richard thought they'd turn off the water and the joke would be over, but the spray kept coming. Finally, he dove after the nozzle, but it kept getting away from him until he got a good hold on the hose. Without thinking, he ran.

"Revenge!" he shouted as he ran around the corner of the house. He couldn't see anyone in the backyard. No one was under the deck or near the stump. A giggle came from off to the left, and when Richard turned he saw the sleeve of a shirt moving from behind an oak. He aimed the hose at the tree and ran toward it. Both Grandpa and Christopher ran out from behind the oak, trying to escape the blast of water and laughing every step.

"Help! Help!" Grandpa shouted. "Attorney on the loose!"

Both victims were entirely soaked when they decided to join forces and jump their attacker. Christopher grabbed Richard's knees and Grandpa tackled his waist, so they all three tumbled down to the ground, the hose still blasting between them. They rolled around on the ground, shouting and laughing, the hose was wrapping itself around them until they were hopelessly knotted up.

Grandma came running out onto the deck.

"Hey. Hey, you boys!" she shouted. "Stop that! Listen to me!"

The three dripping-wet generations of Carson men stopped their wrestling. Christopher finally thought to turn off the nozzle, but it still took them a minute to untangle themselves from the hose. The three stood side-by-side, in order of age, looking up at Grandma like boys caught with a bat at their feet and a broken window behind their backs.

"That's better," Grandma said. "I can't believe you three, acting like children. Now, do me a favor and roll around in the flower beds. They need some water." She smiled. "And they'll get plenty of fertilizing from you three as well."

She turned to go back into the house, and they looked at each other, nodded, and then Richard took the nozzle and turned it on, aiming right for his mother.

"I was always completely alert and on top of things," Richard said as he walked into the living room. While he finished up the dinner dishes, he'd heard his mother talking to Christopher about when he was a boy. "Don't believe anything your grandmother tells you."

"Too late, son," Grandma said. "I've got the pictures to prove it, and he's looking at them with me as we speak."

Richard sat next to them. "Lies. All lies."

"Your daddy used to always do that as a boy," Grandma said to Christopher, pointing to a photo of Richard as a four-year-old. "Sometimes I'd walk through this room and see him just sitting on the couch, in his own little world. An hour later I'd walk by, and he'd still be just sitting here. 'What are you doing?' I'd ask. 'Just thinking,' he'd say, when I finally got his attention."

"I do that too, sometimes," Christopher said, leaning over to get a better look at the picture.

"Well, you and your daddy are a lot alike."

"I know." Christopher smiled and nodded, looking down at a picture of his father as a little boy.

Grandma looked over at Richard and they smiled at each other.

"So what have you been thinking about, son?" Grandma asked.

"I don't know, I guess Carol. I wish she could have come with us."

"It would've been fun to spray her," Grandma said, laughing.

"Mother!"

"Well, it would have. I know I enjoyed getting all wet."

"You and Carol aren't alike," Christopher said.

"Maybe not," Grandma said, "but we may be more alike than we are different." She pointed to another picture. "Ah, this is one of my favorites."

"What's that thing he's sitting in front of?" Christopher asked.

"Oh, that's our old Underwood typewriter. It was actually my mother's and she gave it to us. It was ancient even back then. Sort of like a computer, but people had to be real careful when they poked at the keys because it was so hard to correct mistakes. And you didn't have to turn it on and off. And it didn't have a screen."

"Doesn't sound much like a computer to me."

"You've seen typewriters before, haven't you?"

"I don't think so. At least not one that looked like that. If there isn't a screen, how do you see what you've typed?"

"See the paper there? When you typed, the letters appeared on that paper, not a screen. Then, when the paper was full, you just pulled it out and you had what you wrote."

"Did he write very much when he was little?"

"Oh, yes, even as a little boy your daddy loved to write," she said. "He loved to write short stories. One time he divided the paper in fourths and typed on each fourth a short story about knights and castles. Then, after he'd typed several pages, he cut each sheet of paper into four pages, stapled them, and had himself a little book he'd written all by himself."

"Hey, little buddy," Grandpa said, coming into the room carrying *Winnie-the-Pooh*. "Ready for some Moose Tree Corner?"

Christopher jumped up.

"I forgot to tell you about that," Richard said.

"Let me guess." Christopher took a deep breath. "When you were just a kid Grandpa had a dream about walking in the forest and finding a giant tree full of mooses sitting in the branches reading books," he took another breath, "and so from then on every time your family wanted to sit around in the family room and read someone would say 'Let's have Moose Tree Corner' and you'd each grab a book and start reading." he stopped to catch his breath. "Is that about it?"

"Close."

Christopher grabbed Grandpa's hand and led him out of the room.

"Grandpa loves that book," Grandma said to Richard. "Hasn't read it for ages."

"I always used to think of our house as being right in the middle of the Hundred Acre Wood," Richard said, looking up from the album. "And in a couple of days I have to drag my own little Christopher back into the city. Doesn't seem right, does it?"

CHAPTER
THIRTY-FIVE

The last three days had been the best vacation Richard had ever had. The family meals, hikes, games—just what both he and his son needed. But now they were at the small train station in his parents' town. Miles down the track was Penn Station and later would be Grand Central. Time to leave. There were only a few people at the station, but they all acted like they knew each other. Several people smiled at Grandma and Grandpa as they walked along the platform behind Richard and Christopher. Richard stopped and placed the bag down next to him. He looked at his watch, then at the station clock, worried.

"We got here in plenty of time, son," Grandpa said. "If the train's on time, it won't be here for another fifteen minutes."

"Now will you tell me what's in the bag?" asked Christopher, pointing to a large canvas bag his grandfather had been carrying ever since they'd left the Jeep.

Grandma pulled out two gifts. They were both meticulously wrapped in the same red paper, with gold bows and ribbon.

"Honey," she said as she handed both gifts to Christopher, "here are a couple of little things we wanted you two to have. This heavy one is for your Daddy, and this big one is for you."

175

"You didn't have to do that," Richard said.

"If we'd had to," Grandpa said, "it would've taken all the fun out of it."

"Don't open them until you get on the train and want something to do, okay?" Grandma said.

Christopher nodded. Grandpa coughed two or three times, a sure sign he was trying not to get emotional. Richard looked at his watch and then glanced around the platform, hoping the train would be late.

"I hate good-byes," Grandma finally spoke up, "but I hate worse having to rush them just because some dumb train pulls up."

They all hugged each other and said their goodbyes. Christopher was trying to be a big boy about it all; he even coughed a couple of times like his grandpa.

"You take good care of your daddy, okay?" Grandma said.

The train pulled up, and a few people started getting off. An older couple a few feet away waved as two children and their parents—both the mother and father—got off the train. They all ran toward each other and hugged and kissed. Richard wished he was saying hello. Just looking forward to such a greeting at the other end of the tracks would make this good-bye tolerable.

"Come on, Christopher," Richard said. "We'd better get on the train."

Richard and Christopher were heading for the train when someone shouted, "Hey, it's not going to leave without you! Hold up!"

All four turned to see David running along the platform toward them. Christopher, Grandma, and Grandpa turned to Richard to see his expression. He was smiling. "I called him last night," Richard said.

"I've got to start getting up earlier," David said as he got to the family.

"I wasn't sure you were going to make it," Richard said.

"I always make it, I'm just never on time."

The conductor announced it was time to board. David held out his hand to his brother, but Richard pushed it away and hugged him. Christopher smiled as he jumped up and down. Grandpa had his arm around Grandma and they both smiled like they'd just woken up and found out it was Christmas morning and they were six again.

"What you told me on the mountain made me do a lot of thinking," Richard said. "You were right and I was wrong."

"Not the first time, big brother," David said, then smiled. "Do you know who I am, Christopher?"

"Of course, you're David!"

"Nope, I'm Uncle David to you. And you're the only person in the world who can call me that!" David knelt down and hugged his nephew. "I tell you what, I'm going to make it to Manhattan sometime this summer, and I'll bring my guitar. Maybe I can teach you a few licks."

Christopher looked like he wasn't sure what he was going to be taught, but he smiled anyway. He and Richard quickly said good-bye to everyone again and climbed aboard the train just as the conductor made the last call to board.

They found a seat and both crowded the window, watching Grandpa, Grandma, and David waving as the train made its way down the tracks, back to Penn Station.

"It's almost like we're standing still and they're moving away," Christopher said.

"It looks that way," Richard said, "but we're definitely the ones leaving."

CHAPTER
THIRTY-SIX

"What should we do now?" Christopher asked, yawning and stretching from his nap.

"I don't know. We could take another nap, or read a magazine, or look out the window. Or, if you really wanted to...we could open our presents!"

"Now?"

"Right now!"

Christopher didn't wait a second before he started tearing the paper. When he got to the plain brown box, he ripped open the top and looked in.

"Oh no!" Christopher said.

"What? What is it?"

"I can't believe it!"

"What is it?"

Christopher pulled out a Winnie the Pooh bear and hugged it. "They found it!"

"I think I used to have a bear like that."

"This is it! This used to be yours. See how old it is?"

"It's not that old."

Christopher hugged Pooh again.

"I never knew you wanted a bear that bad."

"I didn't—not until I found out about this bear."

"Winnie the Pooh?"

"*Your* Winnie the Pooh." Christopher stood up in his seat and hugged his dad, then kissed him on the cheek. "This is so great, Daddy! Thank you!"

"Wow," Richard said. "Thank *you*, son."

"Grandpa read me the stories when he tucked me in. He told me you named me after his friend, Christopher Robin."

"Yes, I remember."

"Why didn't you ever tell me?"

"I used to tell you. When I'd rock you, I'd tell you all the Pooh Bear stories. But you were too young to know what I was talking about."

"Don't be so sure about that."

"You know, I bought you a Winnie the Pooh bear when you were a baby. I even insisted they let you take it to the school with you."

"What happened to it?"

"I don't know," Richard said. "I kept asking about it, but everyone said you never had one."

Christopher picked up the other present and handed it to his father. "Here, open yours."

"I wonder what it could be."

"I think I know."

"Did they tell you?"

"No, but I can figure it out. Go ahead, open it."

Richard tore the paper off the box and opened it. He pulled out a photo album. "This is one you and Grandma kept looking at. I wonder what I'm supposed to do with this."

"Look at it, silly."

Richard chuckled. "Why didn't I think of that? Let's take a look." As Richard opened the book, Christopher scooted closer to him, still holding the bear. "I don't have the slightest idea who this is," Richard said, pointing to one of the photos.

"That's Bobby. You two were best friends until he moved away in third grade."

"Yeah, I remember Bobby."

Christopher turned a couple of pages and pointed to another picture. "Then, in fourth grade, Andy moved from New Hampshire and you two became best friends." The photo showed Richard and Andy standing in front of some of the trees behind the Carson home. "And that place behind you, that's where you used to go underneath all the branches and pretend it was your clubhouse."

"Oh, I have great memories of that clubhouse. That's where I used to always take Pooh Bear when I was about your age."

"Yep." His smile returned as he turned another page or two. "This is Denise, your first real girlfriend. You took her to your clubhouse and kissed her there for the first time." Christopher laughed.

"How did you know that?"

"Grandma told me."

"Well, how did she know that?"

"I don't know. Parents are supposed to know things like that."

For the next two hours, Richard sat next to his son and listened to him talk. He remembered a lot of the pictures Christopher explained, and his memory seemed to be improving with each photo. Still, he wanted to hear everything and anything Christopher had to say.

When they grew tired, Christopher put the album away and, holding Pooh Bear close, laid his head in his father's lap and fell asleep.

Only a few minutes had passed when the conductor came by and checked their tickets. Richard knew it was a waste of time for him to try to sleep. He wasn't sure if it was a matter of transitioning from the country to the city, or worry about having to confront Carol and her feelings about the sabbatical, but he felt a lost, trapped sense inside him—almost a panic—that increased each mile closer to Manhattan.

Each mile closer to Newman.

CHAPTER
THIRTY-SEVEN

Richard turned over, looked at the alarm clock, then sat up. "What's wrong?" Christopher stood next to his parents' bed, dressed for the day.

"Christopher! How long have you been standing there?"

"Long enough to wonder if you were ever going to wake up," Christopher said.

"It's past eight. I've got to get going!"

"Where?" Christopher grabbed his father's hand. "I know you usually write in the morning before I get up, but it looks like I'm already up. And Carol's already gone to work. Let's do something together."

Richard rubbed his eyes and thought for a moment. "You know, you're right. What should we do?"

"Remember, we just need to ask ourselves what Grandma and Grandpa would do." Christopher didn't say anything for a moment, then smiled. "Let's chop some wood."

They smiled, then raced to the kitchen. As they ate a couple of bowls of cereal and some toast, they kept comparing their cereal to the waffles and pancakes and eggs they'd grown accustomed to during their short visit to Grandma and Grandpa's. Grandpa's pancakes were the most fun to eat, they agreed, since the middles were never quite done. "Cream-filled," they told each other.

"Now we have to go see the world," Christopher said.

Their first stop for the day of chopping wood was the American Museum of Natural History, across from Central Park. They'd been by there two or three times, and each time Christopher would ask about that mysterious building and Richard would promise they'd go there someday. His favorite area was the dinosaur bones, and he kept complaining about how badly his legs wanted to climb over all the dinosaurs.

"I think their bones are talking to mine, telling mine to climb, climb, climb," he said.

After spending the morning in the museum, the two walked outside and decided they were hungry. "Where would you like to eat?" Richard asked.

"I don't know. Where do you want to eat?"

"Anywhere you want to."

"Okay...how about if we buy some hot dogs and eat in the grass?"

Richard stopped for a second. "Sounds good to me. We'll eat the longest dogs in the tallest grass in the world!"

They took a cab to the former IBM building on the corner of 57th and Madison. Richard spotted a street vendor and bought two large hot dogs, some potato chips, and a couple of Sprites.

"Where's the grass?" asked Christopher.

"Follow me."

Richard headed for the atrium at the side of the building with Christopher close behind. As the two walked in, the little boy was astonished to see the giant shoots of bamboo reaching up to a ceiling that seemed miles away.

Between bites, they talked about anything that came to Christopher's mind. Will they someday build skyscrapers in Central Park? Did people use to ride their horses down all these streets? Why doesn't this little island sink from all the tall buildings? Did people use to ride their horses down the subways?

Richard told Christopher he had a special surprise for him and led him out the door, west on 57th, then north on Fifth Avenue. Christopher was so busy asking where they were going he didn't notice when they'd arrived, standing next to a man dressed up like a toy soldier. Richard pointed to the store: FAO Schwartz.

"What is this place?" Christopher almost shouted.

"A toy store. They sell nothing but toys here, the finest around. Do you want to go inside?"

"Are you kidding?"

The toy soldier opened the door and Christopher ran in, his father not far behind. He turned in circles several times, probably getting dizzy trying to see everything at once. Light, playful music—like the music from a child's music box—filled the air with "Welcome to Our World" and a happy excitement.

Christopher stared at the giant clock that reached up to the second-floor ceiling. He studied each of the different toys along the side of the clock tower as it slowly turned. Then he noticed what appeared to be a life-sized castle tower. He watched as a part of it moved up on a giant pole.

"An elevator! There's another floor?" he asked.

"Sure."

"And that's just toys, too?"

"Nothing but toys. Do you want to go up?"

"No. Let's see everything down here first."

Christopher touched every soft, stuffed animal he saw: lions, bears, dogs, cats, tigers. He ran over to what seemed like life-sized stuffed animals and stroked the giraffe a number of times, looking along its long neck and up to its jaw. Every minute or two Christopher would point to something else—"Daddy, look at this!"—and Richard would follow him to the next toy. They spent an hour on the first floor alone, making certain there wasn't a single toy left untouched.

"This is unbelievable!" Christopher said. "I think I need to rest."

"Well, okay. Or, we could go upstairs now."

Christopher smiled and ran toward the elevator. When he saw the escalator off to the side, he made a detour and headed for a stuffed animal named "Spanky," a brown bear sitting in a bright red miniature BMW at the foot of the escalator. Richard waved his hand over a word on the information board and Spanky announced where the sports equipment was located. Another wave of the hand, and the bear talked about the trains.

"Let's go!" Christopher shouted.

He jumped on the escalator, his excitement building each foot closer to the second floor. He headed first for the sleek, red miniature Ferrari. His father told him to climb in it, but he couldn't believe that it was a real car for children. There was also a miniature Jeep, a Batmobile, and a Barbie convertible. Christopher went to great lengths to make sure his father understood he had no interest in the convertible.

"Christopher, you've got to check these out. They were my favorite."

Richard led his son over to the large Legos area full of displays. Christopher looked enthralled with the pirate ships, the space stations, the castles. Tub after tub of Legos lined the top of the shelves next to the ceiling, and beneath them were rows of building kits.

"Let's build something," Richard said.

"Is it all right?"

"Sure. That's what these tables are for."

They sat at a red and white table covered with Legos and started building everything that came to mind. A tower. Cars to crash into the tower. A rough replica of the large pirate ship they'd seen on display, though their crow's nest looked more like a miniature telephone pole. They'd been building with the Legos for a half-hour when two identical twin boys, about Christopher's age, sat next to them. Christopher glanced at his father and started to get up, and Richard was going to get up as well, but then he pretended not to notice his son's movement and remained seated, still building the small house he'd started. Christopher sat back down and concentrated on his staircase. Christopher and his father had been talking and laughing with each other, but now everyone at the table was quiet, working on his own project. The twins didn't even talk to each other, but were busy constructing what appeared to be two robots. Their nanny stood several feet away, talking on her cell phone.

As Richard built, he kept an eye on the three boys. He realized he'd never seen his son with other children before. Of course, he'd seen Christopher with other residents, but not with other children who could act like children. He watched as the twins finished their robots just about the same time Christopher completed his stairs. The twins had their robots fight each other, crashing them together and making battle noises with their mouths. Then, one of the twins had his robot run away.

Christopher moved his stairs very slightly toward the robots, but it was enough to let the twins know everything was okay. The one robot ran up the stairs, the other closely following, and the two battled it out at the top of the stairs. Christopher held onto the stairs to help keep them together, but after a minute of fighting, he got into the act by shaking the stairs and making them collapse under the weight of the fighting robots. The three boys laughed and started building something else together.

Richard was fascinated with how quickly Christopher had learned to come up with things that would delay going to bed. They had to build one last robot with the new Legos, and read one of the books they'd bought at The Strand Bookstore that afternoon, then another book, and now, for the past ten minutes, Christopher had been making up games that they would play someday.

"Okay," Richard said, "just one more."

"How do you play the bobbledy-goop ball game?"

Richard smiled. "I don't know. How?"

"You get about thirteen or fourteen people in a circle. They need to be good friends."

"Yeah."

"Then one person stands in the middle and starts bobbling around with a big orange ball. A square ball."

"Okay."

"When he finally sits down on the ground, everyone—"

"Picks up some goop and throws it at him?" Richard asked.

"They all yell 'goop' and run around in a circle."

"Of course. How do you win the game?"

"By having fun."

They both laughed, then Richard gave his son a hug. "We had a week's worth of fun all in one day."

"I've never had this much fun. Not even in Vermont."

Richard smiled. "I'm glad you had such a good time. And remember, Uncle David and I worked it out so he could visit us next week for a couple of days."

"Now I'll never be able to get to sleep," Christopher said.

"We chopped a lot of wood, didn't we?" Richard said, then bent down to kiss Christopher. "Good night, son."

"Good night, Daddy." Richard was at the door before Christopher spoke again. "I love you."

"I love you, too, son. Sleep tight."

This felt good. This felt like being a dad.

CHAPTER
THIRTY-EIGHT

Richard closed the door and stood by it for just a minute, waiting to see if Christopher was going to call him back in. When he didn't hear anything, he walked down the hall to the office. He looked on his desk for the notes he'd made in Vermont. He had had a few ideas for his novel and was excited to tackle them now. The most he'd ever written was about fifty pages before scrapping them and starting over. He heard that one of the big mistakes of first-time novelists was writing about something they really didn't know anything about, so he had decided a long time ago to write about growing up. He'd write about a boy growing up in New England, and how the people he knew and the choices he made shaped what he would later become as a man. Maybe not a best-seller or the seed for a blockbuster movie, but it was a story he wanted to tell. The problem was, he was never satisfied with what he had to say.

But he'd taken some good notes, and he felt different tonight. He thought he'd finally figured out what had been wrong all this time. Up until now, he had a message to send. He wanted to make a bold statement about society. He kept changing his mind about what that bold statement was exactly, but he always knew he wanted to make it. During the past few days, though, watching his son and his parents, and today, playing and eating and shopping and talking with Christopher, something became different. Finally, he knew he had a story to tell rather than a message to send.

He found his notes and sat down with his notebook.

Thirty minutes passed, and so did the feeling that something would be different this time. Watching his son and feeling something different was one thing, putting it into words was another. He kept rereading and rearranging his notes, but he hadn't even written a word, not wanting to put anything on paper that wasn't perfect. Just as he reached for his notebook, not knowing if he were going to file it in the cabinet or the trash, one word caught his eye: porch. He thought of the porch at Andy's house, and the feeling came back, and, without thinking, he began writing.

The porch. What it was made of. When it was built. The games played on, underneath, around it. The talks. A resort for lemonade in the summer, a fort for snowball fights in the winter. The first three pages were just about the porch, and then that led to the house. The type of house, the location of the house, the importance of the house—and of the people who lived there. Page after page about the house and its family. Richard wasn't trying to be poetic, and he wasn't trying not to be, he was simply putting words on paper, much as a sculptor might throw a lump of clay down on his table. It was a lump of clay, with no particular form, no hidden meaning. But over time, with the proper molding and shaping by talented, loving hands, an image would emerge that could transcend the roughness of its origins and bring to the world something it had never seen before.

For the first time, Richard felt like a writer.

CHAPTER
THIRTY-NINE

After writing in their notebooks for most of the morning, Richard and Christopher and his Winnie the Pooh ventured out to Central Park. Richard figured his son would enjoy boating on the lake and going to the zoo, but he was surprised at how much he loved riding on the carousel. He couldn't imagine anything more old-fashioned than a carousel, but his son wanted to ride it again and again.

Richard had promised they'd eat dinner at Grand Central Station. Dinner took a long time because Christopher was so excited to talk about the day, but Richard was in no hurry.

Richard and Christopher climbed the stairs to catch the subway home, Grand Central becoming increasingly crowded and hectic. Richard held tightly on to his son's hand while he looked for signs pointing to the subway they needed. Something felt different, but he didn't know what. Like there was some strange sense of tension among all these strangers. Travelers...homeless... commuters...a man selling yo-yos that lit up...a small band—bass, lead guitar, and drums...a woman selling puppets...a self-styled rapper. It was almost like being at a circus thrown together at the last minute. He felt that unique mixture of fun and sadness he'd always experienced at the circus as a kid. But that wasn't what kept nagging at Richard. Too many people pushing past each other. Too many shadows. Something wasn't right.

"Stay close," Richard almost shouted to be heard. "Our train shouldn't be too far from here."

They turned a corner, but found themselves at a four-way intersection. Richard, just for a moment, wasn't quite sure which hall to take. He paused to get his bearings. Christopher held onto his bear more tightly.

Just as Richard made up his mind and started off to the left, he felt a large force hit him from behind so hard that he fell to the floor. He no longer felt his son's hand in his.

"Christopher!"

He stood up but the crowd was swarming around him and he couldn't see his son.

"Christopher!" he shouted, but no response. He pushed his way through the crowd.

"Christopher! Where are you?" He looked around the intersection and along the walls. He scanned the different halls, wondering which one he should try, or if he should just stay where he was. He could feel his heart beating, faster, faster, and felt sweat forming all over his body, dripping from his forehead and under his arms.

"Christopher!" he shouted. "Has anyone seen a little boy? A little boy holding a bear?"

No one listened.

He went down one of the halls, calling after Christopher, asking anyone who would listen if they'd seen a boy with a bear.

He turned the corner and saw through the rushing crowd a station employee back against the wall, walking slowly. Richard ran up to the man and grabbed him by his shirt, pushing him against the wall.

"Hey, pal!"

"I've lost my son."

"What?"

"I've lost my son. He was with me a minute ago, but now he's gone. You've got to help me find him."

The man asked to see a picture and then messaged the photo and the boy's information to the station police headquarters, promising they'd all help look. Richard headed back down the hall. Madhouse. Where was his little boy in this madhouse? He didn't belong here.

Richard turned the corner into the larger Grand Central foyer and stopped. Thousands. People rushed all over the place, everyone and everything moving around each other, into each other. He looked up into the high ceiling with all its stars and felt himself spinning. Felt the whole station turning around and around. He fell against the wall behind him.

Richard finally saw Al's newsstand and ran up to it.

"Mr. Carson, what is it?"

"Have you seen a little boy around here, holding a bear?"

"No. What little boy?"

"My son—he's gone."

"Let's go," Al said. He locked up his stand. "I'll help you look." He pulled down the metal door until it touched the counter, then came out of the stand through a small door on the side.

"Let's divide up," Richard said. "You take the east side, I'll take the west. He's six years old, about this tall," he held out his hand, "with brown hair. Oh, forget it, just look at this." He showed Al Christopher's picture on his phone.

Richard kept calling Christopher's name, but no one seemed to notice him. He climbed up on a bench, searching the huge cavern. It was impossible to see individual children in the station. If he was lucky, he might see the tops of one or two heads, but he couldn't make out faces. A couple of times he thought he saw a boy that might look like his son, but each time the child was with an adult or a couple. Christopher would be alone. Scared and alone.

He climbed down from the bench, still calling his son's name. When he walked around an information counter, he found a police officer scanning the crowd.

"Officer," Richard said, "I'm looking for my little boy—"

"Right," the officer said, "I am, too." He held up his cell phone and showed the picture of Christopher. "Headquarters sent it to us. We've all got one."

"I don't see how this is going to work," Richard said. "How can we find one little boy in this crowd?"

"I'm not looking for one little boy."

"What do you mean?"

"I hate to bring this up, Mr. Carson, but there's a chance someone took your son. I'm looking for an adult with a boy who looks like he's not very happy."

The officer walked off, cell in hand, looking down a hall.

He was right. As much as Richard didn't want to admit it, maybe Christopher wasn't alone. He changed his focus, searching for anyone with a child. A train must have just arrived because another flood of people came down the hall, parting around Richard and making him feel even more helpless. He pushed his way through the new crowd, getting in front of it so he could get a better view of the station.

He found another bench and stood on it to get a broader perspective. He called his son's name out, realizing it would be almost impossible for Christopher to hear him. As he turned, something caught his attention. A large, bulky man in a dark suit was crouching down near the corner for some reason, a woman standing next to him, nervously glancing all over and tapping the man on the shoulder. She looked frantic.

Why was the man crouching down?

Richard jumped off the bench and started walking over to the couple. The woman saw him, then grabbed the man's shoulder and shook him. Richard ran toward them, pushing people aside.

"Christopher?" he shouted.

"Come on, come on," the woman almost shouted to the man. "He's here. We gotta go."

The man turned and Richard saw his little boy, clutching his bear, standing against the wall crying. Before the man could stand up, Richard ran into him with all his weight, knocking him into the woman.

"Daddy!" Christopher shouted.

Richard grabbed his son and held him. The man stood up, but suddenly fell down hard, right on his face. Al stood behind him.

"We gotta get out of here, Mr. Carson," Al said, pointing to door. The woman was running out to a van with "Shapiro's Coat Outlet" painted on its side. She kept shouting as two men climbed out of the van and started pushing their way into the station.

"Let's go," Richard said, and he moved through the crowd as quickly as possible. He couldn't run—there were too many people—but he soon got lost in the crowd. When he looked behind him, he saw that the three men and the woman had lost track of them and had split up, each scanning the foyer.

Christopher held on to his father's neck with one arm, and to Pooh Bear with the other. He'd stopped crying.

"Follow me," Al said, taking the lead.

They ran up to his newsstand, making sure none of the men had seen them. As Al struggled with the keys, Richard noticed one of the men heading in their direction. He didn't think he'd seen them, but he wasn't sure. Al finally got the door unlocked and the three dove into the newsstand. After he'd locked the door, Al pointed to the floor and they sat down. It was tight, and Christopher sat in his father's lap, still holding onto his neck. They could hear themselves breathing, almost panting, from all the running. A thin sheet of light passed under the metal door and cut across the interior of the stand. Al opened his mouth, but Richard motioned with his finger to his lips not to say anything.

Richard looked down at his watch and wondered how long they would need to stay hidden. He tried to calm down and think things through, figure out what was happening, but his mind raced in just one place.

After about a half hour, Al touched Richard on the shoulder. "I'm gonna go take a look," he whispered, then left the stand.

The next time Richard glanced at his watch an hour had passed. His son rocked back and forth in his lap a little bit as though he were trying to calm down his bear. The door started to rattle and Christopher grabbed his father around the neck.

"I've looked all over," Al said, "but they're gone. The van's gone, too."

"I just want to go home, Daddy. Can't we just go home?"

"Okay, son," Richard whispered. "Everything's going to be all right."

They found a police officer near the information booth and reported what had happened. The officer called for others to come and search the station while he talked with Richard. Richard responded to a list of questions, but nothing seemed to be leading to any answers. The officer did his best to interview Christopher, but all the boy could remember was the man grabbing him and holding onto him while they made their way through the terminal. He never looked up to see their faces because he was so afraid.

"Is there anyone, Mr. Carson," the officer said, "anyone who'd want to kidnap your son?"

Richard thought of Harold Solomon. He knew what Harold would think, that it had to be the school. But he also knew that Harold wouldn't say anything—it was too dangerous. But Harold was paranoid. Besides, what would be the point of their trying to kidnap Christopher? Why would they take such a big risk?

CHAPTER FORTY

After the cab took off from the station, Richard let out a sigh and started to relax a little.

"Is everything going to be okay, Daddy?"

"Yes, son, everything's going to be just fine. Everything's better when the sun comes up."

Christopher snuggled up to his father, still holding on tight to his bear, and closed his eyes. Richard found himself looking in the mirror and off to the sides, seeing if the van was anywhere near. He wondered if he would always be like this, checking people's faces, searching for suspicious cars.

When they got to their apartment building, Christopher was asleep. Richard paid the driver and, with his son in one hand and the bear in the other, made his way up to their apartment. While he fumbled for his keys, the apartment door opened.

"What took you so long?" Carol asked as he came in through the door. "You were supposed to be back a long time ago. I called your cell."

Richard put the bag down and headed down the hall, carrying Christopher.

"He's had a rough day," he whispered. "I'll tell you about it in a minute."

Richard laid Christopher on his bed. He took the little boy's shoes off and covered him with a blanket. When he returned to the living room, Carol was waiting by the couch.

"So, what happened?" she asked.

Richard kept walking through the living room and into their bedroom. Without turning on the light, he sat on the edge of their bed, rubbing his neck.

"You're gone for days and then you come home late," she said. "I'm worried sick, some mysterious thing happened, and you don't have anything to say?"

"When we were at Grand Central today, someone tried to take Christopher."

"Take? What do you mean, 'take'?"

"I don't know. Kidnap, I guess."

She backed up against the wall and covered her mouth with her hand. "Kidnap? Who?"

"I don't know who, why, I don't know anything."

"Is he all right?"

"A little shaken up, but he's okay."

Carol left their bedroom and walked back toward Christopher's room. When she came back, she looked like she was in the courtroom with a hostile witness.

"Do you still think he's better off outside of Newman?" she said, keeping her voice down.

"What? Carol, what happened to the—"

"Richard, start thinking of him." Her voice was low, but he'd never seen her so furious before. "If he were back in Newman—where he belongs—none of this would have happened. You need to start thinking of him."

"I am thinking of him. We need to be with him all the time, to protect him, to—"

"You were with him today, Richard, and that didn't seem to help much."

CHAPTER
FORTY-ONE

Light from the living room window shone on Richard as he lay on the couch. He hadn't bothered to get a blanket, or to even take off his shoes. Three times during the night he'd heard noises and had run down the hall, ready to defend his son again. Each time, once he realized there was nothing to fight, he would check on Christopher, then lie back down on the couch, waiting at least an hour for sleep to come back.

"Daddy."

Richard sat up like an alarm had gone off.

"Are you okay?" Richard asked, grabbing his son.

"Sure. I just wanted to let you know the sun came up."

"Oh." Richard hugged his son, trying to calm down. He could feel his heart beating, stumbling over itself.

"You were right," Christopher said, "everything is better."

Richard smiled, remembering what he'd told him the night before.

"I think Carol is already gone. Your door is open and no one's in there. Why did you sleep out here?"

"Habit, I guess." Richard pulled Christopher close to him. "Listen, son, I want to chop wood with you today, but let's do it indoors. I don't feel like leaving the apartment today, okay?"

Christopher smiled. "Writing in the morning, Scrabble and videos in the afternoon. Sounds like a great day to me, Daddy."

When he heard the front door open, Richard looked at his watch. Nine o'clock. They hadn't talked since the night before. He thought of getting up, but he didn't know what to say. Carol had been so angry with him, like it was his fault someone had tried to kidnap their son. He knew he was supposed to get up, but he couldn't let himself. He kept listening for her footsteps to pass down the hall. They never did. She must be just standing near the front door, not far from the office. There was a knock on the office door.

"Come in," he said.

The door opened and Carol walked in, carrying a couple of bags that filled the small study with the smell of Chinese food. She was smiling. And she'd left her briefcase in the hall.

"Hungry?" she asked.

"Sure, I guess."

He got up from the desk, ready to go into the kitchen, but she closed the door and pulled out two sets of chopsticks from one of the bags. She sat on the floor and leaned against the wall.

"It's been a long time since we ate Chinese take-out on the floor," he said.

"That's the whole point, it's been too long. For a lot of things we used to do."

Richard began eating his dinner, watching Carol as she talked. She told him some of the details of the big Matsushita case she'd been working on, about how it looked like one of the associates would be fired because he wasn't billing enough hours to justify keeping him until it was time to not make him partner, about how one of the senior partners might be retiring, which meant she might get an even nicer office.

At one point she asked about his writing. He talked a little about it, careful not to reveal too much, but she appeared genuinely interested. The more he talked, the more she encouraged him to share, until he ended up telling her all about the porch and its significance.

"That sounds like a powerful metaphor. Are you going to carry it throughout the novel?"

When he said he wasn't sure yet, that he was more or less just getting the first thoughts on paper, she surprised him by suggesting that might be the best way to go.

"Have you been writing all day?" she asked before taking a bite from her egg roll.

"We wrote in the morning, but spent the rest of the day doing whatever came to Christopher's mind—so long as it was here. I just wanted to stay home. Keep him safe." He knew he could've said it better, made it sound more productive and less dramatic, but the words just came out.

"Sounds like a good idea. I wish I could've stayed with you."

Richard shook his head and put down the almost empty carton.

"What?" she asked.

"I'm sorry, Carol, this has been great, but you've got to tell me what's going on."

"What do you mean? We're eating dinner."

"I feel like I'm in a play or something, and nobody's shown me the script of the next scene."

"I just wanted to be with you."

"But this isn't like you." Carol frowned when he said that. "I'm sorry, I didn't mean it that way."

"It used to be like me."

"I guess so."

"Let's go off for a couple of days." She held his hand. "We need to get away from the city."

"Where?"

"The Bahamas? Maine? You name the climate."

"I thought you wanted us to watch our budget, with just one income."

"It was just an idea." She pulled her hand away and started picking up.

"Wait a minute, maybe this is a good idea," he said. "Christopher loved being in Vermont. It would do him some good to get away again."

"I was really thinking of just the two of us going."

Richard stared at her. "Are you serious? Leave him after what happened last night?"

"Richard, we need to work on the two of us if we want to help him."

"No way," he said, shaking his head. "I need to know he's safe."

"There's this place I've heard about, called TempCare. It's amazing. Parents can leave their children there for up to two weeks. Highly recommended and completely certified by all the state and national boards. Great teachers. Lots of learning activities. Better than being at home."

"There's no way—"

"Very safe, Richard. Probably the safest place he could be."

Richard picked up the tablet and said "TempCare." He took a minute to read the website, then looked up at Carol.

"Carol, this place looks like a mini-version of Newman. Why would we want to put him there?"

"He'd have other children to play with," she said. "What are you planning on doing, Richard, keep him cooped up here for the rest of the summer? What kind of life is that for him?"

"I don't like keeping him in all day anymore than you do," Richard said. "But we're together, and that's a good life. For both of us."

CHAPTER
FORTY-TWO

They argued for a few minutes, then Carol went to bed about midnight. Richard felt confused about his wife's suggestion they leave Christopher so they could have a weekend together. Right after he was almost kidnapped? She said TempCare was highly recommended. By whom? Who had she been talking to?

His cell phone rang. Harold.

"I'm sorry about what happened to Christopher yesterday," Harold said. "We're all grateful he's okay."

"How did you know? Never mind, you always know things."

"We've got to meet."

"No we don't," Richard said. "Just let me be with my son. I don't really want to get involved—"

"Richard, this is an emergency. If we don't meet, you may not have much time left with your son."

Harold told him where to meet, but nothing else. Richard ran down the stairs, two at a time, to the lobby. When he got outside, he ran to Park Avenue and flagged down a cab. Richard told him the address, and the driver headed for Washington Heights.

Richard sat in the back, sweating. It was hot, and the air coming in from the window didn't seem to do any real good.

They drove past Columbia and Barnard. A couple stumbled along the sidewalk and into the street past stores, tightly closed and barred against attack. Four cops ran down into a subway entrance, guns drawn. This was a different world from his parents' town in Vermont, and it bothered him that he accepted it all without question or surprise. Then he reminded himself where he was going, to meet with a group of good people who cared about each other. That was New York just as much as the dirty streets and the dangerous shadows.

He paid the driver when they pulled to the curb and jumped out, running up to a squatty brick apartment building of only five or six floors. Richard found the Solomon name, then buzzed the apartment. The door unlocked, and he ran up the stairs. When he got to the third floor, he found Harold standing in a doorway, waiting.

"It's Sandra's daughter," Harold whispered.

"What happened?" Richard asked.

"She's dead."

CHAPTER
FORTY-THREE

Richard followed Harold into the living room. Sandra's husband had his arm around her on the couch. Rebecca sat right next to her, trying to offer what comfort she could, and Joan and Lauren, from the discussion group, were nearby as well. No one spoke or made any sound whatsoever.

Richard still didn't really know anyone in the group, and he suspected it was expected of him, now that he was here, to remain off to the side, quiet. But he found himself walking over to where Sandra and her husband sat and kneeling next to them. He reached out and touched Sandra's hand.

"I don't know what to say," he whispered. "I'm sorry."

Sandra nodded.

Richard stepped back and Harold motioned for him to follow. They left the living room and found Paul, alone, leaning against the kitchen counter, drinking a cup of coffee. Harold poured himself and Richard some coffee and the three men stood there, breathing a little easier away from the living room.

After a moment, Paul spoke up. "I'm glad you came, Richard."

"Thanks. Paul, right? The Columbia student."

"Right." Paul took a sip of his coffee. "I wasn't sure you'd come. I told Harold not to bother calling you."

"Why?"

"You didn't seem all that into it when you met with us. Like you thought we were crazy."

"No, I never thought—"

"Maybe not crazy, but like we'd carried this thing too far. Like the school wasn't as bad as we thought it was."

"I won't argue with that," Richard said. He turned to Harold. "What happened to her?"

"The school said Tanya was having a nervous breakdown, remember?" Richard nodded. "Claimed she couldn't handle the thought of leaving Newman and going home. Tonight, Sandra gets a call from the hospital telling her that her little daughter had died."

"How?"

"They're not sure. Autopsy tomorrow."

"What do you think now, Richard?" Paul asked. "Are we still paranoid?"

"You think the school killed Tanya?"

"Oh, man, I never said it did," Paul said. "I never said it killed Joseph's boy, either. But you can keep your nose clean, avoid all responsibility, and let things happen. And that's just as bad, isn't it?"

They heard something going on in the living room and went to investigate. In the living room, they found Sandra standing up with her husband, and both of them embracing Joseph. The three were sobbing as they held on tightly to one another.

"*They* know what it's like when people let things happen," Paul whispered to Richard.

CHAPTER FORTY-FOUR

The curtains were drawn, and a single lamp on the floor softly shone its light. Richard sat on the floor and leaned against the wall. Harold and Rebecca sat across from him. It was almost two o'clock, and everyone else had left over an hour ago.

"So, what do you suggest? What can be done?" Richard asked.

"We pray," Rebecca said.

"The synagogue is our second home," Harold added.

Richard smiled.

"What is it?" Harold asked.

"You sound like my parents."

"They're Jewish?" Rebecca asked. They all smiled.

"No, Episcopalians. But often attributed good things that happened in our lives to prayer."

"And what about you, Richard?" Rebecca asked.

"Oh, I used to think I was somewhat religious. But things started happening with my younger brother, and I decided life needed more action and less prayer."

"Don't be so sure they're different," Harold said. "Besides, prayer isn't all we are doing. We've got our plan."

Rebecca gave her husband a sharp look.

"What plan?" Richard asked.

"Nothing specific, I guess," Harold said.

"Well, then, generally? What is there left to try? The courts?"

"It's difficult to prove the school does anything illegal. All we have are children with empty eyes."

"And two children who have died," Richard said.

"Think about it," Rebecca said. "The children look happy enough at Newman. They're learning, they're among friends, their teachers seem to love them. It's only when they're home they seem lonely, so robotic. It's hard to make the case to a judge that they're better off with their parents."

"Unless we have evidence that links the school to the deaths," Harold said, "we have nothing."

"Politicians?" Richard said. "What about getting the mayor or someone involved?"

"The mayor's daughter is at Newman. Besides," Harold said, "Newman knows where to send his lobbyists, and his money. There are good men and women in government, but without proof, they can't bite the hand that feeds them."

"Even with proof, some still wouldn't," Rebecca said.

"Then what? What's your plan?"

Rebecca and Harold looked at each other, clearly uneasy about something.

"You can trust me," Richard whispered. "Don't you know that by now?"

"To be honest," Rebecca said, "we haven't always known that."

"At first, we wondered," Harold said. "You accomplished something no one else has ever been able to: you got your son out on the sabbatical. Why were they so willing to let you? But we've talked with you, we've listened to you, we've watched you. We trust you now."

"It's a risk," Rebecca said, "but in desperate times, we must learn to trust."

Harold took a card out of his pocket and handed it to Richard. "Put this number in your cell phone, Richard. If you're ever in any trouble related to Christopher and the school, call it. The person answering will ask you for your account number. If you give the right password, you'll be connected to someone who can help."

"Password?"

"Yes. This week it's 'Jacob.' We'll let you know the new one each week. Keep it to yourself. Maybe this would've been a nice number to have when they tried to kidnap Christopher the other day."

"How did you know about that?"

"We are just a small part of a strong network of concerned parents," Rebecca said. "Not just parents with children at Newman, but parents who worry about what's happening in our schools, who don't like the idea of Newman being the future. We know enough to be scared, but we'll wait until the right time. We don't want to endanger anyone's child."

"Did Joseph call this number when his son was missing?"

Harold shook his head. "Unfortunately, we didn't have it set up then. The only person who's used it so far is Sandra, when she found out about the death of her daughter."

"What did your network do?"

"Tanya had already died," Harold said. "What could we do? We notified the other parents to beware of their child being taken to the hospital."

"One more thing," Richard said.

"Yes?"

"What did you mean when you said 'they' tried to kidnap Christopher? Do you have evidence that the school tried to do it?"

"No evidence. That's always the problem, we have no evidence."

"Then, for all you know," Richard said, "it could have been someone else?"

"And with all you know," Harold said, "could it have been someone else?"

CHAPTER
FORTY-FIVE

Richard closed his notebook and put it away while Christopher placed the new car he'd built into the Legos bucket to play with later. They'd decided to watch a video together when Carol called. She was downstairs, she said, waiting in one of her firm's cars. She wanted them to come down for a surprise. All she would tell Richard was they were going somewhere perfectly safe.

Richard and Christopher got into the back of the black sedan with Carol. One of her firm's drivers was behind the wheel.

"What's going on?" Richard asked.

"You'll see," Carol said. "Trust me."

After about ten minutes, the car stopped in front of a large office building that looked vaguely familiar to Richard. They entered a colorful lobby where there were four chairs and a table in the middle of a room full of beanbag chairs and stuffed animals. Next to a set of double-doors was a large sign: TempCare.

"No," Richard said. "I told you this was out of the question."

"This is the safest place in the country for children, Mr. Carson," a man said as he entered through the doors. "There's nothing to worry about here."

"This is Dr. Hawkins," Carol said. "He doesn't usually gives tours, but I pulled a few strings. Said we needed the best."

"Let's go, Christopher," Richard said, turning to the front door.

Carol stopped him. "Please, just a tour. If you don't like it, then it's out of the question."

Richard took a deep breath and looked down at Christopher. "And if you don't like it, son, it's really out of the question."

"Thank you for taking the time," Dr. Hawkins said, shaking hands. He wore khaki slacks, a blue denim shirt, a tie with tigers on it. Like he was trying not to look like a doctor. He even had stubble on his face. They walked down a short hall to the stairwell and started up the stairs, Christopher holding his father's hand.

"We've been in business about three years, Mr. Carson," Dr. Hawkins said. "Though it may not sound very modest, we've had nothing but success. We're proud of the contribution we've made to the general welfare of children and hope to establish other TempCares in the near future."

"What contribution is that, Doctor?" Richard said.

They turned at the top of the stairs and proceeded down a long, white hall. "Adults were finding it increasingly difficult to accomplish their life-goals and be parents as well. You know the struggle."

Richard didn't say anything.

"Because of our services," Dr. Hawkins said, "parents can now go on business trips, vacations, or simply enjoy a peaceful week or two at home, knowing their children are well cared for." The doctor stopped and turned to Richard, winking. "To be frank, in most cases, better cared for."

"You make it sound like this is an altruistic enterprise. I'm assuming you charge a good amount for your contribution to society." Richard noticed the disapproval on his wife's face, but he didn't mind.

"Nothing worthwhile is cheap. How much is your son worth, Mr. Carson?"

"He's not for sale."

They stopped at a one-way mirror. On the other side were two adults and about twenty-five children, ranging in age from three to thirteen, each wearing a charcoal gray uniform. They were divided into four groups, apparently based on age. The youngest children were circling pictures in their workbooks while the others were writing words.

The doctor explained that every child, or, as he called them, "visitor," wore a uniform during their stay to help eliminate any potential feelings of jealousy. He expounded on their teaching techniques, pointing out that visitors in TempCare actually spent more time in receiving instruction than they did in public and private schools. "Almost as much instruction as one will find in Newman, I'm proud to say."

Christopher was barely tall enough to look through the mirror. "Where are your Legos?"

"Come," Dr. Hawkins said. "I'll show you something we're particularly proud of."

The doctor started walking down the hall. "Excuse me," Richard said, "but Christopher asked a question."

"He did?"

"Yes. Go ahead, son, it was a good question."

Christopher hesitated. "Where are your Legos?"

"My what?"

"Legos," Richard said. "You know, little blocks, all sorts of different colors, that you can connect to build things."

"Toys?" Dr. Hawkins glanced at Carol. "Well, we have a break time in the morning, and one in the afternoon, and we have some toys for the visitors to play with then. Keep in mind, this is a place for children to come and learn. We're not here to baby-sit."

"What kind of toys?" Richard asked. "Legos?"

"Not Legos, but some educational ones."

"They're educational," Christopher said.

"I suppose they might be, if one wishes to work in construction," Dr. Hawkins said. He opened a door and motioned for them to follow.

"I don't think we really have to bombard him with all the questions," Carol whispered.

"We agreed to let Christopher and me check this place out. Part of that is questions."

"You're not even giving this place a chance."

"We don't need this place. Christopher can go with us wherever we decide to go."

They went down another white hall. The doctor stopped at another one-way mirror and pointed to a group of children, each wearing a black uniform. They were also divided into groups and studying workbooks, but they seemed somewhat lethargic. An adult sat in the back of the room, wearing a surgical mask.

"We're proud of this service," Dr. Hawkins said. "Sometimes parents will make their plans, only to be bothered with a child coming down with a cold or flu." He smiled. "We have a separate area for ill visitors, making certain that they study, eat, and sleep separately from the well visitors. If any of them goes into the wrong area, we know right away because of the black uniforms. Mr. and Mrs. Carson, you need not worry about Christopher catching anything while here."

"But, doesn't lumping them together make the sick kids even sicker?" Christopher said.

"Is there anything else you'd like to show us?" Carol asked.

"No, that concludes the tour. Let us go back the way we came, and you can sign the papers at the front desk."

"Doctor," Richard said, "did you hear Christopher's question?"

Dr. Hawkins started walking down the hall, with Carol close behind, but Richard and Christopher both stood at the one-way mirror, watching the children. The one adult in the room was obviously staying as far away as she could in the corner. Several children had handkerchiefs with them, constantly wiping their noses. One little girl, no more than five years old, lay under a table that other children were working on. Her eyes were red and swollen, her nose running.

"Doctor," Richard said. "By the way, what kind of doctor are you?"

Dr. Hawkins and Carol were now at the end of the hall, by the door. "A psychologist."

"Oh," Richard nodded. "Well, Doctor, I'd like to see where the children sleep."

"That's not part of the tour, Mr. Carson."

"I've got to be getting back to work, Richard," Carol said. She pointed to her watch. "Dr. Hawkins, thank you for the tour. Where are the papers?"

"No," Richard said, "I'd really like to see where the children sleep. There's nothing to hide, is there?"

"Of course not. This way, please," the doctor said, sighing.

They followed the doctor up another flight of stairs, no one speaking, and then down another long hall. The doctor pulled out a key and unlocked a windowless door. He walked into the room, with Richard and Christopher, still holding hands, close behind. Carol stood at the doorway.

The room's walls were white and bare. Not a picture or poster to be found. Only beds. Row after row of bunk beds, with a small dresser between each one. Richard guessed there must have been at least fifty beds, each neatly made.

Christopher let go of his father's hand. Richard knelt down beside him.

"If you put me here," Christopher said, "will you come back for me?"

Without saying a word, he picked Christopher up and marched past Dr. Hawkins and Carol, looking dead straight ahead. By the time the doctor locked the door to the sleeping room, Richard and Christopher were almost at the door to the stairway. Carol and the doctor almost had to run to catch up. No one spoke as they descended the stairs, and when they got to the lobby, Richard just went ahead through the front door, still carrying his son.

"We need to talk this through," Carol said when she caught up to them on the sidewalk.

"We agreed this was a family decision, and this two-thirds of the family vote no."

"It's just two days, Richard!"

"Just long enough for Christopher to blend in with the walls. I saw a place like this once when I was a kid."

"He wouldn't be there for long."

"They were called kennels. And my dad wouldn't even put our dog in one."

CHAPTER
FORTY-SIX

Two days after the TempCare fiasco, the morning was sunny. Summer had come, but the slight, cool breeze reminded Richard of spring. He, Christopher, and Carol sat at an outside table at a coffee shop on Broadway. He made sure their son sat closest to the wall, away from the sidewalk, and kept searching the area, watching for anyone suspicious. Except for the visit to TempCare, it was the first time Christopher had been out of the apartment for days.

The server brought their coffees and a cinnamon roll with milk for Christopher, then left.

"I know TempCare was a mistake," Carol said. "Again, I'm sorry about that. But now we're talking about just one evening. He'll be fine."

"I just can't get the train station out of my mind," Richard said, shaking his head. "I ought to call David and cancel."

"No!" Christopher said. "It'll be fun to have Uncle David take care of me, Daddy. And we'll stay in the apartment the whole time. We won't leave even if the place catches on fire."

Richard gave his son a look, and Christopher winked at him.

"David was coming anyway for a couple of days. And it's supposed to be a wonderful play," Carol said, "and Hunter went to a lot of trouble to get the tickets for us. *The Egyptians* is the most popular play on Broadway."

"We should've talked about it—"

"I wanted it to be a surprise," Carol said, touching Richard's hand. "It's the first time we've done something together for a long time."

He knew she was right. He'd been ignoring her. But, still, he couldn't stand the thought of leaving his son even for just one evening, even with his brother.

Christopher reached over and touched Richard's other hand, smiling. "You can do this, Daddy. It'll just take a little bit of courage."

Richard laughed, then nodded. "Okay, you two win."

CHAPTER
FORTY-SEVEN

The lobby of the Imperial Theatre was massive, and elegant. The owners had bucked the trend of other theaters on Broadway to modernize with giant screens and irrepressible sound systems that pierced through you. This place was a throwback to an earlier, more relaxed time. Of course, Richard liked it. He sat in a chair in the lobby, waiting for his wife to come back from the restroom. It was intermission and the lobby was crowded.

Carol came up to him, but didn't sit down.

"Do you want me to get you something to drink?" she asked.

"No thanks," he said, standing up. "I called home while you were waiting in line."

"You did?" Carol seemed concerned.

"David said everything's fine. Christopher's in bed. I never pictured David as the baby-sitter type."

"Maybe he's not." Carol looked at her watch. "But he's the good brother type. He knew how much we needed to get out."

Richard took her hand and led her over to a more secluded area in the lobby. "I know I've been concentrating on Christopher. I hope you haven't felt neglected."

Carol smiled.

Just as he leaned over and kissed her on the lips, the lights in the lobby flashed. They joined the crowd going up the stairs and found their seats. Richard mentioned again how good Hunter had been to let them have the tickets. He held Carol's hand and dreamed out loud about someday writing a book that would be made into a popular musical or Hollywood hit. He laughed about how rich they'd be, and about how she'd be freed up to do whatever she wanted. She said she wouldn't change a thing. She'd still practice law with the same firm.

"You never know what you'd do in entirely new circumstances," he whispered as the lights were dimming. "Maybe you'd only want to practice part-time and spend more time with Christopher and me."

The lights were out, and he was looking at the stage, but for a moment he thought he felt her staring at him. She started moving her hand out of his, but he held on tighter and squeezed hers until she finally let it stay.

CHAPTER
FORTY-EIGHT

Richard put the key in the front door of their apartment, but Carol grabbed his arm. "Did you enjoy yourself?" she asked.

"I had a great time. Being with you tonight was even better than excellent. We need to do this more often."

"The night's still young. David wouldn't mind if we stayed out a little longer."

"I know, but I don't want to be gone too long," he said as he opened the door. "I'm going to go check on Christopher."

"Richard?"

"Yes?"

"I do want you to remember I love you. Very much."

"I love you, too." He turned back to Carol and held her in his arms, kissing her.

He closed the door and she locked all three locks.

He walked down the hall, but slowed down as he noticed the living room was dark. One lamp on the corner table was on, offering limited light, but the room was hidden in shadows. He didn't see David.

"David?" Christopher's bedroom door was shut. "Maybe he's in the bathroom," he said, turning to Carol. She was crying. "What's wrong?"

"Believe me," Carol said, "it's for the best."

"What are you talking about? What's going on?" Her eyes moved, just for a second, to Christopher's door, and he ran around the couch and opened the door. The room was empty, the covers on the floor. Pooh Bear was on the floor in the corner.

"David!" Richard shouted. "David!"

He heard moaning coming from their bedroom. When he opened the door, he found David lying on the floor. He knelt down beside his brother and took his pulse.

"He's fine. They said they'd just use some gas on him," Carol said. "Something to make him sleep through the night."

"Carol?" Richard asked.

"I signed the papers." Her crying made it difficult for her to speak.

"What papers? What do you mean?"

She shook her head.

He couldn't understand anything, like he couldn't think.

"I had them come from Newman and pick up Christopher," Carol said.

"You did what?"

"He's back where he belongs. Safe."

Richard ran down the hall to the kitchen, then down to the office, each time searching for some sign of his son, but there was nothing. No one. He ran back into the living room. Carol was sitting on the chair, looking exhausted and dazed.

"Where is he?" he shouted.

"You were getting too close to him. I knew you wouldn't let him go back at the end of the sabbatical."

"Carol, tell me he's not back at that place."

"And when he was almost kidnapped," she said, with more composure as she stood up, "I couldn't take it any longer. You didn't see the harm you were doing to him. And to us."

"You didn't do it for us. You did it for you and Hunter."

"You know that isn't true."

Richard turned and headed down the hall.

"Where are you going?" she called after him.

"Where do you think?"

"I told you, I signed the papers. The sabbatical's over, Richard."

"You are unbelievable."

"And I withdrew my consent. He's back home, now, for good. There's nothing you can do about it."

"I'm going to get him."

"They won't give him to you, Richard. Remember, I'm a good lawyer."

"And I'm a good father." He turned to unlock the door, but she ran up the hall and grabbed him by the arm. "I'll withdraw him for good."

"You can't—not without my signature."

He stopped dead and turned to his wife. He wasn't even sure anymore who he was looking at.

Richard fell against the wall, rubbing his forehead. Nothing made sense.

"I can't believe this," she said as she turned away. She walked a few steps down the hall, running her hands through her hair, but then turned around. "I've had enough of this. I want to be a family, with each one of us where we belong. But I'm not going to spend the rest of my life playing the role of the wicked mother who imprisoned her son. You decide, Richard, either I stay, or I go. But if I stay, you're going to be my husband, and you're going to act like a husband should."

"What are you saying?"

"Leave Christopher in Newman and you've got a family. Try to take him out, and I'm out of here. I'm gone. I'll file for a divorce quicker than you can write a paragraph. If you try to get him out of Newman, I will fight you all the way. And I don't lose fights."

She turned back around and walked down the hall into the living room. Richard stared at the spot where his wife had stood seconds before. Carol had never talked about divorce before. Things were changing too quickly.

"Carol," he said as he started down the hall. "Wait a minute. Let's talk." All he could see in his mind was his son, in his bed, trusting his daddy.

When he came to the living room, Carol was standing by the window. It had started raining. This wasn't how it was supposed to end, he told himself. This wasn't the summer he wanted.

And this wasn't the family he had worked so hard for.

"You're right, Carol," he whispered, just loud enough for her to hear from across the room. She didn't turn around. "I've been trying to have it both ways," he continued. "I have to make a decision."

Richard took a few steps forward, but stopped in the middle of the living room. "I don't want to gain a son but lose a family. I don't want you to leave."

Carol turned around. "I was hoping you'd see it my way."

"But whether you leave or not is your decision," he said, "not mine. I've made my decision, Carol. I'm going to see my son tonight—let him know I love him. Then I'm going to do whatever I have to—whatever I have to—to set him free."

They both stood still for a moment, neither seeming to believe what he had just said. His wife's gaze hardened into a stare that went through him. He turned around, and walked toward the hall.

"How can you do this?" she asked, on the verge of shouting. "You're willing to throw our family away? You're ruining us, Richard." She followed him to the hall. "I'll fight you on this."

"I will not abandon my son."

"You'll never get custody. I'll beat you."

"Beating me won't be enough, Carol. You'll have to kill me to keep me from bringing my son back home."

"Why can't you care more about us than you do about yourself?"

Richard was at the front door when she shouted this. He picked up her briefcase, her constant, devoted companion ever since law school, and shook it. "This is what you care about, Carol."

He threw the briefcase down the hall. It hit the wall and landed inches from her feet. Dozens of pages of legal documents covered the floor between them.

"You've got your papers," he said. "You've always been married to your work, and these are your children. Talk with them. Play with them. Cuddle with them. And in your old age, you can rock them like the grandchildren you'll never know."

CHAPTER FORTY-NINE

I t was one o'clock in the morning and almost no one was on the streets. Not so much because of the time, but the rain. When the sun rose in a few hours, and the rain stopped, the air would feel cleaner. But now, the dirt in the air was washing down on anyone out on the streets.

Richard jumped out of the cab and ran up the steps to the school, but he still got drenched. He pulled on the door but it was, of course, locked. There was no protection over the door, so the rain kept pounding Richard as he pounded on the door. He studied the carving in the door of the pond and the animals, the lion standing nearby. This wasn't a peaceful scene of animals defying the law of the jungle and getting along. This was the moment before the attack. This was the cunning lion, lulling his prey into complacency just before breaking its trust and going for the kill.

"Welcome to the Newman Home," the computerized voice said. "Please wait here for security purposes."

Richard heard that whirling sound and knew something was scanning him.

"I am sorry, Mr. Carson, but the Newman Home is not accepting visitors at this time." "I want to see my son. Now."

"I am sorry, but you are not authorized personnel."

"I'm his father. Open this door."

"I am sorry, but you are not authorized personnel."

"Then bring Christopher here. Let me just see him. You can at least let me know if he made it here safely."

Silence.

"You have to let me know that."

"Mr. Carson," a man's voice said, "we don't have to let you know anything."

There was silence again. Richard pulled on the door but it didn't move at all. "I'm not done talking with you. Come back here!"

He hit the top one of the door handles and cut his hand on the edge. He pounded the door with both fists, smearing blood on it. He kicked at the door, then threw his weight against it, but his efforts made no difference.

"Open this door," he screamed.

Both of his hands were raw now, bleeding. Streaks of blood ran down the door, but refused to be completely washed off. An intense, bright light cut through the rain and reflected off the door, forcing Richard to cover his eyes.

"Raise your hands and turn around," he heard from a loud-speaker on the street.

Richard turned, with his hands in the air, but when he tried to see who was there he was blinded by the bright light.

"Walk toward the light, slowly. Very slowly. Look straight ahead."

Richard moved forward, feeling with his foot for the edge of each step. The rain kept falling hard, and when he got to the middle of the steps he slipped and fell forward, landing face-first on the sidewalk.

"Get up. Now! Get over here."

Richard stood up from the wet pavement, the light still shining in his eyes. When he took a few steps forward, the light shut off and he couldn't see anything for several seconds.

"Open the back door and get in," the voice commanded.

Richard saw that it was a police car. He climbed in the back as ordered and looked at the officer through the wire divider.

"I hate this rain," the officer said as he slipped the gear into drive and drove off. "Hard to see, you know?"

"I was just trying to see my son, officer," Richard said.

"The guys in there called us up and said some maniac's trying to break down the front door."

"I'm no maniac."

"Course not. Perfectly normal to stand out in the pouring rain, pounding on a door 'till your hands bleed. I do it all the time."

"They kidnapped my son!"

"Save it for the station, pal. Okay? And try not to drip so much on my seat."

When they got to the precinct, the officer got out and ran around to Richard's door and opened it. He threw a pair of handcuffs at Richard and said, "Hurry up and put these on. It's raining, you know."

Richard put the cuffs on his hands in front of him, then the officer pulled him out of the car and ran him up the steps to the station. When they got inside, the officer led Richard to the desk of a man in a wrinkled blue shirt, sleeves rolled up to his elbows. The officer pushed Richard into a chair across from the desk, then left without saying a word.

"Hey, could somebody get this guy a towel?" the man behind the desk shouted. "He's dripping all over my desk." Nobody showed up, so the man told Richard not to move and left. He came back with a small, dingy white towel and threw it at Richard.

"Am I under arrest?" Richard asked as he watched the man go back to filling out some form.

"I'm sorry, Mr. Carson," the man said. "I'm sure you have other plans this evening. How inconsiderate of us to keep you."

"Can I take these off?" Richard asked, holding up his cuffed hands.

"I doubt it, but go ahead and try."

The man finally finished the form he was working on and put it aside. "I'm Detective Stanford, and I'm here to tell you to go home and dry off."

"Wait a minute! They kidnapped my son. I want to file a complaint. They're the ones who—"

"They did not kidnap Christopher. Your wife signed the papers, Mr. Carson, you know that. It's all very legal."

"Listen to me—"

"No, you listen to me." Stanford leaned across his desk. "I know all about your history with the Newman Home, and you need to back off."

"Back off?" Richard shouted. "They kidnapped my son."

"All right, man," the detective said, standing up, "that does it." He walked over to another officer and spoke with her for a few seconds, then she followed him over to his desk.

"This is Officer Martinez. She'll handle the paperwork for your stay."

"I'm under arrest?"

"Yes."

"Nobody read me my rights."

"We were hoping you wouldn't have to be under arrest. The commissioner wanted to keep it simple."

"That's right, I did."

They all turned to see a short, round man in a dark suit, his eyes bloodshot. He was in his early fifties, with quite a bit of gray throughout his dark hair. Reaching out his hand to shake Richard's, he introduced himself as Police Commissioner Moretti. When he asked Detective Stanford for a private room, the detective led him and Richard to the captain's office and left them alone, closing the door after him.

The commissioner sat in the captain's chair behind the desk, but Richard remained standing, his hands still cuffed.

"Look," Richard said, "I don't appreciate——"

"Why can't you leave well enough alone, Mr. Carson? Can't you see you're messing with something much bigger than you?"

"What are you talking about?"

"I don't like getting calls from the Newman Home in the middle of the night. And then, the second I hang up, I get a call from——" he stopped. "Well, from someone else I don't like getting calls from in the middle of the night. Newman is an important place, and people you want to keep happy are starting to get a little irritated by you. Do you understand?"

"What would you do if they kidnapped your son?"

"I'd probably send them a year's supply of Ben & Jerry's. I'd love to get that kid out of the house and into a place as good as Newman."

"Well, I don't feel that way. Kidnapping——"

"You keep talking about kidnapping. Let me ask you something, did you, or did you not, put your boy in there years ago?"

"I didn't——"

"Just answer the question!" Moretti shouted. "Did you enroll him?"

"Yes."

"No one kidnapped anyone. Your wife sent him back, and it's as simple as that."

"I can fight her on it."

The commissioner jumped up. "Go ahead, take her to court, I don't care. Spend the next few years fighting her on it. But trying to knock down their door isn't going to get the boy out. I don't care if you and your wife sue each other until the cows take over Battery Park. Just leave the school alone. Especially now."

"Why now?"

Moretti thought for a moment as he sat back down. "Just leave it alone, okay? There's nothing you can do."

Richard nodded.

"So, since there's nothing you can do, you need to quit doing things."

The commissioner got out of the chair and opened the door, calling for Officer Martinez. He had her remove the handcuffs and instructed her to take him straight home.

"I don't want any more calls tonight, Mr. Carson."

CHAPTER FIFTY

The restroom looked like it had never been cleaned. It smelled even worse. Richard's hands were sore and swollen, his clothes still drenched from the rain. When he was done washing his hands, he stepped out of the restroom and found Martinez waiting. She took him out a side door and to one of the squad cars. They climbed in the front seat and neither said a word except when Richard told her the address.

The rain was still pouring when the police car stopped along the curb outside the apartment building. When he got to the front door, he turned and noticed Martinez was waiting to make sure he entered. He went into the building and watched the car drive off.

"May I help you, sir?" asked a large man dressed in a guard's uniform.

"I'm here to see Hunt."

"Hunt?"

"Yeah," Richard said. "Oh, I'm sorry, Hunter Jenkins. I'm Paul Jenkins, his brother. I just got in at Kennedy a few hours ago. The plane was late, then they lost my bags. Hunt's probably been worried sick about me."

"I'll call Dr. Jenkins and let him know you're here."

"Don't do that. Look how late it is." Richard went over to the elevator and pushed the button. "I've got a key, I'll just go on up and sleep on the couch. I don't want to wake him."

"But—"

Richard reached into his pocket, pulled out a fifty, and walked over to the guard, slipping the bill into his hand. "Let's surprise my brother, okay?" he said, smiling.

The bell rang and the elevator door opened. Richard got in, pushing the nineteenth floor button. He had only been with Carol to Hunter and Tiffany's newest apartment two or three times, but he remembered laughing to himself when he learned their apartment number was 1984. Easy to remember. When the doors opened on the nineteenth floor, Richard headed straight for Hunter's apartment and knocked on the door. He knocked, then knocked again, louder. He heard steps coming toward the door, but pounded on the door again anyway. His hands ached.

The door opened just a crack. "Richard?" Hunter asked, his eyes still half-closed. Suddenly, his eyes opened wider. "Richard!" He started to close the door, but Richard threw his weight against it, knocking Hunter down on the floor. Richard slammed the door behind him. Some light—not from the moon, but from other nearby buildings—shone through the mammoth picture window, revealing Hunter, lying on the floor in his purple silk robe and matching boxers.

"I'm calling the police," Hunter said, still lying on the floor.

"If you do, I'd suggest you talk to Detective Stanford. He already knows all about me."

"Get out of here, Richard."

Richard grabbed Hunter by the robe and threw him across the back of the black leather couch. He landed on the coffee table, breaking some expensive Japanese plate. Hunter stumbled to his feet, but Richard was already next to him, grabbing him by the robe again.

"They won't let me see my son, Hunter."

"You're crazy. Get out of here."

"Just tell me, did he make it? Is he safe back at the school?"

"Yes," Hunter said, "he made it back a few hours ago. And he's going to stay there for the next many, many years."

Richard let go of Hunter's robe, then threw his fist into his stomach. Hunter folded over, coughing and gasping for air, and Richard pulled him up and smashed his other fist across Hunter's face, knocking him to the floor. Hunter's lip started bleeding, staining the wooden floor.

"Get up, Dr. Jenkins." Richard stood over him but Hunter just turned over to his side and moaned. "Get up!"

Hunter crawled over to the piano bench and pulled himself up. He sat on the bench, holding his stomach. He touched his mouth, then looked at the blood on his fingers.

"I bet you've never bled before, have you, Hunter? Didn't know you could."

"There's nothing I can do."

"You're going to call them. You're going to tell them to let me see Christopher."

"They'll never let you."

"They will if you call."

"No they won't. Newman's coming soon. Everything's got to look normal."

"I don't care about some old—"

"You'd better care."

"What's he got to do with Christopher?"

"The superintendent thinks Newman has heard about him."

"What do you mean?"

"Richard, listen to what I'm saying. Christopher was the first resident to leave the home for any length of time—"

"It hasn't even been two weeks!"

"I don't care if it's been two days. Newman wouldn't like having a resident with their parents outside the regular visits."

"Then why did the superintendent let him have the sabbatical if you're so afraid of what Newman would think?"

"He was supposed to be out of the country for months," Hunter said. "We figured he'd never find out."

"But why not just tell us 'no' like you have everyone else? What was so special about us?"

"You're complaining about getting the sabbatical?" Hunter shook his head. "After all you've put me through—"

"Put you through? I haven't put you through anything. You haven't done anything for us."

"Hey, you owe me big time. I was dead set against the sabbatical from the start, but Carol was persistent. Then I had to be even more persistent with the superintendent. And I'm still paying for it. He reminds me every day."

"Carol? Persistent? I figured she just talked to you about it and it was done."

"Look, Richard, you two need to talk."

"Why was she so persistent, Hunter?"

Hunter sighed. "She's right. You never give up."

"What are you getting at?"

"She told me a hundred times you'd never let this go until you got your way," Hunter said. "That if the sabbatical timeframe passed, you'd blame her for the rest of her life for any problem that would come up. 'Christopher didn't get into Harvard? It's because he never had that sabbatical.' 'Christopher didn't get that premier job? The sabbatical.'"

"Carol's the one who cares so much about Harvard and jobs, not me."

"Okay—'Christopher isn't a happy guy, fully self-actualized? Man, he should have had that sabbatical, honey. It's all your fault.'

Come on, Richard, you know you never would have let her hear the end of it."

Richard leaned up against the wall, exhausted. He figured that her agreeing to the sabbatical at least meant she thought it was worthwhile. He thought she was sincerely giving it a chance.

"Well, I guess that's good to know what she was thinking," Richard said. "But what about you? Why did you give in?"

"She promised me it wouldn't last more than a week. Two, at most. And I had to give that same assurance to the superintendent. She knew how difficult it would be for you to be a stay-at-home daddy and try to write. Like she said, 'He's never been any good at either one, so how will he good at both of them?'"

"She never said that," Richard said.

"You don't know your own wife."

Richard lunged forward, grabbing Hunter by the robe and throwing him down to the floor. "How do I get him back?"

"You don't," Hunter said, still lying on the floor. "You can beat me up, you can kill me, but it won't do any good. There's nothing you can do that will help your son."

Richard felt himself losing his balance and walked over to lean against the back of the couch. His eyes went to the picture window, searching the lights of the skyscrapers. The rain had stopped, and he could see the moon appearing through the parting clouds.

"Ooh!" someone squealed. "I thought he'd left."

A young woman, barely in her twenties, with long brown hair, clutched a sheet around herself. She knelt down next to Hunter.

"Are you all right, baby?"

Richard shook his head and turned away from the two, heading for the front door.

"Tiffany left for Los Angeles this morning for business," Hunter said.

"I don't want to hear it."

Hunter sat up, the young woman caressing his shoulders. "It's not what you think."

"Is she your new Carol?" asked Richard, still walking away.

"Nothing ever happened between Carol and me."

Richard stopped at the door. "She never became one more notch on your bedpost?"

"Carol was my hope to find a way to get Christopher back where he belonged and keep him there. That's all."

Richard opened the door. "I'm getting him back, one way or another."

"Be careful, Richard. He's too important to Newman. You're never going to get him back. At least, not alive."

CHAPTER
FIFTY-ONE

Richard closed the apartment door behind him and leaned against it. He rubbed his bloodshot eyes with his hand, swollen and throbbing with pain. When he looked at his wrist to see what time it was, his watch was gone, lost somewhere during the night. It must have been seven in the morning, maybe eight o'clock, but it didn't matter.

He walked down the hall, occasionally touching the wall to keep balance. It seemed like no one was home: no lamp on in the living room, and he couldn't hear any sounds. When he got to their bedroom, though, he saw Carol's suitcase on the bed, still opened but almost full with clothes. Next to it was her briefcase, all the papers back in place.

The master bathroom door opened and Carol came out, surprised to see him. She didn't speak.

"What are you doing?" Richard asked.

She walked past him, making it a point not to look at him, and placed a folded blouse in her suitcase.

"After all we've been through in the last twenty-four hours," he said, "let's not add silence to our troubles. All right?" He pulled his dead cell phone out of his pocket and plugged it in. "Where's David?"

"I don't know," Carol said. "Some friend's place. He didn't want to say much to me."

Richard nodded.

She walked to the closet. "Where have you been all night? You look like you've survived a war."

"I'm not sure about the surviving part." He went into the bathroom and ran the hot water, washing his face and hands, scrubbing hard. It hurt, but it felt good to be cleaner. "So, my good wife, this is something you and Hunter have been planning for some time. You figured I'd just last a couple of weeks."

"What are you talking about?"

"Hunter told me all about it."

"Not now."

Richard rinsed his face, holding his face in his cupped hands. "Were you two behind the kidnap attempt?"

"How dare you!"

"Just asking."

"I would never do that to my own son."

"Well, you just did it, didn't you?"

"This is different. This is getting him back home."

"I don't know what to believe anymore," Richard said, grabbing the towel.

Carol closed her eyes and covered her mouth. "I'm staying at Susan's until I find my own place."

"You don't have to leave. I'll find a place."

"No," Carol said. "I don't want to be in this apartment anymore. I don't belong."

"I know how you feel. Ever since Christopher went to that place as a little baby, we've all just been residents."

Richard dried his hands and face, then went back into their bedroom, unbuttoning his shirt.

"Did you get to see Christopher?" Carol asked.

Richard pulled a clean shirt and jeans out of the closet.

"Maybe I'd better take a shower first," he said. Then he turned to Carol and asked, "I probably ought to shower, shouldn't I?"

"I can't believe this." She walked over to her bag and started nervously rearranging things.

"I can't focus, Carol, I'm going to concentrate on just one thing, so I can make it through the next few minutes."

"And that one thing you're going to concentrate on is a shower?"

"You got it. A quick one."

"How can you worry about a shower when our whole world is falling apart?"

"No, things are finally falling together," he said from the door-way to the bathroom. "I'm getting my son back, I just don't know how."

CHAPTER
FIFTY-TWO

After his shower, Richard left the bathroom with his jeans on, buttoning his shirt. He leaned against the wall, looking at his wife sitting on the bed.

"You know, counselor," he said, "there's just one thing I can't figure out."

Carol didn't turn to look at him.

"If I were to come home to you and announce I had decided to pay another woman to be my wife," he said, "that I was going to live with her and be with her, and just visit you occasionally—you wouldn't stand for it. You'd take me to court, and society would proclaim me an inconsiderate, despicable husband. So why can we get away with doing that to children? Why can we have a child, and then pay other people to be the parents?"

"It's not the same thing."

"How is it different?"

Carol closed her suitcase and zipped it shut. "Susan's expecting me," she said, and she left the bedroom, carrying the bag and briefcase.

Richard followed her into the living room, tucking in his shirt. "It's because children can't fight back, isn't it? They're too little.

They can't stop us by hitting us, or get a divorce from us. All they can do is wait—wait until they're angry adults who fight back any way they can."

"I don't think enrolling our son in the finest school in the world will make him grow up and throw Molotov cocktails in the street."

"If we adopt a pet, we actually plan on taking care of it. At least if we had a dog, I could see it whenever I wanted to."

"You never answered me before. Did you see Christopher?"

"They wouldn't let me. He's their property."

"That's not it," Carol said. "They just see you as…well, as unstable."

"Find out for yourself. Call the school and set up an appointment to see your son."

"I can't do that."

"Because you know they won't let you."

"Of course, they'll let me. I signed the papers. They wouldn't let you because they knew you'd cause trouble."

"Then call. What could it hurt?"

"Christopher's where he belongs. He's safe there. He's learning what he needs to know there. I'm not calling the school, Richard. I don't have time for your game."

She reached down to pick up her bag, but his hand grabbed hers as she touched the handle. His face was only inches from hers. "I don't know what this is, but it is not a game." They both stood back up, slowly. "This is the last thing I'm asking of you before you leave. Call the school. If I'm wrong, and they say yes, then you've lost nothing."

Carol folded her arms, thinking. She took a deep breath.

"Carol," he said. "I know you think I'm being dramatic, but I know a father who tried to get his son out of Newman and the boy ended up dead by the river. A woman wanted to get her daughter out, and the little girl died of a nervous breakdown in the hospital. And they tried to kidnap our own son."

"Come on, Richard—"

"Call. It's the last thing I'll ever ask you to do."

She pulled her cell phone out. "The Newman Home."

"Yes," Carol said as she sat on the arm of the couch. "I'd like to speak with the superintendent."

Carol rubbed her neck.

"I understand he's busy. At least take a message to have him call me. Carol Carson. He knows me."

Richard shook his head. "They'll just put you off and we'll never know."

Carol rolled her eyes up and shook her head. "No, no, I really need to speak with him right away. It's urgent."

Carol sighed.

"Just let him know who it is; he'll talk with me." She covered the mouthpiece with her hand. "I'm on hold."

Richard nodded.

"Yes," Carol said into the phone. "Who is this?"

"Oh, hello, Ms. Garrett. I was trying to get in touch with the superintendent but—"

Carol listened for a moment.

"I don't care if he's meeting with someone very important, I need to speak with him."

Carol stood up in her best cross-examination stance.

"All right, all right. Maybe you can help me. My son returned to Newman last night. I wanted to stop by this morning on my way to work and see how he's doing."

Carol started to pace.

"What do you mean it's impossible? It'll just take a few min-utes, and I—"

Carol started pointing her finger as if Ms. Garret could see her.

"Don't talk to me like that! I simply want to—" Carol dropped the phone from her ear and stared at Richard. "That little nitwit hung up on me! They've never acted this way before."

"Something's going on," Richard said. "I'm not sure what it is. Did they mention the name of the person the superintendent is with?"

"No, just someone important."

"Hunter mentioned something about Dr. Newman last night," Richard said. "Pretty important stuff, I guess."

"You saw Hunter last night?"

"We had a chat."

"Maybe he can help," Carol said as she pressed the button programmed for Hunter's number. "Yes, Hunter, this is Carol. There's nothing really wrong. I just wanted to stop by Newman this morning and see Christopher. Just to make sure he made it safely last night."

Carol looked over at Richard.

"Yes, I know you were there when they brought him in," she said, "but I'd like to visit with him for a minute."

She started pacing again.

"What do you mean, maybe later?" Her eyes squinted as she focused in on her questioning of the witness. "Yes, I heard what you said, but did you hear what I said?"

Carol leaned forward like she was trying to hear something.

"Baby? Who's calling you baby? Who's that woman, Hunter?"

She shook her head.

"Look, Hunter, I want to see him now. I'm his mother." She stared at her cell phone. "Twice this morning. I've been hung up on twice."

"What did he say?"

"He said I was starting to sound like you, then hung up on me." She went back to pacing the living room.

Richard still sat on the coffee table. He rubbed his forehead.

"I don't get it, how can you be so calm about all this?" she asked.

"I'm thinking." Richard had hoped something would wake up his wife to how much power Newman exerted over people. Up until now, Carol saw this issue of power as his problem—something he'd created in his mind. So long as she believed she was in charge, that she could see their son whenever she wanted to, she didn't mind the school refusing his request to see him. After all, she figured his requests were unreasonable. But she was discovering who was really in charge, and she didn't like it.

"I don't like being told no," she said. "Who do they think they are? I'm his mother!"

"But he's their resident. As far as they're concerned, they own him."

"Well, they don't!" Carol shouted.

He went to the bedroom for his cell phone and then headed for the front door.

"Where are you going?" she asked.

"I'll figure it out on the way to the school. I hoped they'd listen to you."

"They'd better start listening to me. I'm going with you."

Richard kept walking, surprised, but pleased. He hadn't planned on her coming with him, but it couldn't hurt. Maybe if they saw a prominent lawyer next to him they'd think twice about not letting him see Christopher.

"Did you just manipulate me?" Carol asked.

"Just a little."

"I'm not sure I like that feeling either."

Richard stopped and turned to her. "I knew I could never win against you. But if you fight them with me, I stand a chance."

When they got to the front door his phone beeped with a message.

"It's the Newman school," Richard said, putting the phone on speaker. "Called when it was charging."

"Daddy?"

Richard stood still. It was Christopher's voice, and he was upset.

"I'm sorry, Daddy. They told me you sent me back here because you were mad at me. They said they'd take me to the basement, but that's a bad place, so I got away. They kept saying they were going to make me a lion. I found this phone and remembered your number. I'll do whatever you tell me to do. I won't make you mad at me. Can't you come and get me? Please come and—"

The voice stopped. There was a loud noise, then the phone went dead.

Richard felt burning inside his entire body. He wanted to grab something and tear it apart. He opened the front door and Carol followed closely behind as he walked toward the stairs. He began walking faster, then faster, until he was running. Carol ran to keep up. He jumped down the stairs, two and three at a time.

"What are you going to do?" Carol said.

"I don't know, but I'm not going to sit around and think about it."

CHAPTER FIFTY-THREE

In the cab, Richard and Carol decided they wouldn't mention the message from Christopher. Knowledge was their only leverage, and they didn't have much of it. If they said too much, Christopher might be in more danger.

When they arrived at the Newman School, someone had just stepped through the front door. Richard caught the door before it closed.

"We're here to see our son," Richard said between breaths. The host behind the desk stood up as Richard and Carol ran into the Newman lobby.

The host tried several times to have the two sit down, but they refused, insisting on seeing Christopher. After the host made a phone call, he told them it would be impossible for them to see their son at the moment, but Ms. Garrett would come out to the lobby to speak with them.

"We're not going to take him out," Carol said. "We just want to see him. I leave my car at a parking garage, for crying out loud, and I'm allowed to see that whenever I want!"

"We do not view our residents the same as automobiles, Ms. Carson," the host said.

Richard grabbed her arm and walked with her to the other side of the room.

"This isn't going to work," Carol whispered. "Maybe we ought to call the police or someone."

"The police? They'll probably arrest *us*, not the people here. They weren't helpful last night at all."

"What do you mean?"

"The police picked me up last night. The police commissioner himself came down and let me know I was on thin ice. Apparently, some people were getting upset."

"Then the courts," she said, still whispering. "I know some powerful people, too. Let me make a few phone calls."

"Before or after he's been in the basement?"

The door behind them opened and Ms. Garrett came into the lobby, followed by a host in a safari uniform who looked more like a bouncer than an educator.

"I apologize for the inconvenience of your coming all this way," Ms. Garrett said, smiling too much, "but as I explained over the telephone, it's simply not allowable to visit the residents today."

"Look," Carol said, "you know me. I'm the one who made the arrangements with Dr. Jenkins to have our son returned last night. I'm on your side. I just want to see our son."

"That would be disruptive."

"Can't we just peek through a one-way mirror someplace?"

"Ms. Carson, you returned Christopher to us so he could be properly cared for. Protected. Trained. Please, let us do our job. We know what is best for him."

Carol's eyes squinted again, the way they did when she was ready for a fight.

"Then let us speak to the superintendent," Richard said.

"He's a busy man, Mr. Carson. I can set up an appointment for three or four weeks from now, if you'd like."

"Let's go, Richard," Carol said. "We're not getting anywhere."

"But—"

"This must be what Dr. Newman was calling me about," Carol said. "I'll call him back when we get to my office. I need to have those files in front of me when I talk to him."

Richard tried to hide his surprise. It was the perfect comment, and he watched out of the corner of his eye as the smile on Ms. Garrett's face seemed to slide off.

"I guess you're right," he said, and they headed for the front door.

"Dr. Newman is out of the country," Ms. Garrett said.

"You need to be better informed," Carol said, not looking back.

Richard pushed on the front door to open it.

"Just one moment," Ms. Garrett said, pulling out her cell phone. She spoke into it for a moment, nodding her head. "I'm sure the superintendent has a few minutes this morning. Perhaps we can arrange something."

CHAPTER
FIFTY-FOUR

She led them down a long hall, followed by the safari bouncer. Richard had been down the hall two or three times before, but it felt strange this time. Eerie. There was something different about the air, the walls. Something was off, even more than usual.

The door to the superintendent's office was open, and they walked past his secretary into his office without stopping. He stood up from behind his desk.

"Ms. Carson," the superintendent said, "Dr. Jenkins told me you and he had a crystal clear agreement."

"I never agreed to being shut out from my own son."

"Ms. Carson said that Dr. Newman returned from his trip," Ms. Garrett said. "That he called her."

"Look," Richard started, "all we want—"

"Dr. Newman called you?" the superintendent asked. "I didn't know you knew each other."

"We're just here to see—"

"Certainly, if you personally knew Dr. Newman, I would be aware of that."

"He'll be interested to know how unaware you are, Superintendent," Carol said.

Ms. Garrett took a quick, deep breath.

"All we want to do is see Christopher," Richard said. "Why is that so difficult? He's here, isn't he?"

The superintendent turned to his computer and typed in a command. He turned the monitor so that Richard and Carol could see it, then typed in "Carson" and pressed enter. A schedule of classes came up on the screen. Richard looked closely.

"We know where your son is at all times. Right now, he's in his physics class. Soon, he'll return to his living quarters," he pointed to a block of time on the screen, "for fifteen minutes of personal time. Then, another class." He pointed to "Room 316."

"Are you certain he's in his physics class?" Carol asked.

"Of course. Where else would he be?"

"Then let us just look through the door," Richard said.

"There's no window, so you'd have to open the door to see him. Then, of course, instruction would stop, your resident would see you, and the entire class would be disrupted."

"Would that be so bad?" Carol asked.

"Ms. Carson, we can't play favorites here. If we allow you to disrupt class, we'd have to allow each and every parent to do the same. How would the residents find time to learn?"

"We're not going to wait until the end of the quarter to see our son," Richard said.

"We'll send you a special video this month."

"That's not good enough."

The superintendent sighed and turned the monitor back facing him. "We don't normally do this, but I'll have my assistant take you to our administrative offices. There, you can complete the necessary paperwork to visit your resident."

Carol turned to her husband and smiled, surprised. "Well, good. That's what we wanted."

"So," Richard said, "when can we see him?"

"First you need to fill out the papers."

"I understand that, but when can we see him?"

"They'll explain all of the details to you in the administrative offices, Mr. Carson."

"This afternoon? Tomorrow?"

"It'll take approximately a month, I believe," the superintendent said.

"What?" Carol shouted.

"The month will go quickly."

"It doesn't matter if it's a month or a minute," she said, "the point is we're his parents and—"

"Forget it, Carol," Richard interrupted. "It's no use."

Carol looked over at her husband in shock, ready to argue with him, but he shook his head in a calm, almost stern, way.

"After all," Richard said, "that's what we came here for, the assurance that we could see our son. It doesn't have to be today." He stood up and faced the superintendent. "You can give us your personal assurance he's all right? That he made it back here safely and is now attending his class?"

"Absolutely."

"Fine. Let's sign the papers. The important thing is that we'll get to see him."

"Good. I appreciate your willingness to conform to our policies, Mr. Carson. Believe me, the resident is receiving the best of care as we speak."

"Just one more thing," Richard said. "What does a little lion cub have to do to become a real lion?" It was a gamble, but maybe if the superintendent knew that Richard was aware of a few things he'd be more careful how he treated his son.

The superintendent's eyes froze on Richard, then he took a deep breath. He motioned to the host waiting near the door and instructed him to show the Carsons to the administrative offices. Without a comment, the host walked past the secretary's desk and into the hall, Richard and Carol following close behind. Ms. Garrett remained in the superintendent's office and closed the door.

They turned a corner and came to a closed door. The host stopped and stepped aside. Richard opened the door and motioned for Carol to walk through, which she did. Then Richard went through the doorway and let the door close partway behind him. When the host reached for the doorknob to follow them, Richard slammed with all his weight into the door, hitting the host in the face and knocking him to the floor. Carol let out a scream, but quickly covered her mouth. As the stunned host tried to get up, Richard ran up to him, using his momentum to kick him in the face. The host fell to the floor, apparently unconscious.

Richard grabbed his wife's hand and started to run down the hall.

"I didn't know you could do that," she whispered.

"It's those old Bourne movies you never wanted me to watch," he said as they rounded a corner in the hall, coming to the large door that led to the lobby.

Richard opened the door slightly. The host had his back to the desk, speaking on the telephone. His first thought was that somehow someone knew what he'd done and was notifying the front desk, but he decided there hadn't been enough time. It was worth the risk.

"Carol," he whispered, "just walk through the lobby like nothing has happened, and don't look at the host. Don't give him any reason to quit talking on the phone. Then get a cab and get out of here."

"Where should I go?"

"Don't go back to the apartment. Once they've figured out what happened, they might go looking for you and I don't want you alone."

"I'll go to Susan's."

"Good. I'll call you when things are settled."

"Richard, what are you doing?"

"Who knows? I've got to find Christopher. Now get going." He looked over his shoulder, hoping no one was coming. "There's no time to talk."

"Let me help."

"They're going to catch me sooner or later. You'll be a lot more help out there than in here. Go!"

Carol walked through the doorway cautiously, keeping an eye on the host. He was still talking on the phone, apparently to some friend by the way he was laughing, with his back to the lobby. Richard remembered the card in his wallet with the telephone number from Harold.

"Pssst."

She didn't hear him.

"Carol," he whispered.

She still didn't hear him.

He looked over at the host, expecting any minute for him to turn around. Richard inched his way into the lobby, but he didn't want to leave the door and have it lock on him. He reached into his back pocket and pulled out his wallet, took the card out, then placed the wallet in the doorway, keeping the door from closing. He walked up behind his wife, who was almost at the front door.

"Carol."

She turned, surprised.

"Call this number when you're safely away from here," he whispered.

"Who is it?"

"Tell them it's an emergency. Explain what happened. You can trust them."

She nodded and turned back to the front door. Keeping an eye on the host, Richard walked back toward the large door to the hall. He sighed as he heard the front door close, knowing that Carol had made it. The host said good-bye and turned to hang up the phone. Richard ran for the door, not worrying about sound. He pushed on the door, catching his wallet as it fell, and headed down the hall without looking back.

CHAPTER
FIFTY-FIVE

Richard ran up the stairs and stopped at the door with the sign "FLOOR #3." He opened the door a couple of inches and looked out. The hall was empty. He opened the door a little farther and looked in the opposite direction, closing it when he saw two hosts approaching. As they walked past the door to the stairs, he heard one of them talk about some fight. Once they passed, he opened the door and headed down the hall from where they'd come.

Richard kept repeating "Room 316" in his mind, trying not to forget it. There was a number of doors on either side of the hall and, despite what the superintendent had said, each had a small window. 308...310...312.... Richard ran, crouching down whenever he went past a window. It wasn't difficult to hear the instructors speaking. In 314 he heard the instructor, a man, yelling at one of the residents, accusing the child of not trying hard enough. Finally, he came to 316.

He stopped at the door, inching up to the window so he could see inside. The room was almost completely dark, but he could hear a woman's voice talking about something—the law of inertia?—as she pointed a laser pen at the screen.

Richard searched the room for Christopher, but he just couldn't make out kids' faces. All the students sat rigidly, looking at the screen in front, sometimes entering something into their tablets. Off to the side, about three rows up and against the wall, was an empty desk. The only empty desk in the room.

The teacher said "next" and an image of the solar system appeared on the screen. Richard opened the door and entered the classroom, standing right next to the door. No one noticed him.

"Christopher Carson, you must come with me. I must take you to the superintendent's office immediately," Richard announced. Everyone turned and looked at the dark figure that had spoken in the back. The instructor stopped and put down her laser pointer.

"Who are you?" she asked.

"The superintendent—"

"You aren't from the superintendent's office. Who are you?" Everyone squinted when the instructor turned on the lights. Richard scanned the room, but there was no sign of Christopher.

"Who are you?" she asked again.

"I am the boy's father. I've come for my son. Where is he?"

The children looked shocked to see a real father in the school. They whispered to one another, looking at the father, then at the instructor.

"I'm calling security," the instructor said.

"Where is he?" Richard shouted this time. Several children covered their mouths, eyes wide open and staring.

"He's not here," a little boy said, barely loud enough for Richard to hear. The boy was sitting next to the empty desk.

"Be quiet," the instructor said.

"They said he was sick," the boy continued, "but I don't believe them."

"I will send the next resident who speaks to the basement," the instructor said. "Now turn around."

As she was trying to get the children back in line, Richard jumped into the hall. He ran down to the next corner, but as soon as he turned left, he spotted two hosts at the end of the hall. One of the hosts saw him and yelled for him to stop. Richard turned around and headed back from where he'd come. When he got near the physics classroom, he saw the instructor standing outside the door, talking with a host.

"That's the intruder," the instructor yelled, pointing at Richard.

Richard turned, but saw the other hosts running up fast from behind. He ran forward, thinking he'd have a better chance with just one host. The host lurched forward, tackling Richard around the waist and bringing him down. The two men wrestled on the floor, the host at least fifty pounds heavier. Richard broke from the host's hold and got up, only to be grabbed by the legs and come crashing down on the hard floor again. The host jumped on Richard's back and pulled out a pair of handcuffs, struggling to grab one of Richard's hands as he kept swinging.

Richard heard children screaming. The kids poured out of the physics class, the instructor trying to keep them back and shouting at them to "remember your training." Led by the little boy who had spoken up earlier, the children piled on top of the host, knocking him off of Richard.

"Leave him alone," they were shouting. "He's Christopher's father." They swung their little fists into the host's stomach and face, giving Richard all the time he needed to get up and run down the hall.

CHAPTER
FIFTY-SIX

When Richard pushed open the stairwell door he paused for a second, then ran up the stairs. He figured if Christopher was supposed to be sick, maybe he'd be in bed. He kept trying to remember where the superintendent had pointed when he spoke about "private time," but he couldn't remember the room number. He came to a door that said "FLOOR # 4," but kept running up. When he got to the next door one flight up, he stopped at the sign, "FLOOR # 5," trying to catch his breath. He pushed open the door. He couldn't see or hear anyone and walked down the hall toward a set of large double doors. He looked behind him, saw no one, then ran. Slowly, he opened one of the doors and peered inside the room.

It was huge. Christopher had talked about what the Newman staff called the "dorm room," and how he got to "sleep in a room with a bunch of other guys," but Richard hadn't thought he meant a place like this. It was crowded with beds only a couple of feet apart. A small dresser and bookcase sat at the foot of each bed. Hanging on each headboard by wire was a small metal sign, like a license plate, with the resident's name stamped on it.

Richard saw someone under a blanket move. He wanted to run as fast as possible to that bed, but he thought better of it and walked carefully, keeping an eye on the dark blue blanket. As he got closer to the bed, he could see that the body was about the size of Christopher. He tried to get a look at the child's face, just to be sure, and the boy opened his eyes.

"Oh no," the boy whimpered as he pulled the blanket tight around his neck.

It wasn't Christopher.

"Do you know where Christopher is?" Richard asked.

The boy didn't answer.

"Do you know where Christopher is?" he asked again.

"I really am sick, sir," the boy whispered.

"Don't be afraid of me. I don't work here. See," he held out his arms, "I'm not wearing a uniform. I'm harmless."

The boy studied Richard's face, which must have been bruised and bloody.

"You don't look harmless," the boy said.

Richard looked down at his shirt. "No, I guess I don't. I've been in a couple of fights today."

"Fights? Why?"

"With the hosts here. I'm a father, and my son is here. I'm trying to find him."

The boy let go of his blanket, amazed. "You are a father of a resident?"

"Yes."

The boy sat up in bed. "How did you get in?"

"Do you know where Christopher is?"

"I don't think I know who he is."

"He was on the sabbatical."

"Oh," the boy said, nodding his head. "He hasn't been here. I heard they brought him back last night, but he never slept here." He pointed over to some beds about fifteen feet away.

Richard headed over there. He found a bed with "C. Carson" stamped on the plate, but the mattress was rolled up and the blanket was folded. There was nothing on the dresser or in the bookcase. Richard looked back at the boy.

"Where could he be?"

The boy shook his head. "I don't want to know."

Richard started back toward the double doors. "I've got to find him."

"Why?"

"He doesn't belong here."

As Richard passed by the boy's bed, he read the name. "H. Jenkins."

"Are you the son of Hunter and Tiffany Jenkins?"

"I used to be," the boy said, lying back down in bed.

CHAPTER
FIFTY-SEVEN

After he closed the double doors behind him, Richard pulled out his cell phone to check in with Carol or Harold or somebody, but there was no coverage. Just as he got to the stairwell door, it opened. A woman in a lab coat came out, but she was going in the opposite direction and didn't see him. He slipped into the stairwell before the door closed. He ran down the stairs to the lobby level. He stood still for a moment, catching his breath, when the door opened. He jumped behind it as a short man in a safari uniform walked past and went up the stairs. Once the man was out of sight, Richard let out a breath and stepped away from the wall. He noticed for the first time another door and found some stairs leading down.

Finally, after three flights of stairs, he found another door. The sign on the door said "AUTHORIZED PERSONNEL ONLY." He reached for the door, but it was locked. There was a black pad next to the door, requiring a security card of some sort to get in. Richard leaned up against the door, pressing his ear against it, but couldn't hear anything. He held onto the doorknob as he tried to listen, and soon felt the doorknob moving in his hand. He moved back against the wall, holding his breath. The door opened and he could hear a man talking.

"No, I don't think that will be necessary," the man said, opening the door a little bit more, but hesitating. He seemed to be talking on his cell phone.

"Okay, I'll be there immediately." The man let go of the door and stepped back into the hall.

Richard caught the doorknob and let the door almost close. He waited a minute, until he could no longer hear the man on the phone, then opened the door and slipped through. He was in a long hallway, dimly lit. He saw a door labeled AUTHORIZED PERSONELL ONLY: POST-PROCEDURE LAB. He tried the door, but, of course, it was locked. When he put his ear to the door, he thought he could hear some noise. Maybe a person talking. Impulsively, he knocked on the door, then listened. The noise stopped. He knocked again, but louder. The doorknob began to turn and Richard stood by, ready to jump. When the door opened, he didn't even wait to see who opened it but lunged forward, crashing into the other person. The two fell on the floor and Richard pulled back his fist, ready for a fight, but the other man lay on the floor, unconscious. He was a small man, wearing khaki scrubs and a surgical mask. No one else seemed to be in the room.

The room was some sort of lab: table, desk, a microscope, scientific instruments Richard didn't recognize, and a computer. The microscope was on, probably what the man was working on when he was interrupted. Richard looked into the microscope and saw what looked like a thin slice of tissue. In the middle of it was something he'd never seen before. He tried focusing the lens. He thought he could identify the cells of the tissue, but embedded among the cells was what appeared to be some sort of tiny mechanical instrument.

A bulletin board above the desk was covered with brain scans, similar to the one Hunter had given him for Christopher. Various colors highlighted different portions of the brain, and lines of light crisscrossed the portions. On each of the scans was written the word "Gazelle."

He lifted up one of the scan images and found another paper with "Seven Cubs" at the top. There were seven animals listed: giraffe, elephant, gazelle, zebra, gorilla, leopard, and lion. The word "gazelle" was circled. That pattern of animals seemed familiar to him. "Cubs." Lions had cubs, but elephants had calves, zebras had foals, and he wasn't sure what the others had. Seemed odd to call them all cubs; was there some meaning here?

Richard closed his eyes, trying to remember where he'd seen that grouping of animals before. The outside of the Newman school...the protective railings on the windows. Each floor had its own animal portrayed in its railings: one was giraffe, the next elephant, all the way up to lion. And the video, of Christopher walking...the pattern on the couch included each of these seven animals. The woman in the video called Christopher her "lion cub." And, of course, there was his son's phone message about someone wanting to make a lion out of him. Now, he was just a cub, but someone had bigger plans for him.

Richard stepped away from the desk, looking for other clues—something that might help him figure out where his son was. If Christopher was the lion cub mentioned on the piece of paper, maybe he was getting closer to finding him. He noticed a door in a dark corner of the room. When he stepped into the room, large lights automatically came on, revealing what looked like several operating tables. The walls were white tile and bare, and the room smelled of some chemical. The tables were empty, except for one which held a small body covered with a sheet. Richard walked over to the table and touched the sheet, hesitant to pull it back. He took a deep breath, closed his eyes, and pulled the sheet down. He was shaking. When he finally opened his eyes, he saw the body of a little girl, probably about his son's age. He was instantly relieved, but then felt guilty for feeling that way. While her body looked like it had not been touched by any medical procedure, there were a number of holes on the top and sides of her head, as though someone had been taking samples from her brain, and a small incision behind her ear. He covered her body back up and stepped away.

There was a tag tied to one of the girl's toes: TANYA.

CHAPTER
FIFTY-EIGHT

Richard left the operating room and checked his cell phone again in the lab—still no coverage. He was badly shaken. Was Tanya ever even at the hospital? Did she really die of natural causes, or did Newman kill her so they could turn her into a research subject?

He scanned the bulletin board again, and the desk, hoping to find some clue. When he turned toward the door, he saw that the man he'd knocked out was gone. He opened the door slightly and saw two men in lab coats who had just walked past.

"It's just the beginning," one said. "I don't think we can call it a success until our little lion makes it to adulthood."

"I'll be happy if he just makes it through today," the other said.

Richard closed the door. He was going crazy an inch at a time. How would he ever be able to find his son in this place? He had to keep from getting caught, but he could spend all day searching individual rooms. And who's to say one room he found empty wouldn't have Christopher in it twenty minutes later? He'd said that he'd gotten away from them, but what did that mean? Had they caught him by now? Was he somewhere in the school, or had they let him get out into the city, like Joseph's son?

He heard footsteps coming and put his ear to the door. When that didn't work very well, he opened the door again, slightly. Two men were walking down the hall. The first was a young man in a lab coat, early twenties, with about two days worth of sparse whiskers on his face. The second man was Hunter. They were deep in conversation.

"How much longer do you think this will take?" the younger man asked as they paused before climbing up the stairs. "He's a tough resident."

"Yeah, his parents are as stubborn as he is," Hunter said. "I'd hoped by the end of the day he'd be rehabilitated."

"What will we do if he isn't?"

"We'll have to augment our therapy with chemical procedures," Hunter answered as the two men started up the stairs. "I hate doing that, it's so expensive."

Richard waited until the men were out of sight, then stepped from around the door into the dark hallway. About twenty yards away some light invaded the hall from underneath a closed door. He could hear his footsteps echo down the hall and shifted to walking on the balls of his feet. He felt his body pulling him to run and throw open the door, to find out if the tough little resident—the resident whose parents Hunter knew so well—was his son. But he knew he had to be careful.

When he got to the door, he paused as he read the sign: AUTHORIZED PERSONNEL ONLY: REHABILITATION CENTER. The door looked like solid metal, and there was no window. Richard pushed on it, but it wouldn't budge. Then he noticed the security card pad to the right of the door, the red light activated.

"Who are you?" a voice shouted.

Richard turned to see the young man in the lab coat standing about halfway between Richard and the stairwell door.

"What are you doing here?" the man said.

Richard stood straight, motioning with his hands like he was going to give a full explanation, but then he started running at the man. The man turned around, heading through the stairwell door and up the stairs. Richard made it to the door before it closed and leaped up the stairs, three at a time, pulling himself up with the rail. At the first level landing, the young man was almost an entire flight of stairs ahead. But at the second level, his lead had dropped to a half of a flight. Richard felt his sides aching. The next landing would be the lobby.

As the man rounded the corner and started up the last few steps, his foot caught on the end of his lab coat, tripping him. He fell back to the landing, but got to his feet and started up the stairs again. Richard barely made it around the corner, grabbing the man's foot and tripping him again. The two fell to the landing. Richard felt a couple of hard blows to his sides, right below his ribs. He grabbed the man by his lab coat and threw him down the next set of stairs, leaping on top of him just as he hit the landing. The man didn't move, but Richard could see he was still breathing. He searched the man's pockets until he found the security card and ran down the stairs.

He tried the card on the Rehabilitation Center door, but nothing happened. Again, he held the card up to be read, and this time the door opened.

Richard ran into a large control room of some kind. It was dimly lit, but he could see a long counter with a panel full of knobs, switches, and lights. On either end of the counter were small color monitors showing a countdown. The count was sixteen.

A small flash card sat next to one of the monitors. The printed sticker on the card said: "The Seven Cubs." He pulled out his cell phone and held it against the card until he heard the beep, indicating that the phone had copied something from the card. Probably encrypted and impossible to read, but it was better than nothing.

On the other side of the counter was a glass wall. He ran up to the glass and looked more closely. He could barely make out that in the center of the dimly lit room on the other side stood a straight-backed, metal chair.

And in the chair sat a very still little boy, his back to the control room.

CHAPTER
FIFTY-NINE

The room was too dark for Richard to see if the boy was Christopher or not. There was no security card reader on the metal door that led to the room, so he pushed on it without stopping. The door opened, and Richard stood still for a brief moment, feeling the silence. He didn't even hear the door close behind him. The room was some sort of sound chamber, the other wall rounded, a half-circle that went from one end of the glass wall to the other. There was a gradual curve at the bottom of the wall, blending it into the floor, and another curve at the top. A little light was coming from above the glass wall, but Richard had a difficult time sensing space and distance. The white walls, white ceiling, white floor, seemed to blend far off in the distance. There was no surface to look at.

The boy in the chair hadn't moved at all. His arms and legs were strapped to the chair, and his head was bowed, straight down onto his chest, like he was praying or sleeping. Or dead.

The light over the glass wall shut completely off. Richard turned to the control room, but could see nothing. He held his hand inches from his face, but couldn't see it either. The chamber was totally dark and silent, and he became disoriented. He wasn't sure where the boy was now, or even which direction he himself was facing.

Richard began to sense something. He didn't know what it was, but he felt his body responding to some sort of motion. Gradually, he heard a deep, low resonating hum. His body sensed it more than his ears could hear it, but the rumble was getting louder and higher in pitch. There was shaking—constant, driving shaking. He wasn't sure if the shaking was the floor or himself or what. The sound got louder and louder, the pitch, higher and higher. His ears hurt and he reached up to cover them. Richard worried for the boy, knowing he couldn't cover his own ears.

The sound screeched throughout the chamber now, pounding away at Richard's brain. He felt the room spinning, and he spread out his legs to try to keep his balance. The screech grew louder, higher, and he felt the room literally turn over. Richard fell to the floor and collapsed into the fetal position, holding his ears and rolling. He thought he felt the room turn over again, and again, and he rolled around on the floor, wishing he was strapped down as well.

The screeching stopped dead and Richard found that he was yelling, without really knowing it. He stopped and opened his eyes. He blinked. Again. He wasn't sure if his eyes were opened or not, so he reached up and touch them with his hands. It was difficult for his hands to find his face, he was so disoriented. He wasn't sure he was reaching up or out or at all. Finally, he touched his eyes and thought he felt they were opened. But he couldn't see anything.

"Christopher," he whispered. "Christopher," he said, more loudly, as he stood up, "are you all right? Whoever you are, are you all right?"

No answer. No sound. No sensation.

Dead. Everything felt dead to Richard.

Then the room filled with a bright, searing light, forcing Richard to cover his eyes and fall to his knees. He felt sweat dripping from his forehead, under his arms, all over. Even with his eyes closed, he could tell how bright the room was, and it kept getting hotter. He stood up because his knees were burning through his jeans from touching the floor, but he still couldn't open his eyes. Too bright.

"Are you okay?" he shouted.

No answer.

He sensed that the temperature of the room was starting to decrease, and the light seemed less bright against his eyelids. He covered his eyes and slowly opened them and began to notice faint images appearing on the one round wall, some sort of slides or movie covering the wall, from one end to the other, seamlessly. The light was now bearable, about the intensity in a normally lit room, but growing dimmer. The images became easier to discern.

A man stood on a neighborhood sidewalk, and, several houses down, a little blonde boy rode his bicycle toward the man. Toward his father. The bicycle was wobbly, like the boy was just learning how to ride without training wheels. There was no sound, but the boy was smiling, pleased with his success.

The lights grew dimmer in the room, until they were completely off and the only light came from the images on the wall. Richard stood transfixed by the image of the boy on the bicycle. The image surrounded him. In front, out of the corners of his eyes, everywhere. All he could do was stand and watch and become a part of it.

The perspective of the image shifted now, to that of the boy, as though he were holding the camera while he rode his bike. Richard could sense how the bicycle was unsteady as the view focused down at the handlebars. The view went up, looking at the father a couple of houses down. The father stood erect, arms folded, oblivious to the joy his son was feeling, judging the boy's skills.

The bicycle fell and the view became shaky and out of focus as it was tossed about. Sky. Grass. Handlebars. Sidewalk. The father ran toward the camera, angry. His face was red, and his mouth opened big as he shouted. The room filled with sound. Loud. Sudden. Intense enough to be felt and heard.

"You idiot!" the father shouted. "Can't you ride a simple bicycle? What's wrong with you? Your brother learned how in half the time. Why can't you be more like him?"

The sound of a boy starting to cry.

"Don't start that, you little crybaby! I don't want all the neighbors to see what a baby you are. It's embarrassing. Now get up! Come on, get up! And this time do it right. Something's wrong with you."

The image started to fade, but the last statement echoed throughout the room repeatedly, fading with each repetition. "Something's wrong with you. Something's wrong with you. Something's wrong with you. Something's wrong with you."

The wall was blank for a second or two, then a montage of images flashed by. They were quick, but long enough to pierce the mind. The father yelling at the son while pointing at a messy room...a mother watching television and ignoring the little boy nearby...the mother and father sitting at the dinner table with the little blonde boy, no one looking at each other or speaking....

Richard stood still, not able to move.

"This is what your life would be if you weren't safe here at the Newman Home," a woman's voice filled the room, soft and gentle. "You would be worse than a pet, kept home by parents who only want you to work for them."

...the father slamming the back door as his son carries two huge garbage bags....

"Why do many biological parents like having their offspring in their house? Because it gives them someone to vent their anger at. Someone to yell at. To blame. To beat."

...the mother throwing the toys of the blonde boy as he watched, crying....

Crying.

Richard stared at the wall.

Crying.

Richard blinked. He heard something. Was it part of the images on the wall?

Crying.

He heard it again. Someone said something about stopping. Someone was crying. Richard blinked again, bowing his head so he could look at the floor. Now he could hear better. The woman's voice was still talking, but he was sure he heard someone crying. Someone real. Suddenly he could think again and remembered there was a boy in the room. He looked up at the boy sitting in the chair. His head was moving back and forth as he cried.

"Christopher?" Richard asked.

The boy kept shaking his head, back and forth.

"How horrible," the woman's voice continued. "What a tragedy for little boys and girls to be treated worse than dogs."

The images appeared on the wall more quickly now, almost falling on top of one another.

...a crying baby left behind, alone in a dark room...the father, slapping the boy against the side of his face, forcing him to the floor....

The boy strapped in the chair jolted, his body jerking up and back as if a powerful electric current had shocked his body. If it weren't for the straps he'd have been thrown to the floor. Two seconds later, he jolted again.

"Christopher!" Richard lunged forward. He knelt between the boy and the wall, looking at the boy's twisted face. The child looked haggard, exhausted, old. Sweat poured out of every pore on his face, and his eyes stared straight ahead, through Richard and at the wall.

The blonde boy from the video was sitting in front of him, passed out.

Richard stared at the boy's face, struggling between feelings of relief and disappointment, then searched for wires. He couldn't find any and fumbled instead with the straps, hurrying to try to unbuckle them. The images came faster, surrounding the two, smothering them.

Another jolt.

Richard felt the electricity burn through his arms, knocking him back, almost to the floor. He went back to working on the straps and finally got the arms undone. He could feel the images around them changing, the woman's voice growing louder, more intense. The strap on the boy's left leg was unbuckled.

Another jolt.

The boy's arms flung up and his upper body jumped forward and then slammed back into the chair. Richard fell back again, feeling like red hot wires were running through his veins. He started on the right leg.

The images cut off and the room became completely dark. Richard couldn't see the strap, but kept working with it. He heard the boy breathing and felt his body go limp.

Soft, relaxing music began to play, and images appeared on the wall. Richard finished undoing the strap. As he reached to pick up the boy, he felt some wires embedded in the metal of the chair.

He held the boy in his arms like a baby. He was heavy, far heavier than what his weight would normally seem, completely limp, with no strength left.

Richard carried the boy away from the chair. On the wall were pictures of the school: residents peacefully studying at their desks...an instructor kneeling in the hall, talking with a resident... the residents enjoying a meal in the cafeteria.

"But at the Newman Home," the woman's voice began, "off-spring are people. The kind instructors and administrators at the Newman Home realize there is no difference between residents and adults—we would mistreat residents were we to treat them like children. We take very seriously our charge to raise up a generation of world leaders. Senators, presidents, CEO's. Such leaders begin as mature, competent, knowledgeable residents."

Without warning, the images and sound stopped. Cut off, completely. The chamber was dark again, and Richard couldn't even see the boy in his arms. He walked forward, cautiously, not sure where the door was, his footsteps echoing. The more he stepped forward, the more uncertain he became of where he was, which direction he was going. Then he heard some clicking noise he couldn't identify, and the room filled with a series of noises. There were so many sounds, echoing on top of one another, he had no idea what they were. He stood still, listening. The sounds weren't coming from the speakers, he thought, but from somewhere in the room. From everywhere in the room.

The lights came on from above the glass wall, and Richard could see he and the boy were surrounded by a dozen hosts, holding their security clubs.

CHAPTER SIXTY

Sweat dripped down Richard's forehead and cheeks. The room burned from the lights, so hot it was hard to breathe. He looked at the glass wall to the control room, but all he could see was the reflection of himself holding the boy, and the hosts standing at attention around them.

"You've caused us a lot of trouble, Mr. Carson," the superintendent's voice said, filling the room. "What should we do with you?"

"This boy needs medical attention right away," Richard said.

The door from the control room opened and the man in a lab coat came in. As he got closer, Richard could see a large bump on the man's forehead. He held out his arms and told Richard to give him the boy.

"Will you have a doctor look at him?" Richard asked.

"We will do what we need to do," the man said.

Richard held onto the boy. "No, you'll have a doctor—a real doctor—look at him."

"You're in no position, Mr. Carson," the superintendent's voice said, "to make demands. Give us the boy, or keep him, whichever you prefer. Will he get any medical treatment in your hands?"

Richard looked down at the little boy. He didn't move, but he was sweating so much his clothes were drenched. Richard kissed the boy on his forehead, then handed him to the man.

"How touching," the superintendent said. "Now, what should we do with you, Mr. Carson? Would a little kiss on the forehead help?"

"Let's call my wife and ask her what to do with me. She's waiting to hear from me."

"Your wife who claimed to know Dr. Newman? I've come to understand what kinds of connections she actually has."

Richard looked up at the ceiling, trying to come up with some connection who could help, but he really had no idea about the people Carol knew. "I think the mayor's office would be interested in hearing from her."

"We like the mayor," the superintendent said. "He serves on our board of directors."

"Well, the governor—"

"Considers us one of his major contributors."

"We have many people we could—"

"Your face is so bloodied, so bruised," the superintendent said. "With all your fighting, there may have been an accident. Perhaps a fatal one. Our first priority is to protect the residents, you know, and a wild man running throughout the halls is a dangerous threat. It would sadden us to explain it to your wife, but the police would understand. They might even give me a medal."

Richard licked his lips, tasting the saltiness from his sweat. "Just bring me my son."

"You can have him," the superintendent said, "if you can find him."

"What do you mean?" Richard took a couple of steps toward the door to the control room, but the two nearest hosts moved in closer, stopping him.

"He's gone. He ran away."

"How could that happen? You've got more security here than the White House."

The superintendent laughed. "Accidents happen."

Richard ran for the door, but two hosts jumped in front of him, and a third came from behind and struck the back of Richard's legs with a club. Richard fell to the floor, holding his legs.

"You're a slow learner, Mr. Carson."

Richard struggled to get up. "Just let me go look for my son. I'll leave you and your beloved Dr. Newman alone."

The door to the control room opened and two more hosts stepped in, clubs in hand. The light came on in the control room and Richard could see the superintendent standing behind a counter. A man, probably in his early sixties, passed through the doorway, his eyes slowly moving about the room, inspecting. He was balding on top, but had longish white hair along the sides and back. He wore the same khaki safari uniform as everyone else, but he wore it differently, not like someone playing safari, but like a regal hunter triumphantly returning.

"This room seems smaller than I remember it," he said, never looking at Richard. "The speakers aren't as loud as I would like. And a bit distorted. Do we need larger ones?"

"I'll look into it this afternoon," the superintendent said over the microphone.

"Good."

The man walked toward Richard, still looking off to the sides. The two hosts followed closely behind him.

"A new coat of paint would be nice," the man said.

"Tomorrow," the superintendent said.

"Today."

There was a pause. "Yes. Today."

The man stopped within six feet of Richard, then finally looked at him, directly into his eyes. The man smiled.

"Mr. Carson, I'm Dr. Newman. I believe you called me 'the beloved Dr. Newman.' I like that." He smiled. "It's a pleasure to meet you."

"I want my son."

"I don't value small talk much myself, but it can be a way to get to know a person."

"Where is he?"

Dr. Newman began walking around the room, closely guarded by the hosts. "Do you know where you're standing?"

"In a torture chamber."

"In a dream. My dream. A place where children can come and grow up properly. Where they can be shaped into leaders—without being slowed down by meddlesome, clumsy parents." Dr. Newman turned to Richard and smiled. "No offense, of course."

"Brainwashing doesn't make children grow up to be leaders."

"The term is relative. Leaders are people who can make others do exactly what I tell them to do."

"Just let me have my son."

"Quite ingenious, don't you think? We have the technology to create videos with any resident we want in them, even their parents—videos of events that never occurred. With the help of those electrodes, the residents actually create memories they subconsciously draw upon whenever we need them to. They remember their fathers yelling at them when they were leaning to ride a bicycle, even though their fathers were never near them for long at that age. And, to be candid, I don't think any of our residents know how to ride a bicycle." He chuckled.

"Is he still in this building?" Richard asked.

"Parents mean well, I suppose," Dr. Newman said, "but what do they know about raising children? They read more about their new car than about child development." He smiled. "Not to mention a multi-billion dollar industry called 'education.' You are talking to the most important CEO in the world, Mr. Carson."

Richard took a step toward Dr. Newman, but a host moved forward, club in hand.

"And you know what's truly exciting, Mr. Carson? When the residents get older, the video changes. They learn about how much they owe this school. About how much they owe me."

"Is he on this floor?"

"And once the details of funding and governmental approval are out of the way, the Newman Home system will expand throughout the country."

"Give me my son."

"Would you shut up?" Dr. Newman shouted, turning sharply to Richard. "I am the winner here, you fool. I am a genius and you're not listening to a word I'm saying. There's a lot more going on here than one resident and his trouble-making daddy."

"He's not just a resident, he's my son."

"You are most correct," Dr. Newman said as he looked at the floor. "He's much more than a typical resident. We always saw he was exceptional. He far exceeded the other residents in testing results at every level. We were counting on him in ways you cannot imagine."

"I'd imagine so. It's not every resident who can become a lion."

Dr. Newman stared at Richard, surprised. He looked over at the window to the control room, and the superintendent shrugged. Dr. Newman smiled, then started walking away.

"What's the incision?" Richard asked, pointing to behind his ear. "What have you been doing to them?"

"It's nothing, really. We tried implanting a small chip in a few residents to see if it enhanced their learning capacity. We'd spent years on that chip, but the increase in capacity was minimal and we removed them. No harm done. We've come up with something much, much better."

Richard stepped towards the doctor, but two hosts grabbed his arms.

"What's the experiment?" Richard asked.

"You know," Dr. Newman said, "we didn't always have a Rehabilitation Room. Everything went fine, in the beginning. But then some of the residents started whining. Always wanting to see mommy and daddy. It was the visits, you know. We should have never allowed so many visits."

"It's torture."

"Remember when the government came up with 'enhanced interrogation techniques'? Well, we've established enhanced discipline techniques. Far more humane than when people beat their students with boards and called it paddling. We don't use them often, and when we do, no one ever gets hurt."

"That boy certainly looked harmed," Richard said.

"That was nothing. If he had been your resident, you would have seen some real fireworks."

Richard lunged forward, trying to grab Dr. Newman by the shoulders. Four hosts grabbed him and threw him down, one striking him across the face with his club. The two hosts closest to Dr. Newman pulled him back, protecting him.

"What should we do with you, Mr. Carson?"

"You can kill me, Newman, but that won't solve your problems. There are other people in the city, just like me. It's just a matter of time before they call the authorities."

Dr. Newman laughed. "What authorities? What authorities do you think don't know what we're doing? What authorities want us to stop? We're manufacturing a generation who will do exactly what they are told to do. Do you honestly believe there is an elected official with any power who doesn't want that? Do you think the CEO's don't want compliant, obedient employees? Eventually, because of me, there really will be no child left behind. At least none worth anything to society."

Dr. Newman looked at one of the hosts and pointed to Richard. Richard turned just in time to see a club coming down on his head.

CHAPTER
SIXTY-ONE

Slowly, Richard's mind became aware of his body. He was lying on something hard, and sensed a brightness through his eyelids. The spinning in his head began to settle. There was no sound. Gradually, he raised his hand to his forehead and rubbed it. Shielding his eyes with his hand, he opened them. When he moved his hand to the side, all he could see was whiteness. There were no contrasting colors or shadows, and the whiteness seemed so far away, and yet right up against his face as well. He wondered if he'd died.

He felt a sharp pain at his side. Then another. Someone had just kicked him.

"Get up," the host shouted.

Richard saw three different sets of legs, all wearing khaki slacks. He pushed himself up into a sitting position and looked around, remembering where he was.

"Mr. Carson," the superintendent's voice said over the speakers, "you are a stubborn man. Our time is valuable. Get up!"

Richard tried standing up. The room started to spin again, and he sat back down. Out of the corner of his eye he saw a leg move back, preparing to kick. "I'm getting up," Richard said. "Give me a minute." The leg stopped.

As he was about to stand, he heard over the speakers the sound of a door in the control room opening and closing, then some muffled discussion.

"What? Impossible!" Dr. Newman's voice said. Then there was complete silence.

Richard looked up at the glass wall, but saw only his own reflection. His mouth was bleeding, his head scraped and bruised. When he moved, he felt a sharp pain in his side, like a rib was cracked.

"Mr. Carson," Dr. Newman said over the speakers, "you are—"

The sound was cut off again.

The hosts looked at one another, not sure what they were supposed to do. Richard tried not to look at his reflection in the glass wall.

"We have wasted too much time already," Richard heard Dr. Newman say in the control room. In the background was the sound of a door opening and closing again.

"Mr. Carson," the superintendent's voice said over the speaker, "we wish you the best in finding your son. We regret he somehow ran away."

"What?" Richard said.

"What are you waiting for? Help the gentleman to his feet."

Two of the hosts stepped forward, each grabbing one of Richard's arms and pulling him up.

"We know how dangerous Manhattan streets can be," Newman said, "especially for a little child. Would you like our assistance locating him?"

"No," Richard said, straining to see something behind the glass wall. "Of course not. What's going on here?"

The man in the lab coat who had taken the boy from Richard entered the chamber, carrying a small first aid kit. He poured something from a dark brown bottle onto a cotton ball and started cleaning Richard's face.

"What are you doing?" Richard asked.

"I'm deeply sorry about your son's running away," the man said without any hint of expression on his face. He finished bandaging Richard's forehead. "We tried everything we could to find him, but he's very clever. Let us help you look."

"No," Richard said. "I'm afraid you'd find him."

Two hosts stepped up to Richard and motioned for him to follow, but they were careful not to touch him in any way. The control room was empty; Dr. Newman and the superintendent were nowhere in sight. Richard and the hosts entered the hall and headed for an elevator. They took the elevator to the lobby level, never speaking. When they got to the lobby door, all but one of the hosts turned around and left. The host waited until the others were out of sight, then opened the door for Richard.

The lobby was empty; not even the usual host sat behind the desk. Richard took a couple steps forward, and the door closed and locked behind him. The monitor on the host's desk was blank—something Richard had never seen before at Newman.

Richard inched toward the front door, listening for any sound that might tell him something. When he reached the door, he paused and studied all around it, not knowing what he was looking for, but trying to be alert to anything out of the ordinary. He pulled on the door handle to see if anything would happen. Nothing. He pulled on the door a little more, opening it about a foot, and peered outside.

"Richard," Joseph said. "We're here."

CHAPTER
SIXTY-TWO

R ichard stepped out, shaking Joseph's hand. He saw Harold and held out his hand, but Rebecca quickly jumped in and hugged him.

"What about Christopher?" Harold asked.

"They threw him out on the streets. Said he ran away."

"That sounds familiar," Joseph said. "We've got to hurry."

"How do we know they're telling the truth?" Rebecca asked.

"We don't," Joseph said. "But if they are, we don't have time to waste. Let's go."

Joseph took one side of Richard, and Harold the other, in case he needed help down the steps. For the first time, Richard had a chance to see the scene. He froze for a moment. Dozens of people, people Richard had never seen before, stood along the steps leading down to the waiting sedan. Everyone was looking at Richard, some were crying, but no one said a word.

Richard slipped on his way down the steps and had to lean on Joseph. When they got to the car, Harold turned around and faced the group of people.

"Christopher is out on the streets somewhere," Harold said. Several people gasped, some shook their heads. "So, we'll go with the secondary plan. Fifteen of you stay here on the steps and an-other ten at the back entrance. We've already got groups assembled at the major media outlets. Joseph's people are working on getting the search warrant, but until then we can at least make our pres-ence known and keep them as honest as we can. The rest of you, go to your designated neighborhoods and search for Christopher. Joan," he said to a woman standing near the top of the steps, "would you call ahead to the church and let the others know we're coming? They'll know what to do."

Harold motioned to Richard to sit in the front seat, but Richard turned to the group. "Thank you," he said. "Thank you all."

Harold helped Richard into the front seat, then he and his wife sat in the back. Joseph hurried to the driver's side and started the car. As they pulled away from the curb, the others on the steps and sidewalk filled in the aisle, leaving no means of going up or down the steps.

"I have never been so glad to see so many people in my entire life," Richard said.

"And we've never been so glad to see one," Harold said. "There's a few other people we didn't bring to the school. We'll stop by and have them help us look."

Rebecca explained how Carol had contacted their hotline. She said there had been some delay, since Carol hadn't known the pass-word, but she'd finally gotten through. Richard had never been more grateful for his wife's persistence. Rebecca had asked Carol to go home in case Christopher decided to return there. Their system had pulled together all the people who had showed up at Newman, along with many others he hadn't even seen yet. Some of these people were parents of children at Newman, but many more were simply New Yorkers concerned for years about the direction education was taking and wanted to help. Many didn't even have children of their own.

Harold then told Richard about the letter Joseph had written and delivered, claiming they knew Richard was being held against his will in the school, even though they didn't. The letter threatened that more people would arrive to stand guard around the school while others contacted the media.

"Where is the media?" Richard asked. "Why aren't they all over this story?"

"Hard to say," Joseph said. "We've got groups putting on pressure, but this is all about business. Not everyone's been bought, but it's difficult to know who's taking the orders and who's giving them."

"To be honest, the fact that they let you out is a miracle in itself," Harold said from the back seat.

Richard looked at the copies he'd made on his cell phone, but the files were unreadable because of advanced encrypting. Harold took the phone and copied the files onto his, then sent them to a techie at his firm. Joseph turned on Amsterdam Avenue. Richard knew finding Christopher would be almost impossible, but he kept searching every sidewalk, every storefront, every cafe, hoping to catch some hint of his son.

They were in familiar territory for Richard now, not far from Columbia. He was about to ask where they were going when they passed Cathedral Parkway and Joseph pulled over. They all climbed out of the car, and Richard looked up the street at a small pizza joint where he and his law school pals used to spend what few bucks they had. Richard walked around the sedan and headed for the pizza place, assuming they were going to meet some people there. Joseph shook his head and pointed behind Richard.

Richard turned around. The massive, grey Cathedral Church of Saint John the Divine loomed before him, as mammoth as some mountain from the Bible. It was Episcopal, his family's religion, and he'd visited it several times as a student. He watched the church like it might move. Or talk to him.

"Come on, Richard," Harold said as he and the others started walking past the Children's Sculpture Garden, on their ways toward the front doors of the Cathedral.

"What are we doing here?" Richard asked, following. "We've got to find Christopher."

"That's what we're doing here."

They walked up the steps and entered through the door just to the side of the great center doorway. The foyer was dark and felt like a castle, old and permanent. Someone was speaking, but Richard couldn't make out the words. Harold led the way. Richard's eyes became better adjusted to the light as they entered the nave, so large and tall and inspiring he almost felt like he was still outside. The air was heavy, almost damp, like he was in some special place of nature—a space created by God rather than people. He began to piece together why they were there.

Before him were row after row of wooden chairs filled with people. Two, probably closer to three hundred people—all looking straight ahead. Before them stood not a member of the clergy presenting a sermon, but a man in jeans and a Yankees sweatshirt, pointing to a map of Manhattan. Next to it was a large television that was turned off.

Joseph, Harold, and Rebecca stepped aside as Richard walked forward, deliberately, as if too quick a movement might destroy the scene before him. The speaker at the front saw Richard and stopped talking. The other people turned and saw Richard for the first time. Without anyone saying a word, they all stood as he walked up the aisle.

One man, standing near the front, raced down the aisle to Richard. "We'll find him, big brother," David whispered as they hugged. "I promise."

CHAPTER
SIXTY-THREE

With David at his side, and Joseph and the Solomons following closely behind, Richard walked up the aisle, his mind absorbing the surroundings. He glanced at the people on his left and right, still standing, but didn't recognize anyone. They were all strangers, New Yorkers who'd never met Richard or Carol or Christopher, but who cared enough to help.

They stopped when they got to the front. Harold walked over to the map and reviewed the plan. When they thought Christopher was still at Newman, they were going to send everyone to march on every television station and newspaper in the city. Now that they could assume Christopher was out, they would keep some people at the school, send some to the media, but have most of them canvas Manhattan in specific search teams, looking everywhere for the little boy. Rebecca mentioned that the police had been notified, but she didn't expect them to help. There were a lot of missing children, the sergeant had explained to her, and this one had only been missing for a few hours.

Harold asked Richard about any special places Christopher might go to. Richard mentioned some of the sites they'd visited together, but he really didn't know where he'd go. Rebecca assigned teams.

Harold checked to make certain everyone had a chance to download the photos and videos of Christopher Carol had sent him. And he suggested some teams take the subways, since they were faster and since there was a whole city underground that had to be included in the search.

It didn't take long for Harold to finish up, then Joseph stepped forward. "I won't be long," Joseph began. "We have a little boy to find, and we must do so before it grows dark. I just wanted to tell you what a good thing you're doing. We're looking for Richard's child, but we're also looking for all our children who are lost, not because they wandered away, but because someone sent them away, in one way or another. It's time to bring them home."

Harold reminded search teams to call in every hour, then everyone started filing out. Richard watched as the people made their way outside to search for his little son. He'd never felt stronger, more capable of finding Christopher, but he still had no idea how it would be possible. Where could he be? And what if he didn't want to be found? Christopher was wounded, thinking his own father had betrayed him. Maybe he wasn't just on the streets, but actually hiding. It might be impossible to find him.

"I think you'd better stay here, Richard," Harold said.

"No, I've got to look."

"If one of the teams finds Christopher and brings him back, he'll be surrounded by strangers until you can get back here. We'll do a good job of looking."

"What about me?" David asked from behind. "Christopher knows his Uncle David. I'll stick around so you can look."

"Thanks," Richard said, smiling at his brother.

"Which team do you want to go with, Richard?" Harold asked.

"I won't need a team—it might slow me down."

"All right," Harold said. "I'm going to be staying here with the coordination team. The city is yours."

Richard asked if Harold had heard anything back about the encrypted files, but his friend at the firm said they were almost impossible to crack. When David overheard, he asked for a copy of the files to see if he could decrypt them himself.

Outside on the steps, Richard paused for a moment and looked up into the sky. It was a dark, overcast day, starting to drizzle. He couldn't see the sun, but there was only a handful of hours left of daylight. The search would be an entirely different enterprise once it turned dark.

He ran down the steps and walked down Amsterdam to 110th Street, Cathedral Parkway. Without thinking about it, his pace quickened, until, by the time he'd turned on 110th and was heading toward Broadway, he was running. His face was wet, and his eyes burned from the polluted drizzle, but he kept running, not sure where he was going. He wanted to be alone to listen to his instincts, sense his feelings. But his instincts weren't saying anything, and all he felt was wet. He crossed Broadway and headed down into the subway station to go south, making it to a train just as it was about to leave.

Where could Christopher have possibly gone? He didn't want to duplicate efforts with the search teams, and he wished he'd paid better attention when Harold was reviewing the plan.

Richard looked at his watch: a few minutes after three o'clock. He'd get off at 79th and go to the Natural History Museum. Regardless of how Christopher might feel about his father, maybe he'd go there to look at the dinosaurs. On the other hand, he wouldn't be thinking about dinosaurs at a time like this. Richard stared out the window at the subway walls rushing by. He couldn't let himself feel hopeless.

The train stopped at 79th and Richard got off, looking everywhere for any sign of a little boy. He headed east on 79th, almost running toward the museum.

He stopped for a moment when he got to the grounds. Nothing out of the ordinary. Richard ran into the huge building and went straight to the information desk.

"Excuse me," he said to the uniformed woman behind the desk. He held out his phone so she could see the photo of Christopher. "Have you seen this boy today? He's six years old, about this tall." He held out his hand to show his son's height.

"No, but another group of people came in about fifteen minutes ago asking about this same boy," she said. "It was a different photo, but it looks like the same boy. Christopher...let's see...."

"Carson."

"That's it. But he hasn't been in all day. We've notified the tour guides to keep an eye out for him. And the group gave us a phone number to call if we see him."

"Thank you. Please let us know." Richard stepped back, looking around the large entry area of the museum. "Do you mind if I go to one certain place, just to make sure?"

"No, go right ahead."

Richard headed down the hall toward the dinosaur display. He knew there wasn't much chance he'd find his son there, especially if no one had seen him all day, but he couldn't leave without checking. There were about twenty people in the dinosaur area, but only three children. None of them was his son. Christopher had talked and talked about climbing all over the bones, half hoping that his father would give him permission. They had spent most of their time at the museum in this very spot, walking among what was left of the prehistoric monsters, trying to top each other's story of how exciting and dangerous it must have been back then. "Sometimes the cavemen would wake up in the middle of the night and see a T-Rex sitting in the cave, staring at them." "Not just staring at them. Building a fire ready to cook them." "He wouldn't cook them. He'd eat them alive!" "But the cavemen would wake up just in time to fight the T-Rex barehanded, and win." Richard shook his head—the stories were over with and now they were dealing with real danger.

When he got to FAO Schwartz, the manager met with him and notified the employees to search their areas for Christopher. He accompanied Richard as they looked throughout the store, ending up in the Lego section.

"We'll keep looking for him, Mr. Carson," the manager said as they took the escalator down. "When you do find him, please be sure to call me so I can have you both come down as my personal guests."

Richard thanked him and walked out onto the street. He'd already been to the old IBM building, where he and Christopher had eaten hot dogs, but no one had any information. He'd talked to probably a dozen people already. At first, they always seemed worried about talking to a man with such a bruised and cut face, but the minute he explained about his missing son, without exception they became concerned about the little boy.

He called Harold. No one had tried to leave or enter the school. Apparently, Newman's people must have been making some phone calls, though, because the police commissioner had personally called them at the Cathedral and said he was coming to talk with them.

"Is that going to be a problem?" Richard asked.

"Not now," Harold said. "We're doing everything legally. We have permits to assemble at Newman and the media offices. We notified the police when we first organized that there was a missing child and we'd set up a search effort. I guess that's how the commissioner ended up getting our number. He can't do anything now, except try to scare us. By tomorrow, though, he might find some judge somewhere who will revoke our permits. As long as Joseph is with us, I'm not too afraid of the legal process."

Richard asked to speak with his brother. David told him he'd just finished talking with their parents. They were worried, of course, and wanted to come down to Manhattan, but David had encouraged them to stay home. They said they'd contact the members of their church and hold a special prayer vigil. He said he'd been working on the files but hadn't hacked into them yet.

"How are you holding up?" David asked. "Want me to meet you somewhere?"

"No, thanks, I'm doing okay. Just keep working on those files and be there if they find Christopher. Any word from Carol?"

"Yeah, she's called two or three times. Worried out of her mind. Blames herself. Said she called her mother. Told her the whole story."

"Oh, great. What did the great Defender of the School say?"

"You won't believe this, but she said she'd contact her lawyer and let him know that no more funds were to go to that place and to look into suing Newman. The rats are jumping ship, brother. I can't believe—wait a minute." Richard could hear his brother say something to someone else. "You've got to go to CNN, Richard!"

Richard went to CNN on his phone and saw a reporter with a quiet crowd of people gathered on the steps of Newman. The anchorwoman in Atlanta asked him the status of the situation, and he explained that the superintendent still refused to be interviewed. He mentioned a rumor that Dr. Newman himself was there, but no one had entered or left the building for hours. The network cut to scenes in front of newspaper offices and television studios while the reporter talked of how the major media outlets were being besieged with concerned parents.

The next image on the CNN report was a photo of Christopher when he was five years old. The reporter said the boy had somehow left the school, and encouraged viewers in Manhattan to help in the search.

CHAPTER
SIXTY-FOUR

The lions stood guard on either side as Richard sat on the front steps of the library, his head in his hands. He rubbed his face, not even bothered by the pain he felt when he touched his bruise. The library staff had been helpful and concerned. A group of people had come in earlier looking for the same boy, they'd said, and the staff had already done a search of the building without disturbing the patrons. They'd placed a security guard at the front entrance specifically to keep her eyes out for the little boy.

Hundreds of people were looking for his son—one librarian mentioned he'd even heard about Christopher on the radio during his break—but something was still missing. They wouldn't find his son by playing the odds or throwing a lot of people at the problem.

He looked at his watch. Six o'clock. It had to quit getting later. The sky was just one huge, shapeless cloud. It had stopped drizzling, but could rain at any moment. He'd been to every place he could think of.... What was missing?

Richard headed down the steps to Fifth Avenue, but stopped. He felt like he should stay there, but it didn't make any sense.

Christopher wasn't going to come running up the steps and say "Hi, Dad." He had to keep moving. Time was running out.

His phone indicated a new text from David.

"Take a look at these files, then call me."

Richard opened the attachment and saw the documents he'd copied at the school. They explained about the Seven Cubs: seven children specifically chosen because of their exceptional aptitude and intelligence for a program designed to exponentially increase their capacity for learning. He didn't recognize all of the names, but Tanya was listed as the "gazelle," Samuel the "leopard," and Christopher the "lion." They'd determined that Christopher had the most potential for responding to their experiment favorably and increasing his learning abilities, so he was chosen to be the last "cub"—the one who would benefit from what they learned by trying their theories out on the other six.

Newman had admitted to the first experiment: implanting a chip to enhance their ability to learn. There was a footnote observing that while no lasting harm had been done, three of the children had manifested residual twitching in their hands in stressful situations.

Richard skimmed a couple of pages, hoping to understand what Newman meant when he told him they'd come up with something better than the chip. He scrolled to the next page, titled "Nanorobotics."

The document noted how Newman scientists and engineers had been working on using nanorobotics to enhance the residents' potential for learning. There were several pictures of microscopic nanobots, designed to be injected into the brain and spread throughout it, building new synapses and strengthening existing ones. These nanobots were programmed to nurture the environment in the brain and develop the greatest potential for cognitive development. The goal was to enhance the residents' abilities to such an extent that there was almost no limit to how much or how quickly they could learn.

Richard closed his eyes. He pictured Tanya on the operating table, imagining what she'd gone through.

Newman had injected six of the seven "cub" residents with the nanobots, but none of the procedures was successful. Richard wondered what had happened to the other children, but couldn't find anything that mentioned how they were doing after the injections. After Tanya, though, the scientists were convinced they'd solved the problem and advocated injecting the "lion cub" as soon as possible. If that phase of the experiment proved as successful as they expected, they could then inject all of the residents.

Richard said his brother's name into the phone and it called him.

"So, this is what they meant about developing minds for the future," Richard said. "I guess I'm glad he escaped. I'd hate for Christopher to be injected with that stuff."

"I'm not so sure he escaped ," David said. "For all we know, they're taking him to the injection lab as we speak."

"We don't know that."

"But we can't assume anything. Time's not on our side."

Richard looked back down at the documents on his phone. "Where's the lab? Does it say where the lab is?"

"New Jersey. That's all it says. No city or hospital or anything was named in the report."

"So now we have to send search groups to New Jersey?" Richard said.

"I don't know, but I don't think they'd let their lion cub run away. He's either still at the school, or somehow they're getting him to New Jersey."

Richard looked out over Fifth Avenue, watching the cars pass by. A juggler stood a few feet from the statue of the watchful lion off to the right, and a small group had gathered around.

"Are we going to find him, David?"

"We've got hundreds of people searching every square inch of Manhattan. People are praying from here to Vermont. There's too much positive energy being sent out for something good not to happen."

"I'd almost forgotten about you and your positive energy."

"Hey, it works. There's a whole spiritual—"

"David, I see it!" Richard stood up, staring at Fifth Avenue.

"Well, it's about time. I was always trying to explain it to you when we were kids."

"There it is!"

"What?"

"The van. The blue Shapiro's van from the other day. The kidnapping."

CHAPTER SIXTY-FIVE

Richard ran down the steps, keeping his eye on the truck. "It's heading south on Fifth Avenue," he told his brother. "I'm going to get a cab. Tell Harold to get the nearest search teams down here."

"Will do. Stay with it."

Richard hailed a cab and climbed in.

"Follow that dark blue van up ahead. The one that says 'Shapiro's Coat Outlet' on it."

"What?" the driver asked as he pulled into traffic.

"Van. Blue. Follow it. Go behind."

"I understand English perfectly. I'm just saying this isn't the movies, you know."

"I'll pay you double."

"Money isn't the issue."

"Look, I think that van has my son in it. He's been kidnapped."

The driver studied Richard's face in the rear view mirror. A determined look came over the driver's face. "Now that is a different story." He sped up within three cars of the van as they approached the Empire State Building.

Richard's phone rang. Harold told him he'd instructed all the nearest search teams to get into cabs and head for Fifth Avenue.

He also sent the team members who'd been patrolling in their private cars to the area.

"The police commissioner got here a few minutes ago, he's been trying to get us to shut down our operation," Harold said. "He changed his tune a little, though, when we told him about the blue van."

"Look, Carson," the commissioner said over the phone, "don't do anything stupid. I can't devote the whole force to your hunch, but I'm sending a couple of patrol cars to the area. Let them handle it."

"No thanks," Richard said. "Newman has friends in high places, remember? And they know your phone number."

"Leaving the school alone is one thing. Kidnapping is another. Just be sure—"

Richard hung up, concentrating on the van ahead. He searched the street for any sign of team members, but all the cabs and cars looked alike. There were no police cars in sight, and he had no idea how he was supposed to know when help had arrived.

The phone rang again. It was Harold.

"I don't want to talk to his highness again," Richard said.

"You won't have to. Are you sure it's the right van?"

"Positive."

"You know, it could've been stolen. Maybe those are the real employees driving it. Or maybe there's a whole fleet of Shapiro vans."

"My gut tells me it's right."

"Pull up alongside it. See if it's the same guys."

Richard asked the driver to get closer beside the van. They were in the same lane, with four cars between them, so the driver changed lanes and tried to move up. He had to change lanes two more times, but he finally got beside the van just as Broadway intersected near Madison Square Park. Richard looked closely at the man driving the van. He was thin and stringy; his head almost touched the ceiling, his long, dark hair pulled back in a pony tail. Richard had never seen the man before.

"Can you see them?" Harold asked.

"Yeah. It's a different guy."

"Oh."

The cab started to drop back, but Richard told the cabdriver to stay beside the van for a little longer. The van driver looked at the cab a couple of times, and seemed to get bothered when he noticed how Richard was looking in.

"You're not exactly James Bond, you know," the cabdriver said.

"I want him to see me. If this van's the right one, something will happen."

"What?"

"I don't know. Something. That guy looks like he's getting nervous."

Harold asked what was going on, but Richard told him to sit tight. Richard could hear the commissioner shouting in the background, but he tried not to listen. He looked behind him and noticed there seemed to be more cabs crowded together than usual. He asked the cabdriver to check in with the dispatcher and find out if anything was going on with the other cabs.

"Something's weird here," the dispatcher said over the speaker. "About ten of them near you said something about following a blue van." Richard and the cabdriver smiled at each other.

At the red light, the cabdriver was careful to see if the van would stop or go through. It stopped, and the cab stopped next to it. The van driver looked into the cab again, then knocked on the wall behind him. A small door opened, and the driver spoke to someone. Another man with deep-set eyes stepped into view and looked directly into the cab.

"That's him!" Richard shouted into the phone. "That guy who tried to kidnap Christopher!"

The man recognized Richard and shouted to the van's driver. Richard opened his door to get out, but the light changed and the van sped ahead.

"We can't lose them," Richard said.

"We won't."

"Where could they be going?"

"I don't know," the cabdriver answered. "We can't let them get near any of the tunnels or bridges, though. We could lose them."

"Carson," the commissioner said over the phone, "don't hang up."

"What do you want?"

"Look, I've got more squad cars coming. Back off and let us take care of it. This is my job."

"And this is my son." Richard hung up again.

"Listen," he said to the cabdriver, "can you have the dispatcher tell the other cabs to get on both sides of it? We want to keep the van on Fifth, not let it turn off."

The driver gave instructions to the dispatcher. After a few minutes, the street became heavy with cabs. The men in the van seemed to realize there was a problem because they kept looking all around them, trying to change lanes, but none of the cab drivers let them. The van sped up, but the cabs did as well. A squad car pulled onto Fifth from 13th Street, and another from 10th, but neither could get near the van because of all the cabs.

Richard looked into the cabs nearest him. He didn't recognize any of the passengers, but he could tell they were from the search teams. Determined. Focused on the van. Even the cab drivers appeared different, like hunters surrounding trapped prey.

Fifth Avenue ended at Washington Square Park in Greenwich Village, and the Park was just a block or two ahead. The men in the van were arguing now. The dark-eyed man was now holding a knife, still yelling at the driver, but not pointing the knife at him. The driver looked straight ahead, and the other man turned back to the small door that led to the back of the van.

"Ram him!" Richard shouted to the cabdriver.

"What?"

"He's got a knife, and he's going back into the van. Don't let him go back there!"

"Man, this *is* like the movies!" the cabdriver said and he turned left sharply, ramming the van. The van driver turned, shocked, like his feelings had been hurt, and the other man fell down to the floor. The cab in front slowed down, keeping the van pinned among all the cabs. The man tried pulling himself up again, his hand bleeding, but the cabdriver rammed into the van once more, this time without being asked. The man fell back down. The van sped up, hitting the rear of the cab in front.

Finally, the van driver seemed to realize where he was headed, straight for Washington Square, and tried to turn to the right, slamming into the cab. The van slammed on the brakes and the driver jumped out, trying to make a run for it, not even looking back at his partner lying on the van floor. He didn't get ten feet, though, before he realized it was hopeless. There wasn't a car in the area—just cabs. The street running alongside the park was full of people—search team members, police, curious bystanders—blocking any chance for escape. Two officers ran up and ordered him to spread his arms and legs while they searched him.

The dark-eyed man stood up in the van. He held his bleeding hand, avoiding the eyes of the dozens of cab drivers and passengers who had gotten out of the cabs and stood in a circle around the van.

Five officers ran up to the van to make their arrest, and Richard and his cabdriver were already pulling on the handles to the van's back door. When they got it open, they found at least ten large laundry bags tied at the top. Richard climbed into the van, picking up each bag and tossing it aside when he realized it was just full of clothes. After about six bags, he came to one he couldn't pick up so easily. He tore at the cord, pulling it apart and opening the bag. Inside was Christopher, weak and exhausted, barely conscious.

"Daddy?"

Richard held his son's face. "Yes," he answered. "Are you all right? Did they hurt you?" He rubbed his fingers through Christopher's hair.

Christopher's eyes opened more, and he seemed to recognize his father. "Daddy!" he said louder, holding out his arms and hugging Richard.

"Thank God you're all right," Richard said.

They hugged each other tighter.

"Do you want me?"

"I always wanted you, Christopher. I never sent you back to that place. I would never do that."

As a police officer and two paramedics climbed into the van, father and son held onto each other, rocking back and forth.

CHAPTER
SIXTY-SIX

"**D**addy, I want to go home."

Christopher was holding his father's hand as they sat, exhausted, on a couch in the police station.

"So do I, Christopher, but we have to wait for the officer to come back," Richard said. "The police commissioner said they wouldn't keep us much longer. We have to help the police as much as we can."

The police were treating him differently this time, probably feeling a good deal of pressure from every newspaper and television and radio station in New York to find out why a school was allowed to medically experiment with children.

"How are you two holding up?"

Richard looked up to see Joseph holding a large bag and smiling. The two embraced.

"So this is the famous Christopher," Joseph said as he knelt down beside the boy. "You've helped a lot of children, son, probably without even knowing it."

Christopher looked up at Richard and smiled.

"Here, I've got something for you," Joseph said. He reached into the Macy's bag and pulled out Christopher's Winnie the Pooh bear.

"My bear!" Christopher grabbed it and hugged it. "I wondered if I'd ever see you again, Pooh!"

Joseph sat down with Richard and explained what he'd found out from the commissioner. The two men in the Shapiro's van were going to take Christopher to a doctor named Boswell who worked for Newman in New Jersey. That doctor was going to inject the nanobots into Christopher. Warrants were being issued for the arrests of the superintendent, Dr. Newman, Hunter, Boswell, and other key individuals for a number of charges, including attempted kidnapping, kidnapping, and the homicides of the six other children who were part of the "Seven Cubs."

"They'd taken Samuel to that doctor in New Jersey for the injection," Joseph said, "but something went wrong once the nanobots entered his brain." He paused. "He died within hours. Dr. Newman made it look like he ran away and had the body put by the Hudson after a few days."

"I'm sorry, Joseph."

"There's a measure of peace in knowing what actually happened."

"I'm just so sorry that happened to your son," Richard said. "No one could've known how bad that place was."

"Everyone knows now."

"Maybe everyone will start thinking about what's best for children. I never like it when people say our children are our most important resource, like they're oil or trees or coal."

"At least the Newman Home won't be able to hurt another child."

"What do you mean?"

Joseph smiled and handed him some papers. "I've got something for you to sign."

Richard looked at the papers. "Is this what I think it is?"

"Absolutely," Joseph said. "I wanted you to be the first. With your signature, you acknowledge that you are receiving custody of your son. Newman is closing down, Richard, and we're getting all the kids back to their parents."

Richard took the papers. All these years he'd fought with Carol just to get his son home for the summer, hoping it might extend to something more. He signed the papers and then knelt down in front of his son.

"You're mine and I'm yours, Christopher. No one can take you away again."

Christopher hugged his father.

"I don't get it, Joseph," Richard said, standing up. "Just because Newman's going to be arrested doesn't mean the school has to give up the children. Why aren't they fighting this? You must be an amazing attorney, my friend."

"Oh, that's where you're wrong. I can't take any credit for this. It took a better lawyer to make this miracle happen so quickly."

"Who?"

"The same person who gave me that bear for your son," Joseph said, nodding towards the hallway. "She's waiting out in the hall so she can get these papers back and process them."

Christopher jumped up from the couch and held Richard's leg.

"She'd like to talk to you both," Joseph said. "Just for a minute."

"I don't know."

Christopher held more tightly to his father's leg. "I'm scared. Isn't she the one who sent me back there?"

Richard knelt down again so they could be at eye level. "I know you're scared, son, but you and I are together forever. You know that, don't you?"

Christopher nodded. "But she wanted to get rid of me."

"She never, ever wanted to get rid of you. She really believed that the best thing for you was to be at that school. Especially after you were almost kidnapped. She loves you so much she was willing to not be with you."

"I almost understood until that last thing you said," Christopher said, then smiled. "Let's see her."

Joseph left the room with the papers. In a couple of minutes, the door opened and Carol peered in. Richard and Christopher stood up.

"Come in, Carol," Richard said.

Carol came in the room and knelt down beside Christopher. She held his face in her hands and looked into his eyes. "I had no idea," she said. "I'm so sorry. You've got to believe me. I only wanted what was best for you." She kissed him on the forehead, then pulled him close to her and hugged him. Christopher kept holding Richard's hand.

"I believe you," Christopher said, looking down at his bear. "But what do you think is best for me now?" Richard could feel his son's grip on his hand tighten.

"To be home with your dad," she answered. "I know that's what's best for you."

CHAPTER
SIXTY-SEVEN

The first week after signing the papers, Richard and Christopher recuperated at Grandma and Grandpa's. David took time off from work to be with the family. The only rule in the house was not to mention anything that had recently happened. For one week, they did their best to forget.

After the week in Vermont, Richard and Christopher returned to their apartment. They enjoyed their days together, but in the evenings, after his son went to bed, Richard kept up with what was happening to the Newman system. All the schools were closed down, by court order, and other schools scrambled to make room for the children. Parents of the younger former residents were busy trying to make new arrangements in this new world where there were no boarding schools for such young children. Doctors and scientists discussed the status of nanorobotics on talk shows, explaining they had been working for years to use nanobots to help with patients, but that they were still years away from being able to do anything like what Newman had tried. Then, of course, other experts followed up with debates about whether they should even try to change someone's ability to learn in such a way.

It was the middle of the first week back home in their apartment, almost noon. The buzzer rang for the intercom at the front door. Richard made certain the visitor was who he was expecting, then pressed the buzzer to open the door downstairs. After a few minutes, there was a knock at the door and Richard opened it.

"Carol, you look great."

She tried to smile, but Richard could tell she wasn't happy. They'd agreed she'd drop by the preliminary divorce agreement while Christopher was with Uncle David at Central Park.

Richard took her into the living room and they sat on the couch.

"How's he doing?" she asked.

"Really well. He's adjusting well and we're having a great time together. And, get this: literally every private school in Manhattan has offered him a slot, all tuition and fees waived."

She smiled. "Well, you know how important a good education is for a child's future."

"So I've heard."

Carol opened her briefcase and pulled out the papers.

"I still believe we're rushing this," Richard said.

She nodded. "You two need to get going with your new life. I don't want to stand in the way."

"But I wonder—"

"It's all there," she said, handing the papers to him. "The child support is very generous."

"That's not the—"

"No, I can afford it. Plus, I want to pay some alimony so you don't have to work too many hours and can take care of Christopher."

"I think we—"

"I've also included a list of—"

"Carol, slow down! I need to show you something. In Christopher's room."

"What is it?"

"Something you need to see before I can sign any of these papers."

Richard motioned to their son's door. Carol opened it, stepping back when she saw Christopher sitting on his bed.

"Hi, Carol," Christopher said.

She put her hand to her mouth, trying to keep her emotions checked. Richard stood by the door. "Christopher and I have been talking a lot lately, and he's got something to tell you."

"I see," she said. "What is it, Christopher?"

Christopher cleared his throat, then looked up at his mother.

"Well..." he said, looking around his room. "I don't know how to start."

"I really like your room," she said. "You've got a lot of fun things in here."

"Thanks," Christopher said, holding onto Winnie the Pooh. "These posters are like the ones Grandma and Grandpa got me when we visited in Vermont." He pointed to the posters on his wall. "Not the exact same. I wanted something a little different."

"They're very nice," she said.

"And I have this great bedspread, with all my favorite cars on it." Christopher patted the bedspread. "Come feel how comfortable it is."

Carol walked over to the bed and touched the bedspread, but Christopher took her hand and pulled her down to sit by him.

"But my very favorite thing in this room is this," Christopher said, reaching for the picture of the three of them in front of the Brooklyn Bridge. He touched each of the faces. "Isn't this a great picture?"

Carol nodded.

"I see it when I first wake up every morning," Christopher said, handing the picture to her.

"This has always been one of my favorite pictures, too." She touched each of the faces, like her son had done. "I'm so sorry. You can't begin to understand how sorry I am."

"I know," Christopher said, taking the picture from her. "You were only thinking of what was best for me. I even thought it was what was best for me for a while."

Carol smiled through her tears.

Richard sat on the bed on the other side of Christopher and put his arm around his shoulder. "That place is gone forever."

Christopher nodded. "I don't miss it at all." He smiled at his father.

"Can you ever forgive me?" she asked.

Christopher shook his head. Richard smiled. He and Christopher hadn't talked about how to answer this question when they were planning together in the morning, but his son was doing a great job.

Carol looked hurt. "I understand."

"Only on one condition. I can forgive you on one condition."

"What's that?"

"Scrabble."

"What?" Carol asked.

Richard smiled as he pulled out the game from underneath the bed.

"I want you to stay and eat lunch with Daddy and me and then play a game of Scrabble with us."

Carol looked over at Richard as if she wanted him to explain what was happening.

"Let's face it," Richard said, "this game is never as good with just two."

ACKNOWLEDGMENTS

Thank you to Denise Swift, Jeff and Sheri Swift, Steph and Peter Ott, and Ben Swift for their encouragement and patience. To Jen Howard for her excellent editing skills. To all those involved in putting this book together at CreateSpace. To the many family and friends who read the manuscript and offered much-valued suggestions. And thank you to the good people who helped with my Kickstarter project, especially my friends Kelly and Kay Taylor and my father-in-law, Donald W. Fry, for their generous pledges to help fund this book.